Like Water and Ice

Tamar Anolic

Contents

Acknowledgements

Thank you to my Kind Critiques critique group. Your feedback on early chapters made this book what it is.

Thank you to beta readers Gregory May and Leslie Cooney for your invaluable feedback on early drafts of my full manuscript. This book is better for it.

Thank you to Tim Whittome, copyeditor extraordinaire.

Thank you to Arcane Book Covers for this book's wonderful cover design.

Chapter 1

T had Moulton raced away from the arena until he could no longer hear the shouts and jeers. It was late—nearly midnight—but the streetlights still twinkled around him on the Nashville streets. Thad rushed as fast as his legs would carry him—away from that crowd, away from that ice rink, away from the banner reading "1997 Figure Skating National Championships!" He ran until his skates, heavy and forlorn, dragged at his arm and shoulder. When he finally slowed down to a walk, the water of the Cumberland River was gliding in front of him.

Damn it, Thad thought as he collapsed onto a bench in front of the water. His skates crashed off his shoulder and hit the pavement at his feet. The thought of ruining a thousand-dollar pair of skates would have once horrified him, but now he was glad. *Maybe I should just chuck them in the river and be done with it.*

Thad leaned against the back of the bench and closed his eyes. For a long moment, the chilly February air dug into his cheeks. Only the pain in his wrist and hip made him open his eyes again. He winced at the memory of landing hard on the cold ice. *I got what I deserved—fourth place.* He thought of the World Championships, coming up the next month in Lausanne, Switzerland. *I just disqualified myself from that.*

Thad shuddered as a cool breeze rose off the water. *I'm done. My career is over and I never want to get back on the ice.*

Footsteps pounded in his ears, and he jerked toward the sound. A second later, his older brother Scott appeared at his side, his blond hair glowing in the streetlights. "Go away," Thad mumbled.

Instead, Scott sat down next to him, and the two brothers stared at the river in silence for a few minutes. Then Scott turned, and his deep blue eyes, so like Thad's own, fixed on Thad's face. "Come on, Thad, it's just one bad skate. It won't kill you."

"No, it's not 'just one bad skate,'" Thad said forcefully. "I've won Nationals every other year because I'm only good sometimes."

Scott clapped his brother on the knee. "Not true. You're an incredible skater."

"Sometimes. The rest of the time I think I might quit." Thad groaned and buried his face in his hands. "How did you even find me here?"

"In front of the water?" Scott pointed his chin at the river. "You're our father's son. We both are."

Thad made a face. "Not what I wanted to hear."

"Then how about this? You made the team for Worlds!"

Thad jumped to his feet. "What? How's that possible? I was *fourth!*"

Scott smiled as he stood up. "Paul Monfils' knee is bothering him again—he was named to the Worlds team but told the judges he couldn't train for it."

Thad stared around in disbelief. The orange streetlights glittered in the same pulsating motion as the confusion moving through his brain. He ran a hand through his dark brown hair to steady himself. Then he looked back at Scott and felt the height difference between his thin 5′8″ frame and Scott's heavier six feet. "Paul just had surgery on that knee last summer. I was surprised he was skating here at all tonight, let alone as well as he did."

"He was really in pain, though. You didn't see him backstage—he could barely walk. I'm not surprised he said he couldn't do Worlds."

"At least he was honest about it." Thad took a deep breath.

"And you're going Lausanne instead!" Scott clapped Thad on the back. "You, Sebastian Adler and Joaquin Sanchez."

Thad shook his head again and opened his mouth to speak. For a minute, no words came. "I can't believe it."

"Come on." Scott waved his hand back toward Nashville Arena. "Let's get back to the rink—you're supposed to meet with the press."

A week later, Thad pulled into the parking lot of the Denver Skating Club just as the news on his radio turned to sports. "U.S. Figure Skating is gearing up for World Championships in Lausanne after last weekend's shocker at Nationals," said the announcer, William Gibson. "Is our team *really* sending Thad Moulton back to Worlds after his disastrous performance?"

"Monfils' knee has been a problem since last season, Billy," said his partner, Hank Shaw. "I was surprised to see him on the ice at all."

"But Moulton is twenty-six already—how much longer is he going to be doing this? Shouldn't he retire already?"

"When he's on, he's great. When he's not, though..."

"It's that second possibility I'm worried about, Hank. Russia's skaters have always been incredible—it's Grigoriy Arsenyev who's projected to win Worlds now, if not the next Olympics."

"The Olympics are still a year away," Hank answered. "Who knows..."

Thad punched the radio's power button and was glad when Hank's voice went off mid-sentence. "Damn them both," he said as he hauled himself out of his car. "Where were these guys last year when I won both Nationals and Worlds?"

Thad struggled to put the sportscasters out of his head as he went inside. It was dark, and only the streetlights lit his way. Most of the lights inside the arena were off too, but the emergency lights provided enough illumination to showcase the huge "Colorado Avalanche—1996 Stanley Cup Champions!" banner that hung over the ice.

Thad rolled his eyes. *You'd never know that a few elite figure skaters train here.*

The nearby clock was just clicking to six a.m. as Thad made his way down the narrow, dark corridors. *These hallways aren't much brighter even when the lights are on,* he thought. Inside the locker room, Thad was greeted by some light, at least, as the overhead lights flickered. He was relieved to see his coach, Trevor Galloway, pulling on his athletic gear.

"Thought I'd never see you here," Trevor joked as he ran a hand through his longish blond hair.

Thad rolled his eyes. "I'm on time."

"It's a start. We have plenty to work on."

"Yeah, I know. I'm unhappy about last weekend, too."

Trevor's dark eyes were serious. "We have room for improvement."

"Even the news is saying I don't deserve to go to Worlds." Thad's teeth clenched.

Trevor dropped an arm around Thad's shoulders as Thad kicked off his sneakers, and Thad felt his coach's warm personality even through his own frustration. "Ignore them," Trevor said.

Surprise rattled through Thad, and his eyes jerked upward.

"I'm serious," Trevor said. "The press has only been on your side when you've skated your best, and sometimes not even then."

"Don't worry, I haven't forgotten. 'Thad Moulton lost gold at Nationals. How could a skater of that caliber only win silver?' And never mind the last Olympics."

Trevor was silent as they walked from the locker room to the rink.

Thad could see the gears of his mind working and waited for him to speak.

"I'm going to put you on a media diet until after Worlds. We'll talk to the press when we can't avoid it, but otherwise I don't want you listening to or watching the news."

Thad took a deep breath. Anxiety swirled within him, making his chest tighten. "That's quite a step."

"But a necessary one. The press isn't your friend. Now, someone like Grigoriy Arsenyev..."

"Ugh." Thad made a face as he stepped onto the ice. "The press loves him."

Trevor shrugged as he skated after Thad. "That they do. But if you beat him at Worlds, maybe the press will lay off."

"Nah, I'd have to beat him at the Olympics too."

"One thing at a time. Worlds are first. You got a pass after a bad performance at Nationals, but the Olympic Committee won't be so nice if you don't do well at Worlds or at Nationals next year."

Thad felt like he was going to sink into the ice.

"Let's warm up and then we can start working on your triple Lutz–triple Salchow combination," Trevor continued.

Thad took a deep breath and began skating around the rink. He moved slowly until his muscles stopped complaining. Then he went faster and faster. After a round of stretching, Trevor joined him back out on the ice. Above them, the "Stanley Cup Champions" banner fluttered in a breeze Thad could not feel. Next to it, an Avalanche banner showcased the team's official colors, and Thad put his back to the burgundy, blue, black, silver, and white as he turned to face his coach.

"Okay," Trevor said. "Jumps, one right after the other."

Thad took off across the ice. His skates glided and he felt free. *If only it were this easy in competition.* He went for an easy single toe loop first, launching off the back outside edge of his right foot without even thinking about it. Then he hit a double Salchow and smiled. *I love the Salchows. There's just something about taking off from one foot and landing on the other—and switching edges—that gets me every time.* A fast triple axel followed, then a double axel.

"Great!" Trevor called. "See? That's all you need to do in competition."

"Easy as pie." Thad rolled his eyes as he rejoined Trevor at the center of the ice.

Trevor looked at him for a minute. "You can do it. Focus on your skating. Ignore everything else."

Thad nodded and headed off the ice. As he reached the side of the rink, Emily Burrows, one of the other senior singles skaters, arrived for her ice time. "Hello," Thad said as he stepped aside to let her make the most of her practice time.

"Hi, Thad," she chirped. "I think we'll be on the same flight to Europe for Worlds."

"That'll be nice." Thad's heart rate jumped just a bit. "Your first senior Worlds?" *Even if I know that already.*

Emily nodded. "I didn't make it last year and I was really disappointed. I'm so happy I'm going this year."

Thad smiled. "You've been skating better." *And she's only twenty. I'll bet she has another couple of years of good skating ahead of her.*

"I've always liked your skating, too, Thad. If you're on, you'll do great at Worlds."

"Thanks." Thad wished he could keep smiling, but uncertainty rose within him like a spike. *If I'm on.* Then Emily took off across the ice, her blond ponytail flying behind her.

Trevor came over. "Enough socializing. Go stretch out."

Thad nodded and pulled his skates off. A few minutes later, he was sitting in a quiet part of the arena and grabbing his toes. He winced as he felt his hamstrings stretch. *Gotta stay loose,* he reminded himself. *It's the only way to stay strong on the ice.*

Chapter 2

The next morning, Thad winced as his alarm went off in his ear. "Oof," he said as he pulled himself out of bed. Memories flashed through his mind of staying up for midnight practice sessions as a kid. *It was the only time the ice at home was available at a reasonable price,* he thought as he remembered the tiny Gloucester, Massachusetts rink he had practiced at.

The sky was completely black on the drive to the rink in Denver, but the streetlights glowed a deep orange over the highway. Inside the arena, the lights were just coming on as Thad used one of the arena's treadmills to warm up. His thighs ached and his calves were tight. *Ouch,* he thought. *I hope my whole workout isn't like this.* It was not until he got onto the ice that his body started cooperating.

When he finished his practice a few hours later, one of the arena's televisions caught his eye. *Is that another rink?* he wondered. Then the camera focused on Sebastian Adler, yawning as he warmed up. The banner of a New York news station flashed across the bottom of the screen. *It must be a local station, covering his practices leading up to Worlds,* Thad thought.

He watched Sebastian skate across the ice in his skintight black pants and a white t-shirt before glancing down at his own looser warmup pants and long-sleeve shirt. Then he rolled his eyes as Sebastian tugged at the black leather gloves he was wearing. *It's always about how he looks.*

Thad reached for his skate guards and pulled off his skates before allowing himself one last glance back at the TV. Sebastian was skating around the ice now, looking down at his hands as he did. Then he started tugging at his gloves again.

Thad made a face without meaning to. *You're the only one on the ice, Sebastian,* he felt like saying. *Who are you posing for?* Then the answer hit him in the head. *He knows the camera's there. Of course.* A second later, Trevor appeared in Thad's peripheral vision, so he made a show of turning away from the TV.

Still, Trevor picked up the remote control, and the TV went black. "Media ban applies in here, too."

Thad swallowed hard, then reached for his water bottle.

"Don't worry so much about what Sebastian is doing," Trevor added. "Focus on yourself."

"I knew you would say that." Thad smiled.

Trevor remained serious. "I mean it. Sebastian is a show-off. He cares more about his appearance than anything else."

Thad shrugged as he stretched out. "We're figure skaters. Half the sport is about how we look."

"There's paying attention to looks, and there's posturing. Sebastian does the second."

Thad looked back at the TV before he remembered it was off. "I don't know, maybe he's not wrong. He gets better press than I do."

"The news is always going to promote a guy's guy in figure skating. Sebastian is just that." Trevor shook his head. "Ignore all of it. You're a better skater than he is, and I want the world to know that."

"Me too." The words resounded through Thad's whole body. "I wish I could just prove that, once and for all."

"And you can. Your jumps were great today. Do that at Worlds, and the positive press coverage will be for you."

The next afternoon, Thad arrived back at the ice just as the Colorado Avalanche was leaving. A few last hockey pucks flew off the ice as the team's captain, Jack Wallace, passed one each to the team's two forwards. Then they all came toward Thad as they skated to the side of the ice. Each of them snickered when they saw him. *Great,* Thad thought. *They all know I lost at Nationals.* He stared straight ahead as the rink's Zamboni began its journey across the ice.

Jack made a point of knocking into Thad as he passed him, and his teammates' snickers turned into outright laughter.

Thad just shrugged as he continued staring at the Zamboni. *I got that all the time from hockey players when I was growing up. They can't scare me now.* Still, he was glad when the Zamboni finished its work and there was a smooth surface under his blades. After another three hours of practice, Thad's whole body ached. He stretched out, then hauled himself to his feet.

"I'll see you tomorrow," Trevor said.

"Of course you will." Thad watched Trevor make his way toward his office. Then he tossed his skates over one shoulder, his duffel bag over the other and headed for the door. Just outside the arena, the cool air met his skin and the smell of the mountains met his nose. Joaquin Sanchez, the third man on the U.S. team for Worlds, was coming toward him. "I don't think I've seen you since Nationals," Thad said. "Laying low for a bit?"

"Ummm..." Joaquin looked at the ground for a minute, making Thad wonder if he had said the wrong thing. Then Joaquin looked back up. "Not really laying low so much as taking advantage of the 'off times' on the ice."

"New practice strategy?" Thad shoved his car keys into his pocket and inhaled another breath of the cold air around them.

"A bit. It is cheaper."

"I understand that."

Joaquin smiled. "Yeah, we both come from working class backgrounds, don't we?"

Thad nodded as he thought of his father, heading out to sea on his fishing boat. "What about your coaching team? You didn't want to skate with Trevor?"

"I asked." Joaquin looked at the ground again. "He said his schedule was full."

Thad thought of the few other skaters that were on Trevor's roster. *That's not true—he could have taken on one more.* "Well, I think you're in the right place to train, at least. This is a good rink."

"I've also been spending more time in the weight room. I hope it'll help my skating."

"Yeah, Trevor has had me doing that too for the last year or so."

"Good idea. Sebastian is spending plenty of time weightlifting, I know that."

Thad rolled his eyes. "He always did."

"Gotta keep up with those hockey guys somehow."

Thad laughed. "I started skating to play hockey with my brother. We still go out sometimes." He thought of the jumble of pucks and sticks, so different from the solitary lines of figure skating, and was glad he had chosen the second.

"You close to your family?" Joaquin asked.

Thad nodded.

"That must be nice."

"Isn't your sister coaching you now?"

"Yeah, she is—that's why I'm even here in Denver. She moved here years ago for her job." Joaquin checked his watch. "I better get inside."

Thad nodded and took off toward his car. He was yawning by the time he arrived home, but his stomach was growling too. For a moment, he stood in front of his refrigerator, trying to decide what to make for dinner. Then he remembered the soup in his freezer.

Oh yeah, Anne made a bunch of that. He pictured Trevor's wife, petite and blond, as he pulled open the freezer and deposited a container of the stuff onto his counter to defrost. A smile twitched at his lips as he headed for the shower and remembered the years he had spent living with Trevor and Anne after they had all moved to Denver. *Anne still acts like I live with them. At least it makes my life easier.*

A week later, Trevor dismissed Thad after a light practice. "I don't want to tire you out too much before Worlds. I'll pick you up at the airport at five a.m. tomorrow."

Thad winced. "We still changing planes in New York?"

"Yeah. Sebastian and his crew won't be on our flight, though—they're taking an earlier flight out."

Thad shrugged. "That suits me."

Trevor eyed him for a moment. "You two have to act like you get along for the press. We're the World team. It's gonna be all three of you up there facing the media."

"I know that."

"But?"

Thad frowned. "But what?"

"There's always a 'but.'"

Thad laughed. "But this is a competition. That pits us against each other by itself."

Trevor smiled. "Bring that attitude onto the ice and you have a good chance of winning."

Thad's phone was ringing when he got home that day, and he smiled at the sound of his mother's voice on the other end. "Are you ready for Worlds?" Rosie Moulton asked.

"As ready as I can be." Thad twisted the phone's long, curly cord through his fingers and felt its cool surface against his skin.

"Good, your father and I are flying out to Lausanne the day after to-morrow."

"Me too!" Thad heard Scott howl in the background. His smile turned into a grin.

"Yes, Scott will be on the flight with us," Rosie said, and she, too, sounded like she was smiling.

Then Thad's father, James, got on the phone. "Good luck, son. I'm rooting for you."

"Thanks, Dad."

"I mean it, Thad. I wouldn't miss this competition for anything."

Then Scott got on. "Take those Russians down! Especially Arsenyev. I can't stand that guy."

Thad laughed. "I'll hit him with a hockey stick."

"No, that's my job," Scott protested. "You just skate your best."

"I will."

The next morning, Emily and her coach, Mia Spencer, were in the back seat when Trevor pulled up in front of Thad's apartment building. Thad wedged his suitcase and backpack into the car's full trunk and climbed into the front seat. Trevor pulled away from the curb before Thad had the chance to put on his seatbelt. "Take it easy, Trevor. Doing away with your top skater won't help our chances at Worlds."

Trevor's smile made his eyes crinkle. "So you're our team's best skater now?"

"We all know that. Despite my performance at Nationals." Thad's stomach sank, even as he continued smiling. *I may never be able to put that competition behind me.*

"Well, you're going to Worlds, regardless of that performance. Make the most of it."

"I will." Thad turned around and looked at Emily and Mia.

Mia's auburn hair caught the streetlights as she stared out the window. Thad examined her profile for a minute and noticed her thick eyebrows and long nose before he looked back at Emily.

Her warm brown eyes met his deep blue ones. She smiled. "This is going to be good."

"You're not nervous?"

"Oh, I barely slept last night. But now I'm just excited."

"That sounds right." Thad smiled.

They were quiet the rest of the way to the airport as snowflakes trickled down around them. It was only when they were sitting at the gate, waiting for their flight, that Thad looked over at Trevor again. "Are Joaquin and his sister on our flight?"

"I don't know."

"Did you coordinate with them at all?"

"No." Trevor looked away, and his gaze went all around the airport until it fixed on the window and the far space beyond it.

Okay, Thad thought. He looked over at Emily.

"I'm going to sleep on the plane," she said.

"That's a good idea," Mia said from the seat next to her. "I don't want you to be exhausted when we get to Lausanne."

"Mia," Trevor said. When she looked at him, he tossed his head toward the open space behind them. A second later, both coaches were walking away from their athletes. Mia tried to match Trevor's long strides as her coat hung off her thin frame.

"What's up with Mia?" Thad asked.

"Nothing," Emily answered.

Thad raised his eyebrows. "That's her normal?"

"Yeah, she's pretty strict and usually in a bad mood, but I've been skating better with her than with any of my other coaches." Emily changed the subject in the blink of an eye. "When did you move to Denver?"

"When Trevor did—about fifteen years ago. Before that, he coached in Boston."

"How interesting! Mia moved here only a couple of years after you did. She was coaching at the New York Skating Club before that."

"That's the club that Sebastian Adler belongs to." Thad made a face.

Emily laughed. "He's so handsome. All the girls I skate with are in love with him. Too bad he's married."

"Yeah, I remember when he got engaged—it caused quite a stir."

Emily looked at him for a moment. "Why don't I think you approve?"

Thad shrugged. "I didn't say that. It's his life. He can do whatever he wants." *His wife is eight years older than him and good friends with his coach. I always wondered what was going on there.*

"His son is cute, though."

Emily's words cut through the buzzing in Thad's brain. "Yeah, he is." Thad swallowed as he stared outside. The snow had stopped but the frost caught the light of the rising sun. Then Emily started speaking again, and her words brought Thad's eyes back to her face.

"I'm a little worried about how Kim or Jenni might skate at Worlds," she said, naming the skaters who had come in first and second at Nationals.

Thad smiled. "Kim's an incredible athlete, and her jumps have always been huge. What about Jenni bothers you?"

Emily made a face. "We've never gotten along. Sometimes I wish she would just disappear altogether."

Thad laughed. Then he looked up as Trevor and Mia returned from their walk.

"Come on, we're about to board," Trevor said.

Thad hauled himself to his feet and picked up his bookbag. Emily took a split second longer to pick up her coffee.

"Let's go, honey," Mia said.

"I'm coming, I'm coming," Emily protested. "I wouldn't miss this flight for anything."

Thad smiled at her, and she smiled back.

When their plane approached Lausanne, Thad caught his breath as the water and mountains came into view at the same time. *Dad will love it here.*

Outside the airport, the group passed under a banner that read, "World Figure Skating Championships, March 16–23, 1997."

"Guess they know we're here," Trevor cracked.

Thad snickered. "I can always count on your humor." He was glad when he got to his quiet hotel room, away from all the hustle and bustle outside. He changed his clothes and dragged his sluggish body to the rink for practice.

Sebastian was already skating on the other side of the ice, and Thad avoided him. It took a few laps for his body to start to feel normal again, and Thad was relieved. *Jet lag can be a nightmare,* he thought.

He went for a few jumps. A double axel came first, and Thad launched into the forward-facing jump, with its extra half-rotation, faster than he had been expecting. His triple toe loop came easily too, and soon Thad was smiling as he glided around the ice. He went into his first footwork sequence, then his second. Before he knew it, he was heading into different spins. He spun faster and faster and felt his breath catch in his throat. Then he dashed across the ice and launched into a triple axel. One rotation, two... Thad hit the ice after the third one and his landing was clean. *Awesome,* he thought. *Maybe I have a shot at winning this competition after all.*

He and Sebastian got off the ice at the same time, but the reporters who were waiting all rushed at Sebastian. Thad disentangled himself from the group and grabbed his skate guards, but he could not miss the questions that were being thrown at his fellow skater.

"Sebastian, are you going to try any of the quad jumps at this competition?" several reporters asked at once.

"Yes, I have a quad toe loop in my arsenal, and I plan on using it," Sebastian answered confidently. "That's the way this sport is going, and I plan on taking advantage of it."

Thad swallowed and began walking away. There were enough cameras around that he hoped his face retained a neutral expression. Then a lone reporter approached him, microphone in hand. "Thad, I was hoping to catch you for a few questions before the short program tomorrow night. Do you have a minute?"

"Sure." Thad smiled.

"I'm Stephanie Chen with NBC News. I've been a fan of yours for years now. How are you feeling about this competition?"

"Right now, I'm glad I got in some practice—the ice always helps center me. My jumps are coming along. I feel looser and more confident."

"That's good to hear. Do you think you could beat Grigoriy Arsenyev?"

"That's the question, isn't it? He's an up-and-coming skater with quite a few good jumps to his name."

"Speaking of jumps, Sebastian is planning a quad. Are you?"

Thad groaned inwardly but outwardly maintained his smile. "Not right now, Stephanie. I've never landed one in practice. I'm not sure it's safe to do it in competition yet."

"Do you think that might give Sebastian an edge?"

"He'd have to land it first, which is far from a sure thing at this point. And the rest of his program has to be solid too. Footwork and spinning are still important."

"You love spinning, don't you?" Stephanie smiled.

"It's why I became a figure skater rather than a hockey player." Thad was glad that his own smile was genuine now. "And the jumps—I always feel like I'm flying."

"Yeah, you don't even need a pilot's license." Stephanie laughed, and Thad joined her. "Well, good luck at this competition. A lot of us are rooting for you."

"Thank you."

"Nice job," Trevor said as he steered Thad away from the cameras. "Your practice looked solid too."

Thad nodded. "I feel pretty good."

"That's a relief. Keep that momentum."

The next morning, Joaquin was on the ice when Thad arrived at the arena. His sister Laura was at the boards, keeping an eye on him. Thad stepped onto the ice for a warmup and gave Joaquin a nod when he got closer to him. "When did you get in?"

"About two hours ago."

"And you're on the ice already? That's fast."

"I don't have much of a choice. The short program is tonight."

"I'm well aware. Did you take a later flight out of Denver than we did?"

Joaquin nodded. "We got into New York just in time for the overnight flight last night. I'm lucky everything was on time."

"You cut it pretty close."

"Not on purpose. The earlier flights were more expensive. We took our chances."

Thad was about to answer when Grigoriy Arsenyev skated toward them. He was coming fast and skating backward. Both Thad and Joaquin leapt out of the way, but Thad's clothes fluttered in the wind that followed Grigoriy.

Thad rolled his eyes, then looked back at Joaquin. His teammate was rolling his eyes too, and his whole body seemed to move with the gesture. Thad burst out laughing, and Joaquin joined him.

"Oh, man," Thad said when he could breathe again.

"For real." Joaquin shook his head. "Alright, I have to warm up."

Thad nodded and took off across the ice. After practice and stretching, he and Trevor left the arena.

"How are you feeling?" Trevor asked as a cool breeze swept up from the water.

Thad tried to take a deep breath, but his heart suddenly fluttered. "Nervous."

Trevor nodded. "That's expected. Let's get back to the hotel. I want you to relax for the afternoon, and we'll come back here ready to roll."

A few minutes later, Thad got out of the hotel elevator looking forward to the quiet of his room. When he pushed his door open, however, sound greeted his ears. Frowning, Thad closed the door behind him and went into the room. It took him a minute to realize the TV was on. *The housekeeping staff must have left it on. How obnoxious.*

He was about to turn it off when he realized that the news was on, and it was covering the World Championships. Thad's stomach sank. *Just what I wanted to avoid.* Then he saw Joaquin's picture in the top right-hand corner of the screen, and his finger moved away from the remote control's "off" button.

"Can Joaquin Sanchez repeat his incredible performance from Nationals?" one reporter asked. "I sure hope so."

"I hope so too," the second reporter answered. "This is a guy who came up from nothing—a poor family from a bad neighborhood, and he's already lost two coaches and a brother to AIDS."

Thad winced.

The first reporter nodded. "And his father died of a heart attack two years ago. It's no wonder he wasn't skating his best, but his phenomenal performance at Nationals put him back on the map."

Thad turned off the TV before the commentary went any further. Then he let out a breath he had not realized he was holding. *I knew Joaquin had it rough, but I didn't realize it was that bad.* He swallowed. *That sure is different from Sebastian—his parents were elite athletes who made decent money as a result.*

Thad put down the remote and sat on his bed. The room was quiet now without the TV on. After a minute, the walls' neutral grays started to quiet the buzzing in his head. Thad breathed more deeply, and the minutes ticked by. When he got up to get dressed for the arena again, he was calm. *I'm even looking forward to this program.*

When he arrived back at the arena, Grigoriy was backstage, but even the sight of his opponent in black pants, a bright yellow shirt, and leather gloves did little to disturb Thad's calm. Joaquin and Sebastian joined him, and Thad was glad for their company as the other Russian athletes joined Grigoriy. "Are we ready for this?"

Sebastian nodded.

Joaquin did too, and Thad saw a flintiness in his eyes. "Let's do this," Joaquin said.

The three Americans and Grigoriy were in the last group to skate, and when Thad took the ice, he was next to last. He had not watched Sebastian and Joaquin skate, and he was glad for that now as the afternoon's calm returned. His heart jumped when his name was announced, and he skated to the center of the rink. His legs felt loose, and relief flowed through him. Then the arena got quiet, and Thad pulled himself into his starting position.

Five seconds later, the opening strains of Benjamin Britten's "Four Sea Interludes" from the opera *Peter Grimes* sounded through the arena. Thad's muscles responded, and his short program started. His skates barely touched the ice as he glided in one direction, then another. *This piece always makes me think of home,* he thought as the sounds of the sea and Sunday church bells reached his ears. He took a deep breath and was sure he smelled the ocean.

Thad gathered steam as the music's tempo picked up. *Triple toe–triple toe combination,* he thought as he picked up speed. He launched into the air and felt the wind around him. Once his blades were back on the ice, he launched into his second jump without hesitating. He landed on one foot and smiled. The crowd around him roared, and Thad knew one good combination was under his belt.

Thoughts of the lonely fisherman at the center of Britten's opera swirled through Thad's mind as his deep blue costume made him think of the water again. He danced across the ice, then went into a spin. Two more triple jumps followed as the music swelled into a storm that pounded the coast.

Thad's energy vibrated in time with the music. By the time he hit his double axel–triple toe loop combination, the audience was clapping along with the drumbeats. His program ended thirty seconds later, after yet another smooth triple Lutz.

Relief warmed Thad's veins faster than his movement had. Now, he could look into the audience and find his family. He saw his mother's face first, even among the thousands of other cheering spectators. He waved and smiled at her in particular, even as his eye caught the signs and banners in the upper stands. "Team USA!" one banner screamed. "Go Thad!" yelled another.

Thad was grinning by the time he got off the ice.

Trevor was waiting for him in the "kiss and cry" area, and he, too, was smiling. "Great job. That was one of your best programs in a while."

Thad nodded as he caught his breath. "How did Joaquin and Sebastian do?"

"Joaquin is in first right now, but I think you'll beat him."

"And Sebastian? Did he do the quad?"

Trevor shook his head. "He's saving it for the long program. He's in third."

Thad looked around and remembered that the cameras that were in his face. He smiled and waved. "Thank you, Mom and Dad, for being here. Thanks, Scott. You're the best."

Then his scores came up: 5.8. 5.9. 5.9. 6.0. 5.9. 5.9. 5.8. 6.0. 5.9.

Thad sucked in a breath as the crowd roared again. "Wow," he managed to gasp.

"That was a great program, Thad." Trevor clapped him on the back. "You're in first place now by a decent margin. Arsenyev is going to have to skate perfectly if he wants to beat you."

Thad's legs ached as he stood and waved to the crowd. Then he made his way backstage. He was out of the crowd's sight before he started to feel like he was catching his breath again. "Wow," he repeated.

Trevor nodded. "Let's see how Arsenyev does, but if you repeat that performance in the long program, the gold should be yours."

Thad swallowed hard and found that his mouth was very dry. Trevor held out a bottle of water and Thad took it gratefully. He was still heaving down huge gulps when his eyes focused on the TV backstage. Every camera in the arena was now on Grigoriy, and Thad was relieved to be out of the spotlight. Then Grigoriy's music started, and Thad's eyes focused on his competitor like lasers.

The Russian hit three beautiful triple Lutzes in a row, and Thad's stomach sank. "He is a good skater, unfortunately," said a voice in Thad's ear. He looked over. Joaquin was standing a few feet away. Sebastian was behind him.

"I know," Thad said.

Sebastian came over and elbowed Thad. "Don't worry about Arsenyev. You skated incredibly too. That's all you can do for now."

"Thanks," Thad said as he watched Grigoriy land a triple toe loop.

When Grigoriy's scores came up, he had all 5.9s and 6.0s. The clacking of Trevor's calculator hit Thad's ears a second later. "He's three tenths of a point ahead of you, Thad."

"That's nothing," Joaquin said. "You still have a shot at gold."

"And you still have a shot at the podium," Thad answered.

Joaquin nodded. "There's enough room for Beau Tremblay to slide in there after the long program, though," he said of the Canadian skater who was in fifth place.

"Anything can happen," Sebastian said with a shrug. "We all have to skate well on Tuesday."

Thad eyed him for a moment. *He's awfully confident for a guy in fourth. I'll bet anything he's counting on his quad.* But he just nodded. "Good luck, you guys. I'm going to find my family."

"Me too," Sebastian said as Laura joined Joaquin.

Thad smiled at both Laura and Joaquin, then made his way out of the arena.

Chapter 3

Thad was relieved when he got outside—until he was besieged by reporters. It was only when he saw Stephanie Chen that he relaxed. "Nice job tonight, Thad," she said.

"Thanks," Thad answered with a smile. "I'm happy with my short program and hope I'll be able to say the same for the long program."

Stephanie turned her microphone toward Trevor. "Any advice for Thad heading into the long program?"

Trevor looked over at Thad. "Keep your head together, stay calm. You have a great long program and you can win this competition." He looked back at Stephanie. "When you're talking about singles figure skating, it's a lonely sport. With pairs and ice dancing, you at least have a partner. For the singles skater, it's just you and all those hours at the rink." He paused and rubbed his chin. "Skating, at the Olympic level, is a bubble in a lot of ways. Some skaters handle that better than others."

Thad was quiet until they were in the car with Emily and Mia in the back seat. "I never heard you say any of that," he told his coach.

"What, about keeping your head together? I'm so glad you've been listening to me these last sixteen years."

They both laughed. Then Thad shook his head. "I meant the rest of it, about skating being a lonely sport."

Trevor shrugged. "You disagree with any of it?"

Thad stared out the window. "No, I just... never heard you say it."

Trevor's eyes locked on the road in front of them. "I've spent my life trying to fill that void for my students as much as I could. I guess I've just been thinking about it a lot lately."

Thad thought of the years he had spent living with Trevor and Anne, and all the time he had spent at their house since moving out. "You've done a lot. I wouldn't have gotten this far in my career without you."

Trevor smiled. "You've pulled yourself up plenty too, Thad. There were times I thought you'd quit, but you always came back."

"Partly because of you, making sure I came back for the right reasons." Thad was smiling again.

Trevor nodded. "You have to love the sport for it to be worth it at this level."

Thad turned and looked into the back seat. Mia was staring out the window, but Emily was looking back at him. Thad's heart jumped as he held her gaze. When they got back into the hotel, Trevor and Mia took off toward the elevators, but Thad and Emily stood in the lobby for a moment and looked at each other.

"Your short program was really good," Emily said.

"The best I could have hoped for."

Emily pointed her chin at the nearby TV. "Look, your parents are being interviewed."

Thad's head jerked in that direction. Then he recognized the arena he had just left. "When did this happen?"

"Before warmups, I think. The reporters were already gone when I got there."

Thad shook his head. "Stephanie's been one of my fans forever. I'm not surprised she would know who my parents are."

"Buuut?" Emily asked, dragging out the word and laughing.

Thad's amusement made his lips twitch upward. "I guess I'm surprised she'd have the guts to interview them. I don't know that I'd have the fortitude to approach someone I didn't know."

"She's a reporter, Thad. It's what she does."

Thad looked back at the TV.

"James, Rosie, your son Thad is about to compete in the World Figure Skating Championships," Stephanie said. "How do you feel?"

"We're very proud of him," Rosie answered. "And we think he has a good chance at the podium."

James nodded. "Thad's been working very hard on some new programs that I think the audience will enjoy. I hope that's reflected in the judges' marks, too."

Thad snickered. "Dad's always focused on the end game."

"Can you talk about what it's like to be here tonight?" Stephanie asked.

"It's amazing," Rosie said. "Thad's been skating a long time, and I have every confidence that he'll skate his best."

"I've always been a fan of his," Stephanie answered. "Even through his low periods."

Rosie nodded. "He had a couple of years in there where injuries kept him off the ice, but he's come back from that in fine form."

"Figure skating is a tough sport—there are always highs and lows," James added. "We're fortunate that we've had a whole community at home in Gloucester supporting us."

Rosie smiled. "The community came together with clam bakes and other events. Thad wouldn't still be skating without it."

James remained serious as he continued talking. "At one point we were within a week or two of telling Thad he couldn't skate anymore—he was about fourteen at the time and we couldn't afford it. We kept it from him as long as we could, but we thought we'd reached the end of the road."

"That was when the community stepped in," Rosie said. "We've been fortunate that way, and it's great that Thad has come so far since then."

Thad shook his head as the interview ended. "I'd already moved to Denver by the time that happened. I didn't even hear about it until years later."

Emily's eyes were bright. "It's rough, but it means you have a lot to fight for." She reached out and touched his elbow.

Thad's face grew warm, but he did not pull away from her. "I have to win this competition. I'm not sure it'll be worth it otherwise."

Suddenly, a number of people surrounded them, startling Thad. It took him a moment to realize that they were all wearing figure skating shirts—and that they were all holding pens for his autograph.

Thad laughed. "Did you come all the way here just to watch me skate?"

"Yes," one girl said as Thad signed the t-shirt she was holding.

Emily grinned too as she signed autographs. "Awesome. It's great to have your support."

It was half an hour later before Thad made it back to his hotel room, but now he was smiling. *The fans are awesome,* he realized. *You're skating well again, and people are noticing.*

The next day, Thad spent as much time with his family as he could. "Your short program was amazing, Thad," Rosie said as they went to lunch. She dropped an arm around her younger son.

"It's too bad Arsenyev is so good too," Scott cracked.

Thad shrugged. "All he has to do is fall in the long program."

Scott laughed. "I know you're hoping for that."

Thad managed a smile. He was glad when their food came and he didn't have to say anything else.

After lunch, they walked along the water. "This is beautiful," James said.

"I knew you'd think so." Thad's eyes went back and forth between the water and his father.

"Think you're ready for the long program?"

"It's always business for you, Dad, isn't it?" Thad hoped his smile looked genuine as nervousness fluttered in his stomach again.

James shrugged. "So? It's why we're here, isn't it?"

Thad took a slow, long breath and looked away. The water, with the mountains in the distance, looked more ominous as Scott and Rosie looked at him uneasily. "Yes, it is." *I don't know what else to say. Dad's not wrong, but...* His thoughts trailed off as he caught sight of Emily and Mia walking toward them. Emily smiled when she saw him, and Thad smiled back. *I do like her,* he realized. "Mom, Dad, Scott, this is Emily Burrows, and her coach, Mia Spencer."

"Yes, of course," Rosie said. "We've been following your skating career for some time now."

"It's nice to meet you," Scott added.

"Thank you," Emily said. "I'm around Thad plenty at the rink. It's good to see the rest of his family." Her eyes stayed on Scott, Rosie, and James as they continued speaking.

"Is your family here to see you skate, too?" Thad asked.

"Oh, yeah, they wouldn't have missed it for anything."

"They're out shopping now, though," Mia said. "Meanwhile, I figured I'd give Emily a few extra pointers before her short program tonight."

"Good luck," Thad said.

"Thanks," Emily answered. "I'm hoping to skate as well as you did." She beamed.

"And I'm hoping I can replicate that tomorrow."

"You will. I have confidence in you."

The following night, Thad arrived back at the arena struggling to control the butterflies in his stomach. He took a few deep breaths and pictured a good program. Then he tried to picture a program with no falls, but nothing worked. It was not until he stepped onto the ice for his warmup that he started to feel his feet under him.

Then Grigoriy Arsenyev flew by him, mere inches away. Thad jumped back. "Damn it," he yelped.

Nearby, Joaquin shook his head. "He's trying to cause a crash, I think."

"He's going to succeed, too."

Joaquin looked amused. "I've never heard you curse, even if I think it's warranted this time."

"It was also warranted the other day," Thad said as thought of Grigoriy's antics before the short program.

Now, Joaquin's amusement turned into a full smile. "If he needs to do that just to skate well, he should find a new profession."

"Yeah, let's beat him."

Once more, Thad was skating next to last, right before Grigoriy. He kept a pair of headphones on as the rest of the skaters went through their long programs. Light jazz flowed into his ears as his turn to skate approached. He faced the wall whenever a set of marks came up. *I don't want to know what anyone else is doing.*

He only removed his headphones when Trevor came to get him. He arrived at the edge of the ice as Joaquin got his marks. *I hope he gets to the podium,* Thad thought as he heard a 6.0 announced among a range of 5.8s, 5.7s and 5.9s. Then he shut everything else out as his name was called.

Thad skated to the center of the ice and looked for his family as the rest of the crowd cheered. For a moment, he caught sight of his mother's bright blue jacket. Then everything else went dark as he focused on his program.

As soon as the first notes of *The Flying Dutchman* came up, Thad swept into his long program. Long strokes across the ice presaged his first jumps as he thought of the Dutchman, cursed to sailing for seven years at a time without a reprieve. *I love this music.* Three triples in a row followed each other: one loop, one Salchow and one Lutz. Thad landed on the ice one footed and confident, surprising even himself.

This is my favorite sequence coming up, he thought as he danced on the ice. *Fancy footwork.* The crowd roared him on, and Thad was smiling as he knocked off three more smooth jumps—two triples and a double—as the Dutchman came ashore and was rewarded with a bride. *I can do this,* Thad thought as he spun around and then went for his last combination: a triple Lutz–triple Salchow. It was not until he had landed them both and heard the crowd's roar again that a smile warmed up his face. One last clean double toe loop led Thad into his last sit spin. By the time he was still again, the crowd was on its feet and cheering. Flowers and stuffed animals landed on the ice.

Thad was still grinning as he met Trevor just off the ice.

"That was fantastic," Trevor said. "And with only Grigoriy left, you're in a great position here."

Thad caught his breath as he sat down and waited for his scores. The crowd continued to cheer as he waited. And waited. Even Grigoriy had appeared at the side of the ice now, ready to skate. "What's taking so long?" Thad wondered.

"I don't know." Trevor's expression was serious.

Thad took a deep breath and wished the cameras were not in his face. Then, finally, his marks appeared. 6.0. 6.0. 6.0. Thad sucked in a breath. 5.9. 5.9. 5.8 5.8. 5.8. 5.9.

"A few 5.8s?" Trevor demanded. "Come on!"

Thad couldn't disagree with him, especially as the crowd booed the lower marks. "That was one of my better skates," he said as Grigoriy's name was announced and his rival skated to the center of the ice.

"I don't know what happened," Trevor agreed. "They must want to leave room for Arsenyev."

That's not fair at all, Thad thought, but he said nothing as he got away from the harsh lights and away from the cameras. "How'd Joaquin and Sebastian do?"

"Sebastian fell on his quad. Stepped out on a couple of his other jumps, too. He's in seventh. But Joaquin skated beautifully—he'll be on the podium. What color his medal is depends on Arsenyev."

"Good for him."

Trevor shrugged. "I'd feel better if it weren't for your 5.8s."

"Me too."

They fell silent as they watched Grigoriy skate his long program on the TV backstage. "Oooh, I think he just stepped out on that triple axel," Trevor said a minute later.

Thad nodded. "I saw that too."

Two jumps later, Grigoriy landed a triple toe loop with both feet on the ice.

"Another mistake," Trevor said. "He's given you some opportunities to take the gold."

Hope rose within Thad. The rest of Grigoriy's program was clean, though, and Thad struggled to quash his disappointment as his rival left the ice. "Damn it."

"Seriously," Trevor said. "He has his antics, but he always pulls out a good program."

Unlike Sebastian most of the time, or even me, Thad thought, and was glad he managed not to say that out loud. He swallowed hard as Grigoriy's marks started to come up. Then he struggled not to curse as those marks were a mix of 6.0s and 5.9s.

"Unbelievable," Trevor mumbled. "He didn't land those two jumps well. You deserved the gold, not him."

Thad swallowed. No words came, however, as disappointment flooded through his body. Then Joaquin clapped him on the back, making him jump.

"Congrats on the silver, even if those scores are whack," Joaquin said.

"For real. Congrats on the bronze."

"Thanks, even if I think my scores should have been higher, too."

"There's a lot of that going around," Thad answered as they walked out for the medal ceremony.

A minute later, Grigoriy grinned as the gold medal was placed around his neck. Then he pumped his fist in the air. Thad struggled to control his disgust as his silver medal was placed around his own neck. Next to him, though, Joaquin was beaming, a broad grin that rivaled his expression when he had taken the top prize at Nationals the month before. Thad, looking at him, managed a genuine smile, especially as he caught sight of the two American flags outnumbering the single Russian one.

"Congratulations," Thad said, and put out his hand.

Joaquin shook his hand in return. "I deserve to be behind you. You skated magnificently."

"Thanks." Thad turned an offered his hand to Grigoriy.

Grigory hesitated for a second before shaking Thad's hand. Still, his eyes flickered toward Joaquin with distaste. Then he turned and left the podium and was surrounded by his coach and teammates.

Thad watched him go before stepping down and rejoining Trevor. A second later, his family surrounded him, and Thad was rewarded with the round of hugs he had been hoping for. "Congratulations, sweetie," Rosie said. "That was amazing."

"Nice job," James said. "I thought you deserved the gold."

"Me too," Scott said as he shot a glance at the departing Russian team.

"Yeah, I was surprised by the outcome," Thad admitted as they all left the arena. "But..." He clasped the medal around his neck. "Silver's pretty amazing too."

"Yes, it is," Scott said. "And you've grown into a better sport than I ever was."

"Oh, I know."

The whole family laughed.

Much as he wished he could go back to his hotel room, Thad followed Trevor to the obligatory press conference. The conference was only for the top three skaters, but plenty of reporters caught Sebastian on his way out of the arena.

"This was not my best skating," Sebastian said. "But I still have confidence that I'll land a quad, whether it's at the Olympics next year or some other time."

A minute later, Thad struggled to keep a straight face as he, Joaquin, and Grigoriy sat at the long table in front of the press room with their coaches next to them. Then the questions started.

"Grigoriy, how are you feeling about your win?"

"I am happy right now." Grigoriy clutched the medal around his neck.

"Thad, do you wish you had won the gold?"

Thad managed a smile. "Of course. I skated two very good, clean programs, which is always a challenge under the pressure of competition. But I am happy with my silv-."

"Do you think your falls at previous competitions made a difference in the judges' minds?" another reporter interrupted.

"No, I don't," Thad answered. "Each competition is always about the two programs in that competition." *Sort of. I do think we're often judged on past performances too.*

"Joaquin, this is your second time on the podium in a month in a huge competition. What's that like?"

"I'm as happy as Thad is," Joaquin answered. "I'm thrilled to have skated my best and it's good to get recognized for it."

The rest of the questions went to Grigoriy, and soon Thad felt invisible. The second the questions stopped, Trevor grabbed Thad's arm. "Let's get out of here."

Thad followed him out the door.

Joaquin and Laura were on their heels. "Yikes, that was awful," Joaquin said as soon as they were out of the press' earshot.

"No kidding," Thad answered.

Joaquin shook his head. "We've got to take Arsenyev down a few notches."

Thad smiled. "Now there's an attitude I can get behind."

Thad rejoined his family after the press conference was over. They were all quiet as they made their way back to the hotel. Thad's frustration raged within him. *Does no one else see that I skated better than Grigoriy?*

It was not until they were in Rosie and James' room that Scott swung his fist in frustration. "Damn that Russian guy. Who does he think he is?"

"He's the best in the world right now." Thad rolled his eyes.

Rosie and James shook their heads. "I don't know what those judges were thinking," James said.

"You skated better than he did, especially in the long program," Rosie added. "The rest of the world just has to figure that out now."

Thad basked in his family's comradery, and was glad for their presence as they sat in the stands the next night to watch Emily's long program. When she came in third, Thad cheered as he watched the American flag being raised twice more—Emily was behind Kim McGrath, who had taken the gold, and Fujita Sakura of Japan.

"I'm so glad Emily medaled," Rosie told Thad. "I always thought she was a graceful skater who never quite skated as well in competition as I thought she could."

Thad nodded. "She's been skating better. It's good to see her put it all together." *I'm glad Kim is skating well too,* he thought. *If she keeps it up, we could have a good team for a while.*

The flight back to Denver, with its layover in New York, was a long one. Thad stumbled off the plane at John F. Kennedy Airport, glad for the space after the packed plane. His eyes had barely adjusted to the airport's interior when they focused on a large banner. "Welcome Home World Championship Skaters!" it read. People in the airport cheered when they deplaned.

Thad smiled. *Perhaps I should have worn my medal around my neck.* His backpack seemed to weigh more from the hardware. Next to him, Joaquin waved at their supporters as they made their way through the airport.

"It would have been better if one of us had actually been champion," Sebastian mumbled.

"Maybe if you'd skated better one of us would have been," Joaquin quipped.

"Especially if you'd landed the quad," Thad added, laughing.

"Maybe *only* if I'd landed the quad." Sebastian's eyes focused on Thad. "You were amazing, and you deserved to win."

"Thank you." *I think that's the first positive thing he's said since the competition ended, other than a simple congratulations.*

Sebastian nodded as he picked up his son. Then he headed for the baggage claim with his wife and coach following him. Thad and Joaquin went to the gate for their flight to Denver. Emily and their coaches were a few steps behind them. Emily sat next to Thad as Laura and Joaquin sat across from them. Trevor and Mia continued walking around the airport.

"Is your dad always such a quiet guy?" Emily asked.

Thad looked over at her and found her looking back at him. "What do you mean?"

"I sat with your family during your long program. He barely said a word all night. Your mom and brother did most of the talking."

"Oh, that's normal." Thad waved a hand at her. "Don't take it personally—he's like that with everyone, even the family."

"His mom's great, though," Joaquin said.

Thad's eyebrows jumped in surprise.

"She was visiting you when I first moved to Denver, and she invited me to dinner. She really made me feel welcome."

Thad smiled. "I remember that."

"Your brother was cracking jokes throughout most of the long programs," Emily said. "He only got quiet when you two and Sebastian skated."

"I'll bet you shouldn't repeat some of what he said."

"No, definitely not."

The whole group laughed.

The next day, Thad had a rare day off. For the first time in months, he slept past sunrise. When he dragged his eyes open, it was after eight o'clock.

"Whoa," he said as he pushed himself into a sitting position and tried to swing his legs over the side of his bed. All of his muscles complained. *Maybe Trevor was right in giving me a day off.*

Thad stopped at his apartment door long enough to get the newspaper. Then he flipped to the sports section. "Thad Moulton Loses World Title to Russian Skater," a large headline read.

Thad winced. "Damn it." He spent an extra second looking at the picture of himself doing one of his trademark spins. Then he shook his head. "I didn't lose the gold, I won the silver," he said aloud, even as he remembered winning gold the previous year. He shook his head and tossed the paper in the trash.

Thad took a deep breath and walked around his apartment. The next thing he knew, he was running his fingers over his silver medal. Its ridges and grooves were rough against his skin. Still, his eyes moved to the gold medal he had won at Worlds the year before. *I deserved to win gold this time, too.*

His stomach sank at the memory of Grigoriy's mistakes and his inexplicable higher marks. *It was like that at most of the Grand Prix events last year, too,* he thought. *Except Grigoriy was flawless for a few of those. If I can't beat him when I skate better, there's no future in this anymore.* Thad bit his lip. *Can I really quit so close to the Olympics, though?*

Thad closed his eyes, and exhaustion coursed through his body. Exhaustion from the jet lag from Worlds. Exhaustion at having just skated at a large competition. Exhaustion from the years of early morning practices, from the falls, the bruises. Exhaustion from the years of injuries and not being able to compete. Exhaustion from being written off and having to prove himself over and over again.

It's time to retire, Thad decided. *The Olympics are soon but they're still a full year away. I don't have the stamina for it anymore.*

Chapter 4

T had was flipping through the newspaper the next afternoon when it went from the city section to the society pages without warning. *How obnoxious,* he thought. He was about to close the paper when a familiar face, staring back at him from a picture, caught his eye. His heart jumped in his chest. *Is that Ashley?*

He stopped flipping the pages and lifted the section up higher. "Cheerleader, society girl marries banker," the headline read. Thad stared at the page for a long time as Ashley Wright's smile jumped out at him from her photo. *She looks happy,* Thad thought as he examined the man in the photo next to her.

His face burned as he thought of the year he and Ashley had dated, finding time for each other in between his time on the ice and her traveling for the Denver Broncos' away games. *She was one of the better cheerleaders they had.* He looked back at the article in front of him.

"Ms. Wright, who was formerly a cheerleader with the Denver Broncos and the Pittsburgh Steelers, is now cheering for the New York Jets," he read. "She moved to New York two years ago and met Mr. MacDonald, a Vice President with J.P. Morgan, only a few weeks after her arrival."

How nice, Thad thought sarcastically. He put down the paper and stared into the middle distance. *I liked Ashley but we didn't have time for each other. By the time we broke up, I was sure she was seeing someone else.*

His stomach sank, and Thad clenched his teeth to keep the pain away. *Skating has been all encompassing. Now I need to decide what else there is for me in life.*

That night, Thad cradled a bouquet of flowers in one arm as he grabbed the bottle of wine he had left in the back seat. He nudged his car door closed with his elbow and was glad when it closed firmly enough to lock the car. Then he headed up the front steps to Trevor and Anne's house and rang the bell.

Anne came to the door and smiled. "How do you always choose the prettiest bouquets?"

"By the talent of the florist at the store."

Anne laughed as they headed for the kitchen.

Thad smiled back. All around him, the house was bright and warm, and an overwhelming desire to stay there flooded through him. *My apartment is much sparser,* he thought. *This feels like a real home.*

In the kitchen, Thad put the bottle of wine on the table as Anne pulled a tall vase from one of the cabinets and filled it with water. She cut the plastic off the bouquet and slipped the flowers into the vase. "There," she said as she put the full vase at the center of the table. "That looks great."

Thad nodded. "Very colorful." The smell of the roast chicken in the oven flooded his nose, but there was also another, lingering, smell. Thad inhaled deeply. *Anne's beef stew. She must have made that recently.*

Then Anne saw the wine Thad had left on the table. "This is my favorite wine."

"I know. That's why I got it."

Anne smiled as she put the bottle in the fridge. "And Trevor doesn't like it, so I get to have it all by myself."

Thad's eyebrows came together in a frown. "I remember him drinking at least a glass of it every time you opened a bottle."

Anne shook her head. "He hasn't recently."

Then Caleb King, the ten-year-old skater who was living with Trevor and Anne, bounced down the stairs and into the kitchen. "Thad!" he yelped.

"Caleb!" Thad answered. He gave Caleb a light whack on the shoulder, and Caleb grinned.

Trevor came into the room too. "Hi, Thad. I don't see you enough at the rink."

They all laughed.

Caleb tugged at Thad's arm. "Trevor got a new set of boxing gloves. They're down in the basement."

"Why don't you show me?" Thad said.

"Yeah!" Caleb bounced toward the staircase that led to the basement, and Thad followed him, laughing.

It was cooler in the basement than it had been upstairs, and darker, too. Thad flipped the switch at the bottom of the stairs and was rewarded with a golden light that flooded the room. He followed Caleb into a smaller room and grinned as Caleb pulled out a pair of boxing gloves.

"These things are awesome!" Caleb said.

Trevor and Anne came downstairs. Trevor went over to a second pair of boxing gloves and pulled them on. Then he and Caleb started swinging at each other. Anne laughed as they purposely hit air. One of Caleb's punches landed on Trevor's shoulder, and Trevor swung back at him. The light blow grazed Caleb's ear as he ducked away.

Thad smiled as he watched them. "My dad and brother used to box each other all the time. I always wondered who would win."

"Even though your dad was a lot bigger than Scott?" Anne asked.

"Scott got in a few good punches as he got older."

"I'm sure he did. I've learned not to underestimate Scott—or your father."

Thad had to think about it for a minute before he nodded. "I suppose you're right."

Anne smiled. "I'm glad this still feels like home to you."

Thad dropped an arm around her shoulders. "Me too." He thought of the small, second story bedroom of the tiny house in Gloucester that he had shared with Scott. Its sloped ceilings and small windows jumped out in his mind. "I've always been lucky to have two homes, and two close families."

A few minutes later, Trevor was smiling too as he pulled his boxing gloves off. "Come on, let's eat."

Dinner was almost over by the time Thad got his tongue to work again. "Listen, Trevor, I'm thinking of retiring from competitive skating."

The room became silent in an instant.

"You'd go pro?" Caleb asked.

Thad nodded, even as his insides crumbled. "I never thought I'd be able to make this decision, but now I think it's time."

"This close to the Olympics?" Trevor and Anne said at the same time.

Thad looked away from them and was shocked when tears stung at his eyes. "I always assumed I'd go for the Olympics too, but after how badly I skated at Nationals, and even skating well at Worlds and not winning..." He shrugged. "Maybe it's just time."

Trevor put his fork down and swallowed. "You've always overcome the type of performances you gave at Nationals, and your medal at Worlds shows that. I know you're disappointed now, but I think you should reconsider."

Thad just looked at his plate.

"Take some time to think about it," Trevor repeated. "Don't do anything definite now."

Anne nodded. "Your skating at Worlds was beautiful. You can beat Arsenyev, I know it."

"Yeah," Caleb said. "You can't get off the ice now. Not with the Olympics so close."

Thad glanced over at Caleb and wished he could smile. Then he looked back at Trevor.

"Don't make any decisions now," Trevor repeated. "To the contrary, let's go over your programs from Worlds and see what we think about moving forward."

Thad and Trevor spent the next day watching recorded versions of the World programs. "Emily's skating was beautiful, but she didn't have as many triples as the ladies who came in ahead of her," Trevor said.

Thad nodded as he watched Emily's short and long programs in quick succession. "And I think she gets tired at the end of her long program."

"Yeah, she and Mia have been working on that. Mia said she's been impressed by how much Emily has been improving in that area."

Thad thought of how much time Trevor and Mia had been spending together, at the airports and at Worlds. *I wonder if Anne knows about that,* he thought. *I can't be the one to ask her, though. She's too much like a mother to me.*

"Emily skated much better than Jenni Newell," Trevor said. "I know they were rivals in the junior circuit, but Emily's started to pull away from her, and this is the first major competition that's showed that."

"Rivals?" Thad repeated as he watched Jenni step out on one of her jumps.

Trevor nodded. "Jenni was precocious as a young skater—very good, very early on. She won most of her competitions through the junior circuit. Both she and Emily trained in the same place for a few years and it was always about them against each other."

"Kind of like me and Grigoriy." Thad made a face.

"Yeah..." Trevor drew out the word as he switched the tapes in the VCR.

A minute later, Thad leaned forward as Kim McGrath's short program played. "She's always been a great jumper. I was glad when the team decided to send her to Worlds."

"They sent her because she was amazing at Nationals. And about time, too—she's always been athletic, but she's never had any discipline."

Thad nodded. "She's on—what, her sixth coach in eight years?"

"Something like that." Trevor rolled his eyes. "Leo is doing a great job, but Kim needs help in everything—hair, makeup, her dresses." He made a face. "Yuck."

"She's not all bad in those departments." Thad looked back at the TV and watched Kim skate for a minute. Her blond hair had been braided back into a French braid that Thad thought was pretty. Bright red lipstick jumped out at him, though, and bright blue eye shadow worked its way from Kim's eyelids toward her eyebrows.

Okay, her makeup is garish, Thad thought. Then something that he could not name welled up within him. He stared at the TV so that Trevor would not see whatever it was written on his face. *I feel bad for her,* he realized. *She's so talented. She deserves much better.*

"Seeing people with talent like that but no discipline always brings tears to my eyes," Trevor said.

Thad stared at his coach. "I've never seen you cry over anything."

"I didn't say those tears spilled over and came down my face."

Thad snickered as his eyes went back to the screen in front of them. "Kim and Sakura Fujita are both great athletes," he said, naming the Japanese skater who had taken the silver medal. "I've always wanted to see them go head-to-head when both were skating well."

"And there's the rub. Sakura is consistent in her skating. Kim has never been. But in Lausanne, they were barely a point apart—and pretty far ahead of Emily."

Thad nodded. "I know that."

Trevor took the tape out of the VCR and put in the tape of Joaquin and Sebastian's programs. He pointed out the slight flaws in Joaquin's programs but did not have to do that for Sebastian's long program.

Thad watched as Sebastian launched into his quadruple toe loop and sprawled on the ice when he landed. "Oof, that looked painful."

"It was. Everyone in the audience sucked in a breath. I was almost surprised that he got back up and kept skating."

"He's tough. We all are. Those falls hurt, but what else are you going to do besides get up and keep going? You can't just lay there on the ice."

"Believe me, I know," Trevor answered. "I just wish the whole world knew that."

Thad thought of the press and then of the Avalanche players, their snickers and their insults. "Yeah, wouldn't that be nice?"

"Okay, and these are your programs." Trevor put one last tape into the VCR.

Thad bit his lip as he waited. "It's always weird watching myself."

"But necessary if you're going to learn from your mistakes." Trevor smiled, and his warmth turned Thad's grimace into a smirk.

Then Thad frowned. "Oh, this is before the long program."

Trevor nodded. "I want you to hear what the announcers have to say about you."

Thad braced himself, and his skin pricked. *If it's what the papers always say, I can do without it.*

"Thad Moulton will be skating next, and this is a skater whom so many people in the audience have come to see," said Terry Gannon, one of the commentators.

Next to him, Dick Button, the more famous of the two, nodded. "This is a skater who was once too shy to even look up into the audience as he skated. But his last few programs have changed that, including his short program here at Worlds."

"Yes, that short program was magnificent, but that's not always been the case," Terry said. Next to him, a picture of Thad and Trevor in the "kiss and cry" area at the last Olympics came up onscreen.

Thad winced at the image of himself, sitting next to Trevor and covering his face in his hands.

"Thad's long program at Nationals was reminiscent of his last Olympics," Dick agreed. "Many people in the skating community wondered if he could redeem himself here at Worlds."

"He did that in the short program," Terry answered. "Let's see if his long program is as good."

The camera cut to the ice, where Thad was taking his opening pose at the center. Thad winced again.

"What?" Trevor asked. "Your long program was amazing. The announcers cheered for you the whole way through."

Thad struggled to breathe as he watched. "I still lost."

"I don't agree with the results. I told you that when it happened."

Thad crossed his arms over his chest as he watched himself land one clean jump after another.

"I know you're unhappy with the silver, but your skating was great. If you skate like this at the Olympics, you could win."

"How?" Thad asked. "Grigoriy made mistakes, I didn't, and he still won."

"We'd have to come up with a plan."

"Or I could just go pro, like I said."

Trevor took a deep breath. "I still think you should take some time to decide. I'll support whatever you end up doing."

"But what do you think I should do?"

"The same thing I said back in '93 and '94, when you were struggling with your back injury and not sure if you should skate anymore—you should keep going if you love the sport. The Olympics are a big deal, and they are so close."

The next day, Thad's certainty sat in his stomach like a rock. He picked up a pad of paper and a pen, even as he pictured the large computer sitting on the desk in his spare bedroom. *I'll type it up later*, he thought. *I need to go old school for now.* Then he smiled. *I've barely had that computer for a year. Maybe I'm just not used to it yet.*

A few minutes later, he was sitting at his kitchen table, his pen hovering over the paper. "After a long and illustrious career, I have decided to retire from competitive figure skating," he wrote. Then he stopped.

His chest tightened and his hand cramped. He stared out the window for a moment, hoping it would help him regain his concentration. *I have to do this,* he decided. *I've already made up my mind.* He turned back to the paper in front of him.

"After three National titles and three World medals, it is time to stop competing and start skating professionally. I have enjoyed travelling to each competition at which I have skated, and the fans that have cheered for me have helped sustain my career. But even more than that, having my family's support has made the last twenty years worthwhile. Figure skating has been an incredible experience, and its memories will be forever etched in my mind."

When he was done writing, Thad got up and dumped his pen and paper next to his computer. Suddenly, a huge maw opened up in front of him, sucking him in. Everything around him seemed to spin, and Thad grabbed the chair in front of his desk for balance. *What am I going to do now?* he wondered. *I've never given much thought to my retirement. I guess I'll tour with Stars on Ice or something, but I can't do that forever.*

Thad took deep breaths until he felt like he was standing on solid ground again. Then he shuddered as he thought of the article he had seen on Ashley and her impending wedding. *Would any of this be easier if I were still seeing someone? I can't even tell anymore.*

He paced around until his eye fell back on the pages that he had placed on his desk. *I'll type that up tomorrow and have Trevor send it out to U.S. Figure Skating and the media. Maybe then I'll be able to decide on everything else.*

Despite his decision, Thad made his way to the arena the next day for another practice with Trevor. When got out of the weight room, he saw Emily coming off the ice with a blond guy next to her. Emily was talking excitedly about her new short program, and the guy was smiling. Neither of them noticed Thad as they went to a different part of the arena. Thad's uncertainty welled within him. *Is she already seeing someone else? This is the first I heard about it, and there's plenty of gossip in this arena.*

"That's her brother," Trevor said from a foot away. "He's visiting for a few days."

Thad jumped at the sound of his coach's voice, but he kept his eyes on Emily until he could not see her anymore. Then he looked at Trevor. "How do you know?"

"Mia told me."

Of course, Thad thought.

"They kind of look alike, don't they?"

Thad shrugged. "Not so much that I'd know it's her brother."

"I think they do—same curly blond hair, similar look to their faces..."

"Sounds like you got a better look at him than I did." Thad glanced back to where Emily had disappeared as he pulled his skates on.

"Don't get too caught up in Emily's life," Trevor said. "Focus on your skating."

Thad smiled. "Are you ever going to say anything else?"

"After the Olympics. If you decide to go."

They both laughed. Then Thad hauled himself up and went out on the ice.

That night, Thad was watching television when NBC's sports reporting came on. "The news this evening is that World Champion Grigoriy Arsenyev is hosting an invitational meet in St. Petersburg to showcase the best

Russian skaters, and the best skaters from all over the world," the reporter announced. "This event will take place in May, we're told. Invitations have gone out, and preparations are underway. Mr. Arsenyev says he's looking forward to hosting this event and hopes it will be watched worldwide."

Invitations? Thad thought as the broadcast ended. *I'm sure I never got one of those.* Still, he put on his shoes and went downstairs. His mailbox was as empty as it had been that afternoon, and Thad shook his head. *So much for inviting the best skaters. I wonder if any of the Americans got one.*

The next morning, Thad looked at Trevor as he pulled on his workout clothing. "So, that invitational that Grigoriy is hosting..."

"Yeah, I heard about that. I assume you weren't invited?"

Thad shook his head.

"I wouldn't hold your breath on that changing."

"Who else is going to be there?"

"I have no idea." Trevor thought for a moment. "Do you want me to call Cheryl to see if Sebastian got invited?"

Thad nodded as he pictured Sebastian's coach. "That would be great." He warmed up and then got on the ice. He was almost done for the day when Joaquin skated over to him.

"Going to St. Petersburg?" Joaquin asked with a wry grin.

"Are you kidding? I doubt Grigoriy would even say hello to me, much less invite me halfway across the world."

"Yeah, same here. Except that I'm not even bothering to check my mailbox."

"You're better than I am." Thad smiled.

"Skating wise, not really. You deserve to be there."

Thad shrugged, even as anger rose within him. "If he's inviting the best skaters, maybe. But I don't need another meet at this point. I just want to know who else will be there."

Trevor had an answer to that later that afternoon. "Sebastian was invited. So was Paul Monfils."

"Is Paul even able to skate?"

"I doubt that's the point." Trevor draped an arm around Thad's shoulders as they left the arena. "I think Grigoriy's trying to send a message as to which skaters he prefers—the ones who have less of a chance of beating him."

Thad swallowed and thought of his statement announcing his retirement. Heat rose in his cheeks, turning them pink.

Trevor stopped walking and looked at him. "I know that look."

Thad nearly choked his words out. "Damn Grigoriy."

"I agree." Trevor smiled. "Use it to fire your skating. You have every ability to beat him."

He's right, Thad thought as he was driving home. His anger was still raging within him as he pulled into his building's parking lot. *Damn Grigoriy and all he stands for.*

Thad stormed into his apartment and into the room where his retirement announcement lay. He ripped the pages from the pad, crumpled them into a ball hurled them into the trash. *I'm better than Grigoriy and I have to prove it. That means going to the Olympics next year and beating him—that's what I have to do.*

Thad heaved a breath and wasn't even surprised when it sounded like a snarl. *I'm not a quitter. I won't leave this sport until I have the top prize.*

At the rink the next day, Trevor gave Thad a nod. "You've made a decision, haven't you?"

"How can you tell?"

"You have a determined look on your face, and you're walking straight to the ice—you're not hesitating at all."

Thad smiled. "You know me well."

"I've been coaching you for sixteen years, Thad. It's a long time." Trevor took a deep breath. "So, returning to the ice?"

Thad nodded. "I want to go to the Olympics. I wanted that even before I made the decision to retire, I just didn't think I could hold on long enough to get there."

"I had a feeling you'd say that." Trevor was smiling now too. "But we need a plan." He waved his arm. "Come on."

Thad followed him into the stands, and they sat overlooking the ice. "What do you have in mind?"

"Your Worlds performance was spectacular—I think we need to continue some of the new stuff we started last year to make that happen."

"Such as?"

"Your off-ice training. You're physically stronger than you have been in years. Your program also engaged the audience and was to music that you chose. I want you to think of music you want for next season, as well as why you want to skate to it. You obviously connected to your Worlds music, and I want that to continue."

Thad swallowed. "But all that stuff was in place for Nationals, too, and look how that worked out."

"Which brings me to my last idea—you know Brianna Butler, right?"

Thad nodded. "She's offered to coach me a few times, even when I was at my worst after my back injury. I was impressed."

"She's very smart—she's a sports psychologist who was a competitive skater herself. She's combined all of that into a successful coaching stint."

"You want to bring her in to help me?"

"Yes." Trevor's eyebrows jumped as he spoke. "You have the talent and the dedication to be standing on the podium in every competition you've been in, and I want you to be on that podium."

"Including at the Olympics."

"*Especially* at the Olympics. You've already decided that's what you want. Let's make it happen."

Thad nodded. "Have you called Brianna already?"

"Not yet. I wanted you to decide your future first. Now that you have, I'll help you in any way I can." Trevor took a deep breath through his nose, and Thad knew there was more coming. "I also want you to connect with your fans more. There are always a lot of them at your competitions, and they're always cheering."

Thad told Trevor of the fans he had signed autographs for at Worlds. "That was fun." To his surprise, he was smiling.

Trevor smiled back. "I remember how surprised you were when you started being recognized off the ice."

"Yeah, I was in a grocery store after I won Nationals the first time, and a bunch of giggling girls ran up to me." Thad laughed. "I looked behind me to see who they were interested in."

"Yeah, I remember that." Trevor was laughing now too. "But you need to harness that to counteract the negativity you get from the press. I think it will help your mental state and focus."

Thad became serious as he thought about it. Then he nodded. "The thought of being surrounded by thousands of people during a competition wants to make me hide half the time, but you're right. A lot of them are there to support me."

"Including your family. Use that to your advantage."

Chapter 5

That afternoon, Thad arrived home thinking of his performance at Worlds and the tapes he and Trevor had watched. In his living room, he pulled a specific section of the newspaper from the stack near his trash can. He flipped to the sports from the day after Worlds and found the articles on the ladies' figure skating. "Burrows Takes Bronze as Childhood Rival Drops," the headline read.

Guess Trevor was right, Thad thought as he read the article. *Other women are in the mix besides Emily and Jenni—like Kim McGrath. Maybe the press should drop the rivalry thing.*

Thad almost laughed at himself as he thought of Grigoriy. *The press would make something up there even if our scores were nowhere near each other. They're not going to just walk away from Emily and Jenni, either.*

For a second, Thad stared out his window and raised his hand to shield his eyes from the incoming sunlight. His thoughts went back to the medal ceremony in Lausanne. *I've made my decision to keep competing and I'm not going back on it, whatever the press says.* He swallowed. *I just have to make sure I beat Grigoriy next time.*

When his workout was over the next day, Thad followed Trevor to the office that was upstairs from the rink. Trevor turned on a small fan to get the room's stale air moving, and Thad wished the weather were warm enough to open a window. He watched white puffy clouds move across the deep blue sky as he sat in a chair facing Trevor's desk. *If I didn't know better, I'd think it was summer.*

Trevor sat down opposite him. "I hope Brianna's number hasn't changed." He picked up the phone. A minute later, Thad heard a woman's voice coming out of the receiver, and Trevor looked relieved. "Good afternoon, Brianna, this is Trevor Galloway. I hope I'm not interrupting any of your practice sessions."

"Don't worry, I just got out of one," Brianna answered. "Otherwise you would have gotten my voicemail."

"Well, I'm glad to have gotten you instead. Do you mind if I put you on speakerphone?"

"Depends on who else is in the room."

Thad laughed.

"Don't worry, it's just me and Thad." Trevor looked amused as he hit the speakerphone button and dropped the phone back into its cradle.

"Oh, good," Brianna answered, and her voice echoed through the room now. "I'd rather talk to him than you."

"Tough." But Trevor was smiling.

"Hi, Brianna," Thad said. "Thanks for taking our call."

"Oh, I'm glad I picked up the phone. It's good to hear your voice, Mr. Silver Medalist. What can I do for you?"

"Well, I've decided to continue training so that I can go to the Olympics. I'm happy with how I skated at Worlds but was hoping for a different color medal. Trevor and I remembered how you called a couple of times a few years ago, interested in coaching me. I wondered if you're still interested?" Thad took a breath. "I'm hoping an extra set of eyes would help me fill in the gaps in my training."

"Oh, I'm interested," Brianna said. "Your skating in Lausanne was wonderful. I'd love to do whatever I can for you."

The words could not have been more welcome to Thad's ears.

"Great," Trevor said. "We're hoping your psych degree and work with other elite athletes will make a difference here."

"I'm also hoping your choreography skills come with that," Thad added.

"Absolutely," Brianna said. "I have ideas for you already."

"Are you still out in California?" Trevor asked.

"I am, but I can get to Denver. I have to warn you, though, that Joaquin Sanchez's sister has asked me to do some of his choreography as well, so I'd be working with both of you."

"All the more reason to come to Denver," Thad said, even as Trevor made a face. Thad sent a quizzical look in his coach's direction.

"You're very gracious," Brianna said.

"I like Joaquin's skating, and I've always thought he got lower marks than he deserved."

"Both he and Laura think that too. That's why they called me."

"Sounds like we're in a similar boat."

"Don't worry, Thad, I'm sure you weren't happy with Nationals, or with your placement at Worlds."

"Right on both."

There was a slight pause. "And you've always been a man of few words." Brianna sounded like she was smiling.

"I would have said the same of my dad." The words were out before Thad could stop them. He groaned.

"Don't worry, that's not a bad thing. Your mom did all the talking for him anyway every time I've spoken to them."

"That's always been true."

There was a moment of silence on the other end before Brianna spoke again. "Alright, I'll fly out to Denver. I'll let you know when I get there and we can start working together."

"Thank you so much for doing this, Brianna," Trevor said. "I want to see Thad on the Olympic podium, and for him to get a certain color medal."

"We all want that," Brianna said, and Thad could only nod in agreement.

Thad was in the checkout line at the grocery store the next weekend when a familiar face caught his eye. When he looked more closely, Joaquin's picture stared back at him from the cover of *People* magazine. Thad smiled and picked up the glossy publication. He flipped through the pages until he found the piece on his friend and saw that it was an extended interview. *Good for him,* Thad thought as he dumped the magazine in with his cucumbers and peppers. *He's finally getting the attention he deserves.*

At home, Thad unpacked his groceries and collapsed into a comfortable chair in his living room, magazine in hand. Then he started reading.

<u>Kayla Lee, Journalist</u>: You've been through several coaches in your skating career, and you moved here to Denver to find a new one. Is it strange that your sister is now coaching you instead?

<u>Joaquin</u>: No, I'm happy with everything that's happened. I think it's appropriate for Laura to be coaching me now, and it's an arrangement we're both comfortable with. She was a figure skater before I was—she's the reason I took up skating to begin with. And she was a good skater. She went to Nationals several times and to Worlds once.

<u>Kayla</u>: Does she skate much nowadays?

<u>Joaquin</u>: Not as much as when she was competing. Even her last outing at Nationals, she was struggling with a hip injury. When the competition was over, it was just time for her to stop.

<u>Kayla</u>: Tell me about your family dynamic. You have a brother, don't you?

<u>Joaquin</u>: I had one, yes. He died three years ago.

<u>Kayla</u>: That must have been rough.

<u>Joaquin</u>: It's been very tough, yes.

For a moment, Thad stopped reading and stared across the room. He pictured a pause in the interview as Joaquin looked down and swallowed before looking back up. *I've never heard him say anything about his brother,* Thad thought. *His whole family situation has been tough.* He went back to reading.

Kayla: What was your brother like growing up?

Joaquin: He was the first-born son in a Mexican-American family. I thought I had it hard growing up, but it wasn't any easier for him. He was always the macho one, playing basketball in the neighborhood yards, getting into fights when we were young.

Kayla: And when you got older?

Joaquin: *(pausing)* Um, I don't know. By then, it was more drugs and alcohol, and it was hard to get him to stop. My sister was always girly—figure skating was a good outlet for her. I took after her more than my brother. I loved wearing her outfits, skating around the rink with her. *(Laughs.)* It's probably why my parents let me get into skating too. It must have been easier to watch me when I was always where my sister was. That's why it feels natural to have her as my coach now, going back to your earlier question. Skating was something we always bonded over, and it's nice to have that again now.

Kayla: Now that you're nearing the end of your career, where do you see yourself going from here?

Joaquin: Who said my career is over? Did I say that? *(Laughs)* I still have a lot of fire in me, it's just a question of how to direct it. I've been skating my best recently, and I want to see where that leads me. If it's Nationals next year and the Olympics, that's wonderful. But I need to be the one to decide.

Good for him, Thad thought. *He isn't letting the press push him into retirement, or whatever they think he should do. He's right—he's in charge of his career, not them.*

Two days later, Brianna arrived at the rink with Joaquin and Laura in tow. The cool spring air also seemed to follow her all the way to the ice. Trevor gave her a nod, and his eyes fixed on Brianna, as if Laura and Joaquin were not there. "Thanks for coming."

Brianna smiled. "Two world class figure skaters, both calling me for advice? Don't worry, I wouldn't miss it for the world."

Trevor shot a disparaging look at Joaquin, and his attitude hit Thad like a brick. He opened his mouth to say something, but no words came.

Brianna looked back and forth between Trevor and Joaquin for a moment. "I'm here for both skaters, Trevor. I don't want to get in the way, but I won't have you bulldozing over any of us, either."

Trevor rolled his eyes and pressed his lips into a thin line.

"You know, I came here in part because I agree with something you said at Worlds."

"Oh yeah? What is that?" Trevor's eyebrows came together in genuine confusion—confusion that Thad felt swirling through him, too.

"At the end of the day, the real job is when the skater takes the ice. A coach can do everything in his power, but it's the athlete that's alone at the center of rink. Like you said on the phone, we all want the same thing—for our athletes to reach the podium in the sport's biggest competition."

Trevor took a deep breath, and his hostility lessened. "You're right. Let's get started."

Brianna looked at Thad as they got on the ice. "What do you think happened to you at Nationals? Or at your last Olympics?"

"At the Olympics, it was the pressure. I wanted to win so badly, and there was so much hype."

Joaquin nodded. "I remember all of that. I was almost glad I hadn't been selected."

Brianna looked back at Thad. "And at Nationals?"

"I'm not sure. I thought I had everything together, and..." Thad shook his head.

"Okay," Brianna answered. "We can work on that."

Practice was over for the day when Trevor got Thad's attention again. "By the way, I've entered you into that new meet the Capital City Figure Skating Club is hosting."

"By the way?" Thad repeated as he shielded his eyes from the sunlight that was flowing through the windows. "Thanks for the warning."

Trevor shrugged. "It's April—time to start thinking about that stuff. The ISU has given this meet a temporary sanction for now, so a few of the top skaters have entered. Sebastian will be there. So will Grigoriy."

Thad's stomach dropped at the sound of his Russian rival's name. "When is it?"

"It starts July 2."

"Oh, right after the season begins." Thad looked over at Joaquin and Laura. "Will you guys be there?"

They both nodded.

"It'll be a good warm up," Trevor added, and Thad turned back to him. "You can test out the programs we've been working on before a competition that really matters."

"I'm game," Thad answered with a shrug.

"Good, because you're going."

Thad threw his eyes toward the ceiling. "And if I hadn't wanted to?"

"Tough. I entered you, and the fees are nonrefundable."

"You really know how to stick it to people."

"You included. Now go stretch out."

Thad laughed and got moving. By the time his fingers were touching his toes, Trevor was laughing too.

Later that week, when practice was over, Thad made his way back to the locker room. His legs were shaking as he eased himself onto the bench in front of his locker. "Oof," he groaned.

For a moment, he just sat still, enjoying not having to move. When he tried to stand, though, his legs did not cooperate. He winced and reached for his locker door. He managed to push it in just hard enough for it to open. Then he dragged his bag out and pulled out his second water bottle. It was half empty before he remembered that his main bottle sat empty a couple of feet away from him. *That larger bottle is a liter and a half. I went through all of it at practice and I still need more.*

Thad finished his second bottle, then realized he still didn't want to get up to refill either empty container. Instead, he pulled his skates off and stuck his feet into his sneakers. Even after his shoelaces were tied, it took Thad another two full minutes of sitting before he could haul himself into a standing position. He hobbled over to the water fountain and was relieved to have the cool liquid sliding down his throat again.

By the time he got back to his locker, his larger bottle was half empty. Thad contemplated sitting back down on the bench in front of him and staying there for the rest of the day. Then the sound of men's voices caught his ears—lots of them, mostly in whoops and hollers. *What on Earth?* Thad thought—until the sound of hockey sticks beating the walls of the arena reached his ears. *The Avalanche.*

That got him moving again. He shoved his water bottles into his duffel bag and yanked the zipper closed. Then he hauled the bag onto his shoulder and grabbed his skates. He had just reached the door of the locker room when the hockey players reached it too.

The team's captain, Jack Wallace, was at the front of the group, but he was surrounded by two forwards and the team's goalie. Their coach, Michael Perry, was right behind them. "Time's up, figure skater," Jack growled, and the other players laughed.

Thad just kept walking. *They don't want me here,* he thought. *It was like that when Scott played hockey when we were kids.* He winced as he thought of Scott protecting him from the other players' taunts and shoves. *Some things never change.*

He was glad when he was outside in the bright sunlight. The sound of a few birds singing reached his ears. *Spring*. He was several steps further away from the arena when he realized his heart was still racing. *Twenty years later and I thought I was going to get beat up by those hockey players*. He shook his head at himself. *But Jack and the rest of them are just as mean as some of the hockey kids I knew in Gloucester. Things never change*.

A week later, Thad plucked up the courage to ask Trevor a question that had been lingering in his mind. "How come you didn't take Joaquin on as a skater, even after he moved to Denver? What's your problem with him?"

Trevor eyed Thad as he stretched out. Then he took a long breath and looked everywhere else but Thad. When he finally looked ready to say something, he glanced back toward the ice, as if making sure that neither Joaquin nor Laura were in sight. "He's twenty-five years old already. I think he's at the end of his career."

"Half the planet thinks that of me, too," Thad pointed out. "I'm twenty-six, remember?"

"But I've been your coach since you were ten. It's different." Trevor swallowed.

"What?" Thad asked.

"It's only been these last two competitions that I've thought Joaquin could be a solid skater."

"I don't think that's fair." Thad frowned, struggling to put the feelings that were tumbling through him into words. "I've always thought he could do well—maybe with better coaching or more ice time, or something."

"Yeah, *something*. It's always that intangible, isn't it?"

Thad bit his lip. "He's always been a good spinner, and his jumps are good. I've seen some good footwork in a few of his short programs too."

"These last few competitions have been the first time he's put everything together. I've seen him have a good short program or a good long program, but rarely both together."

"I don't know, even the times he has put both together, he hasn't gotten the marks he deserves." Thad hauled himself into a standing position.

Trevor stood up too. Then he shrugged. "I don't know, I guess I haven't looked at it that way. Just that he's always gotten low marks."

"Well, maybe he deserves a second look."

Trevor took another long breath as he thought about it. "I still don't think it's worth it to take him on as a skater at this point, not with Brianna here, helping him. I think he's going to retire soon."

"Oh, I thought he brought Brianna on for the same reason I did—to increase his chances at the Olympics."

"If I were him, I'd be considering going pro. He's very popular right now, and he could be a major draw for shows like Stars on Ice."

Thad nodded. "It's hard to disagree with that."

"Says the guy who decided not to go that route." Trevor smiled.

"I almost did. After the Olympics, we can discuss it again."

"Even if you don't do well?"

"This from the guy who always thinks I should put my bad performances behind me?"

They both laughed. Then Trevor handed Thad his warmup jacket. "I think you're right, training for the Olympics. And yes, don't think past that right now. Your world will look much different once that's over."

As Thad got home that night, Trevor's advice to connect with his fans rang in his head. *How do I find out if any of them are planning on attending my competitions, though?* he wondered. It was not until he passed the room with his computer that he thought of getting online and searching for fan clubs. *I'm still getting used to the World Wide Web.* Then he winced as the loud, tinny sound of his computer dialing up reached his ears. *I wish there were a better way of connecting.*

His fingers drummed along the edge of his desk as he waited for the connection to be finalized. As soon as it was, his fingers flew over his keyboard, going to AOL first and then running a search for his own name. To his surprise, a number of items came up. *Some of these are websites about me,* Thad realized. *Oh my God.*

His heart began to race, and his face got warm. He clicked on the first link and found several pictures of himself staring back at him. *How bizarre,* he thought, but he was also smiling. He continued clicking and found himself in chat rooms discussing his skating and upcoming competitions. *So this is where the fans come to find out more about me and connect with each other.*

He looked away from the computer for a minute and found himself staring out the window. *Trevor was right,* he realized. *I do have a decent fan base out there.* He stared back at his computer screen and thought of Emily. *I wonder if she has fan clubs too.* His fingers flew over his keyboard again.

A number of links came up again, and Thad clicked on the first one. *Another fan page. This is amazing.* Then he began reading. "Emily Burrows is a twenty-year-old figure skater. She's originally from Nashville but now trains in Denver under coach Mia Spencer."

Thad shook his head. *These people are both interested in us and know a lot. No wonder so many of them are in the stands, cheering.* He stood up and stretched.

Then he turned off his computer, and to his surprise, he was still smiling.

On Saturday night, Thad was flipping through the channels in his television before he realized he didn't know what program he was looking for. *Law and Order isn't on tonight. What am I doing?* He closed his eyes for a long moment and felt them burn through his eyelids and into the tender flesh above his cheekbones. *I am so tired.*

When he reopened his eyes, the news had just come back on after a commercial break, and Thad blinked as he recognized the women on the screen. *Barbara Walters and Jenni Newell. Two people I never thought I'd see in the same room together.* He turned up the volume as fast as he could and was just in time to catch the introduction.

"I'm Barbara Walters, and this is a new edition of The Barbara Walters Special program," the famous journalist said. "Tonight I am interviewing Olympic hopeful Jenni Newell, a figure skater who has been at the top of her sport since she was on the junior circuit."

Barely, Thad thought, rolling his eyes.

"Jenni, thank you for being here today," Barbara continued.

"Thank you," Jenni said, and her grin lit up the screen. "I've wanted to go to the Olympics since I was five. I can't believe it's something that might be within my reach now."

"We have a strong field on the women's side this year," Barbara said. "Kim McGrath and Emily Burrows have been skating as well as you have."

Jenni giggled, and Thad made a face. *She's so fake.*

"We'll see if Kim remains this good," Jenni said. "She's a wonderful skater but has struggled with her consistency."

"What about Emily? I understand that she used to skate at the same Nashville club that you still belong to."

"Yeah, that's right. She moved there from some tiny place in rural Tennessee. But I beat her in all our competitions on the junior circuit and I expect that to continue."

Thad made a face. "What planet is she living on? She hasn't been watching any of Emily's recent programs, that's for sure." In front of him, both Jenni and Barbara laughed, and Thad had to stop himself from throwing the remote at the TV.

"Yeah, what's sports without a little rivalry?" Barbara said.

"Emily and I go way back, and we've always skated against each other," Jenni answered. "Neither of us has ever been above friendly ribbing—hiding each other's skates, stuff like that." She burst into laughter.

Thad winced. *How awful. I can't believe she can laugh about that.*

In front of him, Barbara's face filled with mock horror. "You did not!"

"We were competitive—the whole skating club was. We all wanted to win, and both Emily and I had the skills."

"What did she do? Did she ever withdraw from the competition?"

"No, she usually found her skates in time, but there was that one time at a huge junior competition when she had to borrow a pair of skates from someone else so that she could go out and skate."

"Well, that was brave of her, don't you think?" Barbara asked. "I would have been too mortified to skate after something like that."

Jenni shrugged. "We figure skaters are tough—we can compete through almost anything."

"Who won that competition?"

"I did, by a lot!" Jenni grinned broadly again.

Thad's thumb clamped down hard on his remote control's power button without any command from his brain, and he was glad when his TV screen went dark. *Damn her. She's awful.*

The interview with Jenni was still nagging at Thad when he arrived back at the ice on Monday. He stretched out for longer than usual, waiting for Emily to arrive. When she appeared in his line of sight, he made a beeline for her. "So I don't know if you were watching TV at all on Saturday," he began.

Emily made a face. "Yeah, I saw Jenni's interview. Yuck!"

"I know," Thad said, even as he struggled not to smile at her expression. "Did she really steal your skates before a competition?"

Emily nodded. "I had a great program planned and everything, but without the right skates, I barely landed any of my jumps. I did nothing but cry for a week after that."

Thad swallowed hard. "I'm sorry."

Emily shook her head, and Thad felt anger radiating from her rather than sadness. "I almost quit skating after that. It's impossible to skate your best with a rival like that."

"But instead you moved to Denver."

"That was my parents' idea—they had more sense than I did. I'm glad I'm still skating now, but it took a while to feel that way after that incident. I mean, I had a shot at a medal in that competition and instead I didn't even make the podium."

"That's rough." Thad shook his head. "But I recommend having an extra pair of skates on hand."

Emily smiled. "Oh, I've done that for the last couple of seasons. I'm not expecting Jenni to change her tactics, so I will." She whirled around. "At least now I'm beating her, fair and square."

Thad smiled as she took off toward the ice.

Chapter 6

T had had finished going through his short program twice when Brianna skated over and joined him at the center of the rink. "You looked good today," she said.

"Thanks," Thad answered. *What does she really want? With Trevor I could always tell. I don't know her well enough to say that.*

"What were you thinking about as you skated?"

"Ummm..." Thad's voice got lost in his throat. "Why do you ask?"

"I'm trying to figure out how you think. I'm here to help you skate more consistently, remember?"

Thad took a deep breath as he skated toward the edge of the rink. Brianna followed him. "Umm, I guess when I'm running through my short program, I'm thinking of the next element—the next jump, the next spin, whether it fits in with the music." They got to the side of the ice, and Thad stepped off. "I'm also seeing how my body feels—if I'm tired or how my lungs feel."

Brianna nodded. "At Worlds, what were you thinking about while you were on the ice? Was it all about the technical elements?"

Thad thought about it as he removed his skates. "No, it wasn't." Sweat rolled down his face, and he brushed it off with the back of his hand. "I was thinking about the music and what it portrayed. I was thinking of the breeze off the water in Gloucester, and of the lonely fisherman out at sea."

Brianna smiled. "Not unlike your dad."

"I don't know about that." Thad frowned.

"What do you mean?"

"I didn't even think of that. I was just thinking of the water and my childhood." Thad hauled himself to his feet and began stretching. "Where are you going with all of this?"

"I've been looking at videos of your old programs and I think your best skating has been when you connect with the music or with a character you're trying to portray. Your music can't just be background noise—it has to come from somewhere within you."

Thad thought of the *Four Sea Interludes*, and of *The Flying Dutchman*. "Both those stories are awesome."

"And they mean something to you."

"Yeah, well... growing up on the water, I guess I know where they're coming from."

Brianna smiled. "I want to continue with that. Keep your radio on and find something—a story, a character—that you can relate to. I think that will help you skate your best."

For the next two days in a row, Thad kept his radio on to the classical station as he drove to and from the rink. He also stepped onto the ice for his afternoon workout just as the Avalanche were coming off. He got the usual mix of disdainful looks, but now he noticed that Jack was simply staring past him. *He's watching me, he just doesn't want me to notice,* Thad thought on the second day. He could see Jack's eyes on him, even from his peripheral vision, as he skated away. When he looked at Jack directly, though, the captain looked away. *What's he want from me?* Thad wondered.

Much as he kept an eye out for the Avalanche, though, there was a visitor at the rink whom Thad had not been expecting: Grigoriy Arsenyev. "What's he doing here?" Thad asked Trevor as they met at the center of the ice.

"Visiting skating clubs to see if he wants to train in the U.S." Trevor rolled his eyes. "I wish he'd stay home."

"Why wouldn't he stay in St. Petersburg?"

"Things have been changing a lot in Russia these past few years."

"That's for sure."

"Plenty of Russian skaters and coaches have been coming to the U.S. to get more stability in their training routines. It wouldn't surprise me if that continues."

Thad was stretching out—and also contemplating going back onto the ice for another round of jumps—when Grigoriy came over. Joaquin was stretching out a few feet away, and Brianna was on the ice with a younger skater. Grigoriy gave both Thad and Joaquin a nod, but his eyes were focused more on Thad than on Joaquin.

"Is this where you train?" Grigoriy asked, and his Russian accent whacked Thad's ears.

Thad nodded. "I've skated here for more than a decade."

"I just moved here last year," Joaquin said.

Grigoriy kept his eyes on Thad. "I looked at other skate clubs here in the States. The one in New York, too."

"Where Sebastian skates?" Thad asked.

"Yes. I am thinking of moving to this country."

"New York has a large Russian community."

"That is true."

"So does Russia," Joaquin cracked.

Finally, Grigoriy looked at him. "I'd rather stay in Russia than skate near a *pidor* like you."

Joaquin leapt to his feet and gave him a shove. Grigoriy stumbled backward.

Thad, shocked, jumped up and stood in between them. "Stop," he said, holding out his hand in front of Joaquin's chest. Then he looked back at Grigoriy. "You can't come in here and insult our skaters. Maybe you'd be better off in New York."

"Or staying in Russia," Joaquin mumbled.

Grigoriy was already back on his feet. "I will think about that." He glared at both Thad and Joaquin before taking off.

Thad made sure he was out of the arena before looking back at Joaquin. "What was that about?"

Joaquin made a face.

"What did he call you?"

Joaquin's face twisted even further. "The Russian equivalent of *fag.*" He spat out the word like something hot. "I don't speak Russian but I've skated there enough to know that one word." He shook his head, and his next several words were curses. Then he stormed off, back to the locker room.

Thad watched him go, his heart racing. *I hope Grigoriy goes away and stays away. He's bad news.*

The next day, Grigoriy was nowhere to be seen when Thad arrived back at the ice for practice, *and thank God for that.* Joaquin was not around either, though, and that worried Thad. *Maybe it's too early for Joaquin,* he thought as the clock in the arena clicked to six a.m. *He practices in the afternoon as much as he does in the mornings.*

Four hours later, Thad's muscles ached as he dragged himself into the locker room. *I'm just glad another practice is over. Maybe it'll get quiet around here again and Grigoriy will never come back.*

Thad awoke two mornings later with excitement in his stomach. *Scott is flying in today,* he remembered as he got dressed and headed to the rink. *I've been looking forward to that for weeks.* He was smiling when he got on the ice.

Joaquin arrived an hour later, and this time, his sister Laura was with him. Thad watched him warm up as he went through his own series of jumps and spins. As Joaquin joined Laura back at the boards for some advice, an idea came to him. When his practice was over, he skated to the center of the ice, where Joaquin was practicing a spin. Laura was next to him now instead of at the boards.

Joaquin stopped spinning and gave him a nod.

"My brother is coming to visit for a few days. We were thinking of going out to dinner tomorrow—would you like to join us?"

"Both of us?" Laura asked, looking surprised.

"Yeah, both of you."

Joaquin and Laura looked at each other. "You doing anything after work tomorrow?" Joaquin asked.

"I wasn't planning on it," Laura answered.

"Then let's do this." Joaquin looked at Thad. "Where were you planning on eating?"

"I was thinking of Bastien's Restaurant, probably around seven o'clock."

Joaquin and Laura looked at each other. "I could do that," Laura said.

Joaquin looked back at Thad. "We'll see you there. Thanks for inviting us."

It was louder in Thad's neighborhood as soon as Scott arrived, tumbling out of a cab as Thad got home from his afternoon practice. Thad laughed as he helped his brother carry his suitcase and other bags inside. When their hands were empty, Scott opened his arms and Thad hugged him unreservedly.

"It is so good to see you," Thad said.

"Good to see you too. How have you been holding up?"

"Not bad." Thad took off his coat and pulled open the closet door. Then he held his hand out for Scott's coat.

Scott handed it over and bounced into the living room before the closet door was even closed. Then he flopped down on the couch. "Your furniture is comfortable, even if your place is still a bit Spartan."

"Yeah, I can't skate well if I injure myself sleeping on bad furniture."

Both brothers laughed as Scott dragged his suitcase into the apartment's second bedroom. Then they went into the kitchen and Thad pulled out two large pieces of salmon from the fridge. The fish's orange scales jumped out against the white cutting board Thad put them on.

"Awesome," Scott said as he saw what was for dinner. He produced several small bottles of spices from the paper bag he was carrying. "I brought all of these from Gloucester—I visited Mom and Dad just so that I could get them."

"Great." Thad grinned when he saw his favorite seasonings. "I can almost taste those already."

"I still cook fish a lot too." Scott pulled a bottle of red wine from the bag.

"Me too. I don't make cod much, though."

"Really? I do. I cook it so many different ways that I could eat it a bunch and not even feel like I'm eating the same thing."

"Mom used to do that all the time when we were growing up."

"Yeah, well, we didn't have access to much else. And the cod was fresh from Dad's boat."

"I know, I just..." Thad's voice trailed off as he mixed the sauce in front of him. "I think I got sick of it after a while."

"I can understand that." Scott uncorked the bottle he was holding and pulled two wine glasses from a cabinet.

Thad shook his head. "You're gonna have to drink that by yourself. I can't drink much without feeling it, and I have to be up early tomorrow for practice."

"Come on, Thad, are you going to practice the entire time I'm here?"

"No, of course not. I'm taking tomorrow afternoon and the whole next day off." Still, Thad was sure he felt the chill of the ice, mingled with the heat that was coming from his oven.

"How generous of you."

Soon, both brothers were laughing again as they cooked and ate.

Then Scott asked something of a serious question as his eyes fixed on Thad's face. "When did you stop drinking?"

"When did I start?" Thad replied. "I've always had to be on the ice as early as Dad was out on the water. Can't do that after a few drinks."

Scott shook his head. "Don't tell me you've forgotten the time we went out after you won your first National title?"

"Oh, God." Thad leaned back in his chair and felt the wood dig into his lower back. "I had the worst hangover the next day, and it was all your fault."

"Are you kidding? No one was forcing you."

Thad winced as he leaned forward again and picked up his fork. "That night is one reason I've barely drunk since."

Scott made a show of picking up his wine glass and taking another sip. "Do you miss having a normal life?"

"Can't miss what I never had."

Scott stared at Thad for a moment. "You have a point."

Thad shrugged. "How many people have my talent or the ability to skate full time like I do? I've been to two Olympics and I'm trying to get to a third—not many other people can say that. I don't want to do anything to jeopardize it." He stopped speaking and looked back at his plate. He was still holding his fork, but his food no longer looked as appetizing.

"What's the matter?" Scott asked.

"I just wish more people saw me for the hardworking, good skater that I am. The press always turns it into something bad—I've been called a stiff automaton, and worse."

"Yeah, the press is nasty. You have a lot of fans, though. Didn't you see how many people were in the stands at Nationals and Worlds? A lot of them were there to see you, and a lot of them had signs and banners."

"Yeah, I saw that." Thad shook his head. "Still, I... I don't know."

Scott was the one to lean back in his chair now, and his wine glass was still in his hand. "I know what you mean. The coverage of both Sebastian and Grigoriy is a lot more adoring. You're at least as good a skater as they are, if not better."

Thad nodded.

"I think Joaquin faces some of the same issues you do—lack of press coverage, lack of fair scoring on programs. Even if I also think you're a better skater than he is."

"Yeah, he does struggle with all of that."

"And yet I like his skating—he really pours his heart and soul into it. I've always had a positive impression of him."

"Good," Thad said. "Because I invited him and his sister to dinner tomorrow night."

"Awesome." Scott smiled. "I'm looking forward to that already."

Joaquin and Laura were just arriving at Bastien's Restaurant as Thad and Scott walked to the front door of the quaint Italian place. "This is my brother, Scott," Thad said as the smell of garlic and freshly baked bread met his nose. "This is Joaquin Sanchez and his sister and coach, Laura."

"Good to meet you," Scott said with a grin.

Laura nodded. "Thanks for the invitation. We don't get out enough."

"Speak for yourself," Joaquin teased, giving his sister a whack.

"If you disagree with me, you should spend more time on the ice," Laura answered, rolling her eyes.

"Oh, I practice plenty." Joaquin looked around as they were led to their seats. "This is a nice place."

"Ever been here?" Thad asked.

Both Joaquin and Laura shook their heads. Thad was sure Laura wanted to say something, but she held her tongue as they got seated.

Thad took off his light jacket and draped it over the back of his chair as he sat. *It's warm in here,* he thought.

"Maybe we'll have more time for this kind of stuff after I turn professional," Joaquin said, and when Thad looked over at him, he was looking at Laura.

Laura nodded. "That would be nice."

"Are you planning on going pro?" Thad asked. Disappointment knotted his stomach. "I was hoping to continue skating with you."

"Well, that's very kind of you." Joaquin and Laura looked at each other for another moment. Then Joaquin looked back at Thad. "We've been discussing it."

"Would you do that instead of going to the Olympics?"

"That's what we're trying to figure out." Joaquin stopped talking as the waiter came over and handed them menus.

"I'm trying for the Olympics," Thad said as he felt the menu in his hand, heavier than he had been expecting.

"If I were in your position, I would too," Joaquin said as Laura lifted her water glass. "You're more of the establishment than I am."

Thad looked around the restaurant as he collected his thoughts. "That doesn't mean it's easy."

"No, I think we'd have to be more like Sebastian or Grigoriy for it to be *easy.*" Joaquin shook his head and opened his menu.

"Even if both of you skate better than them," Scott said. "Or better than Sebastian, anyway. Grigoriy is becoming one of the top skaters."

Laura nodded. "The Russians have always been amazing. It's their ballet background, and the fact that the Soviet system provided everything for them."

"That's been changing, though," Thad said. "I think that's why Grigoriy was looking to train here in the U.S."

Laura nodded. "I'll bet. But Sebastian is right in his own way—the quad is the future of figure skating."

"He has to actually land it first," Joaquin mumbled. His face was still pointing downward, toward his menu.

Thad took a long, deep breath as he tried to answer that. His napkin's smooth cloth rubbed against his fingers as he played with it.

"The sport is changing," Laura said into the silence. "Toward the kind of athleticism that Sebastian embodies. And the quad is part of that."

"Athletes always push the boundaries," Scott added. "It's not a bad thing."

"It is if it comes at the expense of everything else that skating is known for," Thad answered. "Sometimes I feel like all anyone cares about is Sebastian's quad—that if he lands it, he'll win, no matter what his spins and footwork look like, or anything else."

"For real," Joaquin agreed. "It's one reason I've been thinking of just going pro. Who knows what the sport will look like by the time we get to the Olympics?"

"The offers from Stars on Ice and other places have been nice too," Laura said.

Joaquin looked over at Thad. "You've been making money from skating for a while now—people know who you are and respect you. People are just starting to figure out who I am. It may be worth taking advantage of that."

"Well, I'd have to see some of your shows if you went that way," Scott said. "I've been enjoying watching you perform."

"Thanks," Joaquin answered, and his smile was genuine.

When the waiter returned, Thad ordered one of the restaurant's pasta dishes with tomatoes and other vegetables. Scott ordered the steak and potatoes, and Joaquin and Laura ordered fish dishes.

When the waiter left again, Laura turned to Thad and Scott. "Several times now during competitions, the commentators have mentioned that your father was a commercial fisherman. It's kind of amusing that we ordered the fish and you didn't."

"We cook plenty of fish at home," Thad said.

Scott glanced at him before looking back at Laura. "Yeah, I think both of us ended up ordering stuff we don't cook ourselves."

"You cook meat plenty," Thad said.

"Not steak though. And I never seem to get the potatoes right."

"What are you talking about? Your mashed potatoes are good."

"Those are easy." Scott leaned back in his chair. "These potatoes looked more like French fries—I never get those right."

When the meal was over and the group was leaving the restaurant, Scott dropped back to talk to Laura as Thad and Joaquin left first. "Have you heard much about Grigoriy since his visit here?" Thad asked.

Joaquin shook his head. "The less, the better, as far as I'm concerned."

"Me too."

"But Laura made some calls to her skating friends, especially the ones in New York. They said it looks like he'll end up there."

"Good." Thad smiled. "Let Sebastian handle him."

Joaquin glanced back at Scott and Laura. "Your brother is definitely a guy's guy."

Thad laughed. "Yeah, he was the hockey player growing up. He looked out for me but made sure I got in there with all the hockey players and their sticks. It's one reason why Jack and the rest of the Avalanche don't bother me much."

"You're lucky. It's always gotten under my skin."

Thad thought of Grigoriy and his insults. "I can understand that."

A few minutes later, Scott eyed Thad as they got back into his car. "I never get to meet any of your friends."

"That's because I rarely get to have friends. Trevor keeps a close eye on me and my social life. Same with the other skaters he coaches."

"Is that normal?"

Thad was quiet for a few minutes as he thought about it. "I don't know. Trevor's been my coach since I was ten. I don't know anything else."

Scott made a face.

"I never even thought much of it. I've always just wanted to skate—and besides, we've gotten results. So many of Trevor's skaters have made it to Nationals, Worlds, and the Olympics."

"I know. He has a great reputation that way—but also a reputation as an ascetic."

"An ascetic?" Thad repeated. "What does that mean?" His eyebrows came together as he glanced up at the bright green street signs above them.

"All work and no play."

"Yeah, that's true."

"Well, if you ever get tired of it, you can always go pro like Joaquin."

Thad bit his lip until it hurt. "I kind of wish he would stay amateur for a little longer and go to the Olympics. I mean, it's only next year."

"Yeah, me too." Scott stared out the window as Thad drove the rest of the way home. "I'm glad you've decided to try again. But I think you've got Dad's stubbornness."

Thad's teeth clenched. "What do you mean?"

"You decided to be a figure skater when you were five, and that was it—no one could tell you otherwise."

Thad laughed. "Yeah, I saw people skating at the rink and that was it. I needed to jump and spin just like they were."

"Mom and Dad couldn't believe how hard you were willing to work to make it happen."

"It was fun, and I wanted it badly."

"Yeah, I know." Scott was silent as he stared out the window again.

"What?" Thad asked a minute later.

Scott shrugged. "None of us could have predicted that you'd go this far—the Olympics three times? It's incredible."

"I haven't made it a third time yet."

"You will. I have confidence in you. Ignore the press. It's your life. Do what you want with it."

"That's what Trevor says."

"He's right."

Thad took a deep breath as he pulled into his driveway. "Some days, though, it just gets to me."

"You're allowed to feel that way. The press is obnoxious. But you're better than they are."

Finally, Thad managed a smile. "Thanks."

Chapter 7

T had's house felt emptier after Scott left. The next morning, nothing but silence greeted his ears when he shut off his alarm. *Damn,* he thought as his body refused to move. *I never have trouble getting out of bed.* Still, it was another few minutes before he managed to get up. He was still dragging all the way out to the car and spent the whole ride to the rink yawning.

"Oh boy," Trevor said when he saw Thad moving sluggishly around the ice.

"This is not one of my good days." Thad winced. "Every part of my body hurts."

"Well, in that case I think it would help to run through a complete program, with all your jumps and everything."

"Ooohhh," Thad groaned.

"It's to build your strength, Thad," Trevor said, as if it were obvious.

Next to him, Brianna nodded. "We need to find the tools for you to skate consistently. Knowing you can do it when you're not feeling your best will give you that confidence."

"You've already had times when you've gone onto the ice in competition not feeling your best," Trevor added.

"Yeah, like when I had the flu at my first Olympics." Thad felt like melting into the ice.

"Lucky you were only an alternate then, right?" Trevor smiled.

Thad did not smile back. "Why can no one forget that? I still had to skate after Gabriel Farber withdrew. He was even sicker than I was."

Trevor's smile disappeared. "You're in a fine mood today."

Thad shrugged and looked away.

"Come on, let's do this. I'll put on the music for *Goodfellas*."

"Think about the music while you're skating," Brianna added. "Why did you choose this piece? What do you bring to the program that's uniquely you?"

The first strains of the music got Thad's body moving more than he could have expected. Still, by the end of the day, he headed home feeling drained and unfocused. *That second workout was overkill,* he thought as he got back into his car. *I wish Trevor had given me a break, just once.*

He drove around for a while before realizing that he did not want to go home. Instead, he landed at a nearby café and picked at a salad before getting down a few bites. *At least eat the chicken,* he told himself. *You need the protein.* But the chicken tasted like cardboard, and Thad managed only one or two more bites. He finished the greens before dumping the container in the trash and heading for the door.

He still drove through downtown instead of taking the quicker way home. *What is the matter with you?* he asked himself as the cool mountain air flowed through his window. *You have to get up early tomorrow.* He thought of how hard Trevor had been pushing him and he made a face. *Maybe I'll sleep in.* But he also thought of Brianna and her admonition to dig deep into the music for his programs. *Maybe I'll go home and watch* Goodfellas *again.*

He was about to turn his car around when he felt the womp-womp-womp of a heavy bass. *Oh yeah, a nightclub,* he thought as he caught sight of the tan, industrial-looking building on his left. *I've heard of this place.* He was about to drive past it when he saw someone stumble out of the building, past the bouncers and into the street. Thad pressed his foot on his brake. *That guy's gonna get hurt if he stumbles out into the street.*

Then Thad recognized the stumbling figure. *Oh, damn, that's Joaquin!* He pulled over and parked. By the time he got out, Joaquin had crossed the street and was doubled over, his hands resting on his knees. For a moment, Thad was sure he was going to throw up. He stopped walking. But Joaquin just stayed there, unmoving. Thad took a deep breath and kept walking. "Joaquin!"

Joaquin jumped.

"Are you okay? If you need to puke, go ahead."

"Yeah, that might make me feel better." Joaquin shook his head, but he stayed upright.

"Are you okay?"

"Yes. No."

Thad suppressed a snort. *How do I even respond to that?* he wondered as a few drops of rain hit his face. He looked up at the passing clouds until he was sure it would only be a few drops. Then he looked back at Joaquin. "What's bothering you?"

"The training, Thad. I'm sick of it."

"Yeah, my legs are killing me and I just want to sleep."

Joaquin stared at him. "I never thought I'd hear that from you. The press always paints you as such a workaholic."

"Maybe we both need a rest." *That's why I almost retired.* "Not that you can ever trust what you read in the papers." Thad looked across the street, back at the club. "At least you're having a social life. I ate dinner alone."

Joaquin shook his head, and for the first time, Thad saw tears in his eyes. "Did you know people in there recognized me? For the first time, people want my autograph."

"And you're unhappy about that?" Thad felt dizzy with surprise.

Joaquin's chest heaved a couple of times. "It's a lot to take in, Thad. I went from being a nobody in the skating world to suddenly being on the top."

Thad nodded. "I remember when that happened to me. But now I also want another shot at the Olympics. If you still want to go pro, maybe that's the best path."

Joaquin looked back at the club as a couple of people stumbled out.

Thad watched him, wondering what he was thinking. There was a silence. "What do you want out of all of this, Joaquin?"

"Laura keeps asking me that too. I can't even tell what she thinks I should say—she keeps telling me I'm the one who has to make a decision."

"She's right."

Joaquin made a face. "And here I thought you were going to help me."

Thad smiled. "What did you dream of doing the first time you skated?"

"Jumping. A big triple jump. I didn't even know the difference between a Lutz and a toe loop. I just wanted to do it all." Joaquin's words came faster now.

"And when you landed your first jump, what did you dream of?"

"Going to the Olympics."

"Do you still want that?"

Joaquin swallowed and looked at the ground. A second later, his tears overflowed. "Yes," he whispered. "That's why I called Brianna for the extra coaching. I want to skate on Olympic ice. I want to fly and land all my triple jumps."

"Me too," Thad said. *That's* why I'm still training."

Joaquin swiped at his tears with the back of his hand. "I just wish I had your temperament, the ability to work like you do."

Thad managed another smile. "It's not all it's cracked up to be. Sometimes I wish I had your flair, your temper."

"Two things I would never wish on anyone." Joaquin was almost smiling now too.

"Then let's both bring our respective gifts to the ice."

Joaquin nodded. "I'll remember that when I practice."

Thad woke up the next morning with a lump of jealousy in the pit of his stomach. *Joaquin has more of a social life than I do.* The words clattered through his brain as he drove to the rink. Then Trevor's voice rang through his brain. *You train harder than he does, Thad. You have a better shot at the gold medal.*

Do I? Thad wondered. *We only have seven minutes on Olympic ice. Anything can happen. Plenty has happened to me at the Olympics. And other big competitions.* Thad struggled to put Nationals out of his mind as he went inside.

Trevor and Mia were already in the stands, and Thad looked around for Emily. The arena was empty except for their coaches, however, and disappointment ate at Thad's stomach. *Maybe she's in the locker room,* he thought as he headed to get into his own workout gear.

The men's locker room was as silent as the rest of the arena had been. The fluorescent lights turned on as Thad got inside. *First one here,* he thought as the motion-activated lights banished the shadows around him. *At least the lights aren't flickering again.*

The room's silence hit Thad's ears, and after a moment, his shoulders bent with the weight of it. *Always quiet, always alone.* He got changed as quickly as he could and slammed his locker closed.

Emily was out on the ice by the time Thad got back there. Finally, he smiled. She glanced up at their coaches before smiling back. Thad looked back at the seats in the arena and realized that both Trevor and Mia had come down to the boards. Trevor gestured for Thad to come over, and Thad was gliding over to him before he thought twice.

Automaton. The word flashed through his mind again, and Thad struggled to keep a straight face. *Damn it,* he thought. Nearby, Mia moved off to another section of the arena so that she could give Emily instructions without interfering with what Trevor was saying. Thad looked back at his coach and nodded as Trevor talked about warmups and jumps.

When he was done speaking, Trevor took a deep breath. "How are you feeling? Better than yesterday?"

"A little." *That should have been your first question.*

"Good." Trevor tossed his head at the ice. "Now go skate."

Thad took off again, but his mind was elsewhere. It was not until he had finished his workout that he managed to get a hold of Emily, who was also leaving the ice. "Hi," he said as he pulled on his skate guards.

"Hi," Emily answered. "How was your brother's visit?"

"Great, though I never thought the house was quiet until he came and left."

Emily laughed. "What else is family for?"

Amusement swept through Thad. "Do you want to meet up for dinner at some point?"

Emily looked surprised. Then she smiled. "Yeah, that would be nice."

"When's good?"

Emily thought about it for a second. "Ummm," she said. Then she shook her head. "What am I saying? It's not like I have much of a life outside the rink."

Thad snickered, even as he thought of Joaquin stumbling out of the club late at night and his own jealousy. "We have to fix that."

"Yes, we do," Emily said crisply. "Do you want to go out to eat?"

"Yeah, let's start with that."

Three days later, Thad was putting on his skates just as the hockey players were getting off the ice. Emily was also coming toward him, ready to warm up, and both Trevor and Mia were higher up in the stands. A number of junior skaters were also nearby, waiting for ice time. When Thad looked back at the rink, though, all he saw were a jumble of hockey sticks and skates.

"Alright, everyone, off the ice. Time for the figure skaters," called the Avalanche's head coach, Michael Perry.

Thad was sure he heard an edge of sarcasm in Michael's voice, and he clenched his teeth. Many of the hockey players in front of him were getting off the ice, though, so Thad took a deep breath and decided to ignore Michael.

Most of the players had gotten off the ice by the time Thad stepped on. *This is my ice now,* he thought. Then Jack Wallace stopped right in front of him. The large capital "C" on Jack's jersey stood out in Thad's peripheral vision as he stared at Jack straight in the face.

"Think this is your ice, Mr. World Medalist?" Jack challenged. His voice rang out over the ice, and the Avalanche players around them stopped to watch.

"I know it's my ice," Thad answered quietly.

"It's too bad I can't even call you World champion."

"I should have won, we both know that."

"Yeah, too bad some Russian upstart stole your medal, huh?"

The hockey players around them snickered. Thad didn't need to move his eyes from Jack's face to see both Emily and Joaquin just off the ice. Joaquin in particular was cringing. Thad continued staring at Jack. Then he shrugged. "Get off the ice, Captain. Your time's up."

Jack smiled, but the expression was as cold as the ice around them. "We'll see about that. Think you can outskate me?"

"Yes, I do." Thad was smiling now. *I love a challenge.* He glided across the ice with barely a twitch of his muscles.

Jack's eyebrows went up in surprise. Then he dove after Thad. Thad swirled around him gracefully, and Jack dove into empty space. Jack tried again, with the same result. Then Thad took off across the ice, skating as fast as he could. Jack raced after him, but by the time Thad reached the boards on the other side of the ice, he was way ahead of Jack and not at all winded.

Thad turned around and glided past Jack again. This time, Jack raised his hockey stick. When he swung it, Thad leaned back on his skates. His spread eagle carried him around the ice until he reached the middle of the rink. Jack came after him again, swinging his stick low as if Thad's skates were a puck.

Without even thinking about it, Thad went into his footwork routine from his long program at Worlds. *Flying Dutchman for the win.* Jack's hockey stick never touched Thad's skates as the two men swirled around the ice. Thad was laughing by the time Jack finally pulled away from him. Then he skated a few feet away and tossed off a clean triple Lutz. By now, the figure skaters around the arena were laughing and hollering. Even the coaches were cheering Thad on. The noise reached the arena's ceiling and bounced off the ice.

The Avalanche players were shaking their heads as Jack got off the ice, and Thad was sure at least a few of them were smirking. He waited until the team had disappeared into the locker room before calmly starting his warmup.

Joaquin skated over to him and laughed. "That was awesome."

Thad laughed too. "Even if you looked a bit nervous as the whole thing started."

"Damn straight I was. Hockey players can be brutal. Doesn't your brother still play?"

Thad nodded. "I think he's the only hockey player in North America that respects figure skaters."

"Maybe that will change after today," Emily said as she skated up to them.

Thad and Joaquin shook their heads at the same time. "No way," Joaquin said.

"I wish I could disagree," Thad said, but he was smiling. Then he laughed. "Well, the Avalanche will always look sideways at me, but that was fun anyway."

Two nights later, Thad sat across from Emily at Cucina Colore, an Italian restaurant he had not eaten at in years. The waitress lit the table's small candle as they got seated, and Thad inhaled the match's burning smell. He smiled as Emily looked all around. "Ever been here?"

Emily shook her head. "But it reminds me of this place my family used to eat at when I was growing up—a tiny little place that closed when I was eight or nine. I used to beg my parents to go there."

"Where was this?"

"Pulaski, Tennessee, where I'm from originally."

"Your parents still live there?"

"No, we moved to Nashville when I was eleven."

"Does anyone else in your family skate?"

"My sister does. She's fourteen and will probably go to Nationals in the next year or two."

"That'd be great."

Emily nodded as the waitress returned. She ordered water to drink and a salad as her main course.

Thad thought of how much Scott and Laura had eaten as he ordered the veal. "Is that all you're having?" he asked after the waitress had left.

"Yeah," Emily said, drawing the word out.

"What's going on?"

"Mia has started weighing me more often." Emily's voice dropped as she spoke. She glanced around the restaurant as if she didn't want to be overheard.

"Trevor hasn't done that to me in a while." Thad frowned, and embarrassment roiled his stomach.

"Yeah, well…" Emily played with her silverware. "I missed a few jumps in practice, and…" She shrugged.

"That's what practice is for. You're *supposed* to fall sometimes."

"Tell Mia that." Emily's eyes flashed with tears.

Thad swallowed hard. "What we do for our skating."

Emily shook her head and wiped her eyes. "I was finally skating better and now this. I'm not sure I can do it much longer."

Thad reached out and took her hand. Her skin was smooth under his fingers. "I know you can."

"Thanks." Emily sniffled.

Thad tried to change the subject. "So tell me about that restaurant in Pulaski that you liked."

Emily took a deep breath. "I liked their pizzas. They had a brick oven just outside the kitchen. We always used to try to get a seat near there so that we could watch the cooks use it."

Thad smiled and was sure he could smell the tomato sauce and mozzarella. "That sounds like fun."

"It was. My brother lives a few blocks from my parents now—he said the owner opened a restaurant near them. They eat there a bunch and I'm always jealous."

"Your sister doesn't go with them?"

"Nah, she's living with her coach in Connecticut."

"Skating." Thad shook his head.

"I hear you moved in with Trevor a few years after he became your coach."

Thad nodded. "Yeah, he's been coaching me since I was ten. He was coaching in Philly, then Boston, then here." He looked up as the waitress arrived with their food. It was not until she left that he spoke again. "Trevor is as much of a workaholic as Mia sounds like."

Emily nodded. "That's certainly true."

"Your skating has gotten a lot better since you've started working with Mia, though."

"I know. It's why I put up with her more difficult stuff. I mean, I'm no Kim McGrath, but..." Emily's voice trailed off again, and she took a bite of her salad.

"But you do have more discipline than she does."

"Yeah, I think this is the longest stretch of consistent training I've seen her go through. I wonder if she'll be able to keep this up through the Olympics."

"I hope so," Thad admitted. "When she's on, she's amazing. I'd love to see her skate on Olympic ice."

"I want to make it there myself."

"I do too. But I also want to skate well while I'm there." *It's not worth the work to get there if I'm just going to crash and burn like I did the last two times.* Frustration and anger rose in Thad as fast as a summer storm. He took a deep breath and looked around the restaurant until he had composed himself. Emily looked calmer by the time Thad looked back at her, and Thad tried to sync himself with that cooler energy.

Emily was smiling by the time they left the restaurant. "That was fun."

"Indeed," Thad answered. "We'll have to do it again."

Emily nodded. "I'd like that."

"Then let's see if we can find another time."

Still, Thad was surprised when Emily invited him to her house a few days later. "How about dinner on Saturday?" she asked.

"I'm fine with that," Thad answered.

"You don't have other plans?"

"Skating," Thad said with a shrug.

Emily laughed, and the sound filled Thad with happiness. "Tell me about it. But I'll see you on Saturday."

"That you will."

It was getting dark when Thad drove over to Emily's place on Saturday night. The sun had already disappeared behind the mountains, but an orange glow still spread across the sky. When he found her address, it was a three-story house in a residential neighborhood. *Does she have the whole place to herself?* Thad wondered as he rang the bell. It wasn't until the doorbell's chimes were ringing that he saw a tiny sign next to the bell that read, "Number 1."

Emily pulled the door open a minute later and grinned. "Come in." She held the door open.

Thad went inside and looked around. "I've never been inside any of the houses around here."

"The owners live on the third floor. Each floor is a different apartment."

Thad nodded as he looked at her. She was wearing black tights and a large, bright sweater. *She looks great,* he thought. *Mia needs to lay off her and the constant weigh-ins.*

"Come on, let's go into the kitchen. I have a chicken cooking."

Thad followed her, and the scent of something wonderful hit his nose. "Ooh, that smells good."

"It's my grandmother's recipe. My mother used to make it all the time when I was growing up."

"You miss your family?"

"Yeah," Emily said slowly as she opened the oven door and examined the chicken inside.

Thad smirked. "That wasn't the most enthusiastic answer."

Emily closed the oven and faced him. "It's a tough question. Living with them was easier in a lot of ways—I didn't have to plan my own meals or get myself to the rink, but as my training got more intense, it took away from the rest of the family and no one ever let me forget it."

Thad winced. "Even with your sister skating too?"

"She's a few years younger, so we were always on a different schedule. My brother is into sports too, but he didn't get driven everywhere because my mom was too busy taking me to the rink."

"She couldn't drop you off and drive him somewhere else?"

"He always had to be on the other side of town at the same time."

Thad rubbed his chin. "My brother was into sports too and somehow it always worked out."

"Mine didn't play any of the winter sports—it was always soccer or basketball or whatever. Wasn't your brother a hockey player? Wasn't your mom driving you to the same rink?"

"Yeah, but not always at the same time. I went out of my way to sign up for the strange practice times because they were cheaper."

Emily nodded and opened the oven again. "The expenses ate at my parents too. My brother ended up working to help pay for everything."

"It was tough on my family too," Thad acknowledged. "My mom did a lot of random work to make ends meet, whether it was knitting in the gas line or driving other skaters whose parents paid her for it."

"Gas line?" Emily asked as she went to set the table.

Thad smiled at the memory. "Yeah, you're six years younger than I am, so maybe you don't remember, but it was the '70s. Gas was scarce. We had to wait in long lines at the pumps."

"That sounds awful."

"I never felt it, somehow. My mom always made light of it." Thad helped Emily arrange glasses and silverware.

"And your brother seems gracious in how your career took off over his own athletic ambitions." Emily shook her head. "I wish it had been that smooth for me."

"Your family seems supportive now."

"Yeah, they are." Emily nodded as she thought about it. "Moving to Denver was good that way. My sister is also out of the house, so it's not as crazy, and my skating has improved. Things have been getting better overall."

"That's good."

Emily nodded. "What about your dad?"

Thad tensed. "What about him?"

"You didn't say whether he was supportive of your skating."

She's observant, Thad thought. "I guess he is now, but there was this one time when I was seven that there was a commotion outside the house. This was up in Gloucester, before I moved here. My dad went outside to see what the fuss was about, and I followed him. A bunch of the neighborhood boys were running away, but they'd left a pink tutu on the front stoop for us to find. There was a note pinned to it—with my name on it."

"Oh, my God." Emily shook her head. "What did you do?"

"My dad threw it in the garbage. But he couldn't look at me for a week after that. I thought I'd done something wrong." Thad looked down at the floor.

"Did he ever go after those boys?"

"I don't think so. But he did ask me if I'd be willing to give up skating and go back to hockey." Thad's cheeks burned with shame at the memory.

"What did you say?" Emily's voice was softer than normal.

"I said no. What else could I say?"

Emily smiled.

"It wasn't until I started winning competitions that he started coming around to his son being a figure skater."

"That's rough." Emily bit her lip as she pulled a bottle of sparkling water from the fridge.

"There's still a part of me that expects to see that pink tutu every time I go to back to Gloucester."

"Have you?"

"No." Thad shook his head. "My dad threw it out. I'm sure it's been sitting in some landfill for the two decades."

"That sounds like a good place for it."

Thad's stomach was growling by the time Emily finished making a salad and removed the chicken from the oven. *I hope she eats more than the salad,* he thought, and he was relieved when she took a few bites of chicken. "This is good," he said, after he had eaten a few bites himself.

"Surprised?" Emily asked, but she looked amused.

"I shouldn't be. I cook okay myself, but I think my family is surprised by that."

"Yeah, we have to eat somehow, and we can't go out all the time." Emily looked out the window. "Do you ever wish we could do normal stuff, like go out more often, and not just for dinner?"

"You don't think we could?"

Emily took another bite of her salad as she thought about it. "It's never felt that way. I've always been so busy skating that it doesn't leave much time for anything else."

Thad nodded. "Me too."

Emily smiled. "It'll be different when we have Olympic medals hanging around our necks."

Thad wished he could smile back, but his stomach was suddenly churning. "I hope that happens. If I crash out like I did at the last Olympics, I'm not sure I could handle it."

"I don't think you will. You have been working so hard, and you've changed your routines, bringing Brianna in and everything."

Thad swallowed. "But people like Sebastian Adler are already married with a kid. It makes me wonder what I'm doing wrong."

"Nothing. He married young. He's still only twenty-four."

Emily was adamant again, and Thad wanted to listen to her. He dragged his eyes back to her face.

"Sebastian's wife's is older and was probably ready to settle down. He's just in a different situation."

Thad nodded. He wished he could say something, but his throat closed around his words.

Emily eyed Thad for another moment. "You're still thinking of the stupid press coverage you've gotten!"

"Yeah."

"Forget about that. You skate better than Sebastian. Maybe his wife and kid are distracting him."

This time, Thad's smile felt somewhat genuine.

They had finished eating when a car, blasting music, went by the house. Thad was sure it stopped in front of the house for a few extra seconds, and the beat of the bass coursed through his veins.

Emily rolled her eyes. "That happens every once in a while, more on the weekends. The worst is when it's in the middle of the night and it wakes me up."

Thad went to the window and lifted the shade. There, the noise hit him even harder. He winced and leaned back as Emily joined him at the window. A car in front of the house was bouncing in time with the music. A minute later, it drove off, its engine roaring. Thad had to wait several seconds before he was sure he could hear. He made a face and looked outside again. Then his heart stopped.

"What's the matter?" Emily asked.

It took Thad a moment to realize that his jaw had dropped. "Trevor is sitting in his car, across the street."

"What?" Emily peered out the window.

"The dark Chevy, right across the street."

It took another second for Emily to see Trevor, but when she did, shock coursed off her in the same waves that were moving through Thad's body. "Is he watching us?"

"Sure looks that way."

A second later, Trevor gunned his engine and the car sped down the road.

"Guess he saw us." Thad shook his head and dropped the shade. He tried to get his tongue to work again, but he was too stunned.

"I can't believe it," Emily said. "Doesn't he see enough of us at the rink? What's he think we're going to do? Pull a muscle?"

Thad swallowed and forced his tongue to work. "I don't know—but he needs to get a life of his own."

Chapter 8

The next morning, Thad woke up ready to get to the ice. *How different from after Worlds,* he thought as he drove to the arena. The rink was silent when Thad arrived. He stood at the boards for a moment, looking around. *No Trevor. That's not like him.* He went to the locker room to change and was already on the ice with Brianna when Trevor came skating out toward him.

"Let's start with warmups," Trevor began. His voice was normal, as if nothing had happened the previous night.

"Trevor," Thad interrupted quietly.

"After warmups, I want to work on a few of your jumps," Trevor continued, as if he hadn't heard him.

"Trevor," Thad said, louder this time.

Trevor looked away.

"What were you doing outside Emily's place last night?" Thad saw Brianna frown out the corner of his eye. *Good,* he thought. *If she's uncomfortable too, that's further proof that Trevor's out of line.* "Were you following me?"

"Of course not." Trevor continued to stare at the ice.

Thad felt the chill from both him and the rink. "Then what were you doing there?"

"Nothing."

"You just sit out in front of her house for kicks?"

"Of course not. I was hoping Mia was there."

"Are you lying to me?"

"What do you want from me, Thad?"

Thad's heart raced in his chest, and his face was burning. "You were watching us, weren't you?"

"Of course I was keeping an eye on you. We're not far out from the Olympics. I don't want you getting distracted."

Thad burst into sarcastic laughter. "The Olympics are eight months away. I'm allowed to have dinner with a friend."

Trevor shook his head. "You need to maintain your focus."

"Give me a break. All the other skaters have some outlet to relax."

"Like Joaquin going out to clubs until he drops? He's not going to make the podium like that, if he even makes the Olympics."

"He's been more focused at practice—maybe you should take notice." Thad's voice was rising. He was shocked by his own anger, *but I can't even stop it.*

Trevor shrugged. "Maybe I haven't noticed because it isn't happening. You're different—your work ethic could take you to the Olympics if you let it."

"Yeah, it's all work and nothing else, right? Automaton, just like the press says."

Finally, Trevor met Thad's gaze, and it was in the form of a glare. "I told you not to read what the press says about you."

Thad glared back at him, and his anger felt hotter than a summer day. "This isn't about me anymore, Trevor, it's about you. You shouldn't have been following me and waiting outside Emily's house. It's too weird. Don't you have a life of your own?"

"My life is here at the rink, Thad, you know that." Trevor began skating off the ice.

Thad followed him. "What would Anne say about that?"

"She supports me to the fullest—and she supports you too. Have you forgotten that?" Trevor glared at his pupil again.

"I haven't. Have you? Did you even make it home last night?"

Trevor shook his head and skated the rest of the way off the ice. "This conversation is over."

Thad wished he could punch something. *That solved nothing,* he thought. *I'm not going to be able to leave the house from now on without Trevor following me.* He skated back toward the center of the ice and began warming up.

Nearby, Brianna was still frowning. "Come on, let's get through a workout. Let's see if you can control your emotions enough to do this."

As if on cue, anger and frustration exploded through Thad like a volcano. Any tightness and fatigue that had chased him earlier in the week was gone as he attacked one jump after another. He landed thirty jumps cleanly, with only two falls, before he felt like his heart rate and breathing were finally slowing down.

It's about time, he thought as a modicum of calm began to creep into his bones. *Even if I wish some of my competitions were that clean.* He skated toward the boards, and was already thinking of his stretching routine, before he caught sight of Joaquin on the other side of the ice.

A second later, Joaquin skated over and smiled as they both stepped off the ice. "Great practice. I haven't seen that kind of energy in you in a while."

Thad rolled his eyes. "I was fighting with Trevor."

"Yeah, I heard. You weren't the only ones here early." Joaquin swallowed and looked down for a moment. When he looked back at Thad, his eyes were serious. "Sometimes that passion can be a good thing, especially if you translate it well on to the ice."

"Only if you don't become distracted and fall along the way." Thad's amused smile lit up his face as he took his skates off.

"You didn't during practice, did you?" Joaquin started pulling his skates off too. "All the best skaters manage to project that kind of emotion."

Thad thought about it. "A lot of them are extroverts, though. I'm the opposite. I can't really play the showman."

"You've been able to do it plenty," Joaquin said with a smile. "And with jumps like what you showed just now..." He tossed his head toward the ice. "You should be doing that more in competition, not less."

It was silent for the next several days that Thad practiced. He and Trevor barely spoke to each other, and for the first time that Thad could remember, he glared at his coach every time he looked at him. All through it, he was glad for Brianna's calm presence, and for her pointers at times when he thought everything was going to fall apart.

At the end of that week, Thad closed his eyes for a few seconds as he glided around the ice. His eyes burned, and the few seconds of darkness against his eyelids did little to assuage that. *Eight months until the Olympics,* he thought. *I hope I can make it that long.*

That afternoon, he pulled himself off the ice just as the Avalanche players were getting on. Most of them sent amused looks in his direction, but Jack stared past him as if he wasn't there. *That suits me,* Thad thought. He got off the ice and began removing his skates. When he looked back at the ice, Jack was watching him.

Thad raised his eyebrows. Jack's face turned red. Then he looked away and skated off to the other side of the rink.

Joaquin sat next to Thad and began taking his own skates off. "He doesn't know what to do with you," he said, pointing his chin in Jack's direction. His amused look turned into a smile.

Thad shrugged. "At least he's leaving me alone."

"I'll bet he's getting hell in the locker room from the other players, though. You may be in for round two at some point."

"I'll keep an eye out."

A little while later, Thad dragged himself home and promptly landed in bed for a nap. Only the ringing of the phone woke him up two hours later. Thad groaned and pulled himself out of bed. Not one part of his body felt like moving, and each of his muscles felt sluggish. Somehow, he reached the phone before the call went to his answering machine.

"Hello?" he said into the receiver.

"Ah, Thad, I wondered if you would pick up," Rosie said on the other end.

"Hi, Mom." *I'm not sure I feel like talking, though.*

"Your father's on, too," Rosie said.

"Yeah, I'm upstairs," James said.

Thad pictured his father in his parents' bedroom, the phone pressed to his ear. "What's going on?" he asked.

"We haven't heard from you recently," Rosie said. "How's your training going?"

"It's going." Thad sank into the nearest chair, even as he had to stretch out the phone's long cord to do it.

"How's the extra training with Brianna going?"

"It's been helpful." Thad was glad to be honest about that, at least. "She balances out Trevor's moods."

"How is Trevor doing?" Rosie asked. "We haven't heard from him in a while either."

Thad shuddered, and his mind went blank. There was a long moment of silence as he tried to figure out what to say.

"You still there, Thad?" his mother asked a minute later.

"Yeah, I'm still here."

"Awfully quiet today," James said.

I must get that from somewhere, Thad thought. "Yeah, I... don't have much to say." *I don't want to talk about Trevor. Please don't ask again.*

"Well, how's Trevor doing?" Rosie asked. "He usually calls occasionally, and we haven't heard from him."

Thad struggled against the anger that was building within him again. "I don't know. We haven't been speaking much."

"What?" Both James and Rosie spoke at the same time now.

"Aren't you still skating?" Rosie asked.

"Of course I am. I want to make the Olympics."

"How do you plan on doing that without a main coach?" James asked.

"He's still coaching me. But Brianna's been picking up a lot of the slack." Thad tried to get the image of Trevor sitting in his car out of his mind and failed. He inhaled a breath and wished he could smell more than the stuffy air in his apartment.

"What's going on, Thad?" Rosie said. "This isn't like you. Or like Trevor."

"Nothing," Thad mumbled.

"I know *that's* not true," Rosie said. "Talk to us, Thad."

Thad sighed. Then he told his parents about seeing Trevor outside Emily's house. "It was just strange. And he took off when he us saw us looking back at him."

"And he won't acknowledge anything?" Rosie asked.

"No," Thad answered. "I don't even know what to make of it."

"Be direct with him," James said. "Clear the air."

I knew he would say that, Thad thought. "I don't know. I already tried to talk to him and he blew me off."

"Yeah, I've rarely seen you raise your voice," Rosie admitted.

"And it didn't work this time."

"Maybe neither of you is really good at confrontation."

"I don't know, I saw Trevor yell at Evan Parker a couple of times. It's been at least ten years now, and I still haven't forgotten this one fight in particular."

"Evan deserved it," James said.

"Yeah, he was legendarily hard to work with," Rosie added. "The drugs, the alcohol. It's not a surprise he left competitive skating."

"It is a shame, though," Thad said. "He was *so* talented."

"No discipline whatsoever, though," Rosie said.

"I know," Thad answered. "It was painful to watch."

"But you're the opposite. Maybe you should talk to Trevor again. It would be a shame not to be able to work things out—you've been together for so long."

"I'm sure he has reasons for doing what he did," James said, and the reasonableness in his voice calmed Thad down a bit.

"Buck up, Thad, you've been through worse," Rosie said. "You'll get through this."

"Thanks, Mom." Thad almost felt better as he hung up the phone, but when he pictured Trevor, he shuddered. *Maybe I'll deal with him some other time.*

That Saturday, Thad flew out to Gloucester for some much needed rest. He spent some time at home, feeling the ocean's breeze wash over him before he followed Scott into Boston's South Station. "How often do you get to travel for work?" Thad asked as he kept an eye on their surroundings.

"I've only gotten to go a couple of times now—I hope they let me do it more. Travel usually goes to the senior people."

"You've been there a couple of years now."

"It's literally been two years, Thad. And government work is such that people stay there forever."

"But why should you stay if you aren't getting more opportunities?"

"Because I haven't been there long, and I like the work." Scott looked around as they got into the station's main concourse. "Besides, NOAA is right in Gloucester and is exactly the type of work I wanted to be doing when I decided to get my Ph.D. I didn't have to move across the country or change my life's work."

The brothers stopped at the large board listing train departures and scanned it until they found their train and gate listing. Then they started moving again. "Still, you seem way more familiar with this train station than I am," Thad said. "I can't even remember the last time I was here."

Scott smiled. "I took the train into New York a bunch when I was at Boston University— both as an undergrad and while I was getting my doctorate. My friends and I got cheap tickets because we were students, and New York is awesome! It was a great way to blow off steam."

"I've competed in New York a few times," Thad answered, smiling now too. *Scott's enthusiasm is contagious.*

"You could go train there. Sebastian has trained there forever and Grigoriy is there too now. Maybe it's worth it to be there permanently instead of sneaking in to spy on them."

Thad laughed.

"I mean it," Scott said. "The city has so much energy—maybe that would help you in your training."

Thad thought about it as their train's boarding announcement sounded through the station. Then he stood up and grabbed his bag. "I don't think so," he said as he and Scott made their way to the train, tickets in hand. "I need the quiet. All that action would tire me out."

Scott nodded. "I know. Even as a kid you needed your quiet time." They were on the train and in their seats before he eyed Thad again.

"What?" Thad asked.

"You've always been an introvert and I think it affected your skating early on. I remember a lot of the commentators mentioning during your early programs—and this was years ago—that you didn't engage the crowd enough."

Thad turned and looked out the window as his stomach sank. "Yeah, I wish I had learned that earlier. It's something Trevor and I have been working to fix, but..."

"Don't worry, I think you've been succeeding." Scott gave Thad a whack on the shoulder as the train started moving.

"Yeah, I think so too." *Whether it's enough for me to medal at the Olympics will be another story.*

Once they were in New York, Thad left Scott at their hotel and headed downtown to the skating club where both Sebastian and Grigoriy trained.

People teemed all around him as the subway cars rattled forward. At the rink, Thad snuck inside and made his way to the top seats. *I hope no one sees me,* he thought as he scanned the ice.

It took him a few minutes of looking to realize that he did not see Sebastian or his coach, Cheryl Turner. Grigoriy was on the ice, however, and his tiny coach, Tatiana Lenkova, was next to him. So was another woman whom Thad did not recognize. Grigoriy's wild arm movements told Thad his rival was upset. He strained his ears, wishing he could hear what Grigoriy was saying.

He watched until Grigoriy stormed off the ice. Then he made his way through the seats and went outside, keeping an eye on the ice to make sure that Tatiana did not see him. Tatiana looked annoyed as she left the rink. Both she and the woman Thad did recognize removed their skates and headed outside. Thad followed them at a small distance. Tatiana was still shaking her head as they got outside.

Thad raced down the small hallway in front of him and opened a different door a crack. Wind rushed into his face, and he took a deep breath. Then he stuck his head out the door and looked around. Tatiana and the other woman were half a block away from him, and their backs were to him. Grigoriy's back was to the building, and he looked everywhere but at his coach. Thad did not dare open the door any further.

"We need to get back on the ice," Thad heard Tatiana say a minute later, her Russian accent obvious.

Grigoriy shook his head. "We'll do it tomorrow."

"Grishka, I already paid for the ice for another two hours, and for Lori's time!" Tatiana's exasperation whacked Thad's ears.

"Is that all you care about, the money?"

"I wish you cared more about it! How are you going to afford to continue skating?"

Grigoriy shrugged. "In Russia, everything was always arranged and paid for."

"Do you want to go back to Russia?" Tatiana spat. "It isn't even like that anymore!"

Lori nodded. "The Soviet system is gone, Grigoriy. This is how we do things here."

Grigoriy shrugged again. Then he turned and walked away, calling out something in Russian as he left.

"What did he say?" Lori asked as Grigoriy disappeared.

"That he'll be back on the ice tomorrow." Tatiana shook her head. "I hope he means it."

Thad closed the door in front of him, made his way to the rink's main entrance, and left from there. Outside, he looked around to make sure that Grigoriy was gone and that Tatiana and Lori could not see him. Then he made a dash for the nearest subway. He tried to remember how to get back uptown as his head spun with confusion.

Grigoriy is frustrated with how skating works here, he thought. *He's used to the Soviet system.* He fumbled with his MetroCard and somehow managed to get it through the millimeter-sized opening in the turnstile. *But Tatiana was right about one thing—Grigoriy won't find the Soviet system in Russia anymore either.*

Thad took a deep breath and savored the feeling of air rushing into his lungs. *She's right about something else too—I don't know a skater here in the U.S. who isn't frustrated by how expensive skating is. I wonder if Grigoriy will skate through the changes he's facing?*

Thad watched a train pull into the station. *Yeah, he will,* he decided as he boarded. *The whole skating world is touting him as the anointed one—he's not going to walk away from that.*

Another week went by without Thad being able to say anything directly to Trevor. *Maybe today,* he thought, but when he got off the ice, all he wanted to do was leave the arena. He hauled himself back into the locker room and was glad for its silence, even with the flickering lights. He was just slamming his locker door when movement in his peripheral vision caught his attention.

That must be Trevor, he thought. When he looked over, though, he saw Jack Wallace. "Oh, God," he groaned. "I thought I'd seen the last of you."

Jack hesitated for a moment. Then he took a deep breath and came over. "And I thought I'd find you here. I know you skate early."

"So you're stalking me now?" Thad fixed Jack in a cold stare.

"No, I..." Jack looked away for a moment. Then he clenched his teeth. "Look, I'm sorry about the other day, challenging you and everything."

Thad softened. "Oooh, an apology. Not what I was expecting." *Even if that was longer ago than just the other day. He's been avoiding me.* Thad put his bag down on the bench in front of him and continued staring at Jack. To his surprise, Jack met his gaze. Then amusement made Thad's lips twitch upward. "Are you sorry because you lost?"

Jack almost smiled. "No, because I should leave the showing off for my own practices." He looked away and heaved a breath.

He has more to say, Thad thought. He waited quietly.

"The truth is, I follow your career. I think you should have won gold at Worlds."

Surprise hit Thad like a winter gale off the water. "You know enough about figure skating to say that?"

"I've watched plenty of skaters in my time. Besides, Sebastian Adler fell on his ass—even I could see that. And the announcers all said Arsenyev had a couple of jumps that weren't clean."

Thad smiled. "All of that is true."

Jack looked away again. Then his words tumbled out of him. "I had to watch your long program alone in my hotel room—we were on the road for several games while you were skating. I almost missed my flight to Boston to play against the Bruins because I wanted to watch your short program and there was a delay on NBC."

Thad sat down on the bench on one side of his bag. "But you got to see it and the long program?"

Jack nodded and sat across from him, on the other side of the duffel bag. "We had one night off in between our second and third games. I watched the long programs in my room as the rest of the guys went out."

"Your teammates stood for that?" Thad was teasing, but he couldn't stop himself.

Jack shrugged. "I found them afterward. They didn't know what I was doing. I couldn't tell them. I would have been the laughingstock of the team."

"That much I know." Thad was serious now. "My brother is a hockey player. Growing up, he got teased because I skated. Everyone thought I was a sissy."

"I got into hockey to prove to my dad I wasn't. I was hoping to prove that the other day, too." Jack winced. "I'm sorry I came after you."

"Apology accepted."

Jack bit his lip. "What's your dad think of your skating? He wish you were a hockey player?"

"When I was growing up, yeah, he did."

"But now he comes to all your competitions. That's more support than I ever saw from my parents."

"Really? You guys are Stanley Cup winners and your parents don't deal with you?"

"Oh, they do now, especially if they can get something out of it, but it's taken me winning the Stanley Cup for that to happen."

Thad shook his head. "I can't even picture that. My parents sacrificed a lot for my skating. It's crazy expensive, and I grew up poor. A lot of skating families are like that."

"Not mine. I was a latch-key kid. My parents never knew where I was. Luckily for me, I was always at the rink. You're lucky you got along with your parents."

Thad rubbed his chin as he thought about it. Then he took a deep breath and smelled both sweat and bleach. "My mom, brother, and I have always been close. My dad..." Thad stopped talking as he thought of James' quiet presence. "I don't know. Growing up, I thought we were like water and ice, existing at the edges of each other but never quite getting along."

"That's not what I see now. The cameras like to show your family as you skate. Your dad's always watching as intently as your mom, and he cheers too when you land a jump."

Thad smiled. "Sometimes it's easier to see that from the outside."

"Yeah, how can you see anything when you're spinning the way you do?"

Both men laughed. Then they looked at each other for a long moment. It was Thad who spoke again to break the silence. "What is it?" he asked.

Jack looked all around the locker room. The silence grew again.

"Talk to me, Jack."

"Are you into any of the other skaters?"

"Emily Burrows. I think it's easiest to date another skater. But our coaches keep strict watches on us and our social lives." *That's an understatement.*

Jack looked away again. "Not what I was expecting."

"Yeah, everyone thinks figure skaters are gay." Thad kicked the side of a locker in frustration.

"You're telling me Joaquin isn't?"

"No, I know he is. But guys like Sebastian Adler go out of their way to prove they're not. It's hard to find a middle ground."

"Yeah, I don't like Adler at all. Him or Arsenyev. Too many airs."

Thad thought of Arsenyev's visit to the arena. "You and me both."

Jack looked at Thad for a long moment. "Emily Burrows, huh? She's cute—but Kim McGrath is the real athlete on the women's side. I think she's going to hit the roof every time she jumps."

Thad laughed. "Me too. I just keep hoping she lands cleanly."

"Yeah, she doesn't look like a figure skater."

Thad's eyebrows came together. "What do you mean?"

"Look at the rest of the girls, Thad. They all look like twigs. McGrath has muscular thighs and real curves." Jack shook his head. "I always root for her, and I always think she gets way lower marks than she should. I was surprised she did so well at Nationals and Worlds."

Thad nodded. "Me too. I'm hoping this is the start of something better for her."

Jack took a deep breath. "But I get it. She's like me and a lot of guys on the hockey team."

"What do you mean?" *I really want to know,* Thad realized.

"Blue collar background, wrong side of the tracks. She'd fit in better in hockey."

"Should I tell her she has an invitation to join the team?" Thad laughed.

Jack laughed too. "I'd love to see her in a pair of hockey skates. That would be hot."

"Until she outskates you." Thad laughed harder.

"Yeah, that's a risk. I see that now." Jack shook his head. Then he stood up.

Thad rose also and hauled his gym bag back onto his shoulder. "I'm sorry I couldn't help you much."

"Don't worry, Thad, you've done plenty." Jack put out his hand.

Thad smiled as he clasped Jack's hand in return.

The rink's chill became a cool silence for several more days until Thad couldn't stand it anymore. *I still can't bring myself to talk to Trevor,* he thought. *But I may lose my mind in the process.* He was relieved to see Joaquin across the ice more days than not. The other skater's smile lit up the arena when Thad himself was feeling so low.

"Laura managed to get a more flexible position at her company," Joaquin said. "She has more time to work with Brianna."

"That's good." Thad was not sure what else to say.

But Joaquin just nodded, and he did not seem to expect more. "I think it's helped me on the ice."

"I also saw you on a cereal box at the grocery store." Thad's smile finally felt a little more genuine now.

"Oh, yeah, I've gotten a few more endorsement deals. The cereal, Campbell's soup... I'm trying to stick to the tame stuff until after the Olympics."

"I think that's smart." Both men were laughing now.

"It's done wonders for my bank account, though." Joaquin became serious again as he spoke.

Thad nodded. "Tell me about it. I couldn't afford my own rent until I started doing endorsements like that a few years ago."

"It's amazing what a difference it makes."

"For real."

Thad was even happier to see Emily getting onto the ice a few minutes later, even if Trevor and Mia, standing together at the boards, made his spirits sink just a little. Thad made sure Trevor was looking away from him before he started speaking to Emily. "Do you want to come to my house for dinner this weekend?"

Emily smiled. "Yeah, I do." She glanced up into the stands. "I won't bring Trevor this time."

Thad laughed. "Sounds like a plan."

Chapter 9

On July 1, Thad flew out to Sacramento with Trevor, Emily, and Mia in tow. Joaquin, Laura, and Brianna were on a later flight. *Probably a cheaper one too,* Thad thought. *But they get in so late at night—I can't say it's worth it. I'm always amazed Joaquin skates as well as he does.* It was a quiet ride to the airport, but for once that silence didn't hold the tension that Thad had been feeling the last few weeks. *I'm looking forward to this competition,* he realized. *Maybe a change in scenery will help fix what's been going on.*

The following morning, the haze that foretold the day's heat turned the otherwise bright sunrise into pastel hues. Thad awoke early enough to watch the pinks fade into the deep blue sky of early morning. Then he spent the first day of the competition watching the women skate their short programs. He was happy for Emily when she came in second, *even if she was behind Jenni. Kim looked slow and sloppy. I'm not surprised she's in third place by a lot.*

It was not until they were driving back to the hotel that Trevor surprised Thad by starting the conversation. "I'm sorry," he said.

Thad looked over at him.

Trevor glanced around the now quiet car, and Thad was certain he had let Emily and Mia go back to the hotel in a separate car on purpose. "I shouldn't have followed you to Emily's."

"What made you realize that?" Thad asked, trying not to roll his eyes. *I still don't think it's something a normal person would have done.*

"I was talking to Anne about it. She's always had more wisdom about this stuff than me."

Thad looked out the window as the traffic light in front of them turned green and Trevor stepped on the gas. "And what did she tell you?"

"She said not to worry about Emily." Trevor smirked. "That you could do worse and see someone completely outside the skating world."

"Oh, yeah, that would be bad." Thad groaned.

"Anne thought that seeing another skater might help keep you both focused."

"And that's all you care about."

"Seven months before the Olympics? You'd better believe it."

Thad shook his head as they arrived back at their hotel. "I never thought I'd be the one saying this, Trevor, but you need to relax."

Trevor nodded. "Maybe we both do."

When it came time for his own short program the next night, Thad warmed up and felt loose on the ice. Then Grigoriy landed a clean quadruple toe loop, and Thad's stomach sank.

"He's been landing a few of those in practice," Sebastian said from nearby.

Thad shook his head in frustration.

"Every time I think I can start ignoring him, he pulls one of those." Sebastian pointed his chin in Grigoriy's direction.

"Damn," Thad mumbled. *Maybe I should have retired after all. I'm not sure I can keep up.*

When warmups were over, Thad got off the ice and mentally ran through his short program. When the music for *Goodfellas* came up almost an hour later, he smiled. *I'm so glad I'm trying this program out,* he thought. Almost immediately, though, he turned his first triple jump into a double.

His stomach quivered with frustration. Then the rest of his mind took over. *Forget about it,* he told himself. *It doesn't matter.*

He took a quick breath through his nostrils. In an instant, he focused on the rest of the program. Everything else was clean, and Thad found himself happy with a string of 5.8s and 5.9s. He did not think of the double jump again until he was waving to the crowd when his program was over. *Wow,* he thought.

"Good job refocusing after that jump," Trevor said as they left the side of the ice so that Grigoriy could skate.

Thad nodded. "Yeah, Brianna and I have been working on not fixating on my failures. Though maybe it's easier so early in the season."

"No, I think it's more the first thing. There's a reason I wanted you to work with her."

"Yeah, I was surprised to see it work so easily."

"Apply it to Nationals and the Olympics."

Thad looked at the floor. "The stakes are so much higher there. This feels like nothing in comparison."

"I know. That's why we've been working on it." Trevor looked over at the nearest monitor to watch the last part of Grigoriy's short program.

Thad looked in the other direction. It was not until Grigoriy had finished skating that Thad forced his attention back to the ice.

"He had a few bobbles too," Trevor said. "I'd be surprised if his marks are higher than yours."

I'll reserve judgement until I actually see those marks, Thad thought. It was not until a string of 5.7s and 5.8s appeared that he smiled. "I'm in first place."

Trevor smiled back. "I'm glad we did this meet."

When Thad stepped onto the ice for warmups before the long program, his heart quickened. *I really want to win.* The words were no sooner formed in his head than his right foot hit a raised patch of ice. In slow motion, he began to fall. The arena spun around him. The other skaters—first Emily, then Sebastian—swayed in different directions. Thad crashed onto the ice on top of his right shoulder, which popped out of the socket as he landed. "Oowww!" he screeched.

He tried to get up, but he could not move his arm. His left hand clutched his right shoulder as pulsating agony moved through his shoulder like an electrical current. Thad gritted his teeth and managed to sit up, but his shoulder hurt too much to attempt to get to his feet.

All around him, the other skaters moved to the boards and eyed him. Then Trevor stepped onto the ice, and Thad was relieved to see his coach. He was even happier when a couple of the arena's medics followed him.

"What happened?" Trevor asked when he reached Thad. His words were calm, but his eyes betrayed his concern.

"There's a bump in the ice over there." Thad pointed his chin toward where he had tripped. Even that motion sent bolts of pain through his shoulder. "Oohhh."

Trevor glanced around at the other skaters. "Come on, let's get you off the ice." He reached out one hand.

"I can't move my arm at all, Trevor."

One of the medics knelt next to him. "This is going to hurt."

Thad cringed as the medic felt his shoulder. Then, with a quick motion, the medic popped the errant shoulder back into its socket. Thad yelled in pain. His voice rattled off the ice and bounced around every inch of the arena. He winced again as his eardrums complained. A single glance up into the arena told him that everyone was watching him. It was so quiet that the silence scared Thad.

Then Trevor held out his hand. "You should be able to get up now."

We'll see about that, Thad thought, but he reached out his left hand to his coach. A second later he was indeed on his feet and skating off the ice.

In the medical area and away from the prying eyes of the other skaters, Trevor grabbed a package of ice and applied it to Thad's shoulder. "That looked brutal."

"It really hurt," Thad admitted.

"I can't believe there was still a bump in the ice—the Zamboni's been over the rink more than once."

"He must have missed a spot."

Trevor eyed Thad for a moment. Then he looked at his watch. "I don't know if I think you should skate with an injury like that, and without a warmup."

"I've gotta win this meet, Trevor."

"It's just an invitational. If this were Nationals or the Olympics, I'd agree with you, but it isn't."

Thad wished he could shrug, but he didn't want to take the risk. "I'm still in first place. I need to beat Grigoriy at least once."

"I'd rather you beat him at the later competitions—like the Olympics."

"Oh, I plan to." Thad smiled.

"I think you're crazy."

"That's a possibility, too."

More than an hour later, though, Thad began to question his judgment as he prepared to go onto the ice. *I'm the last skater to go, and then this meet is over.*

"Grigoriy's marks were a little low, but he's still in second place," Trevor murmured as Thad got close to the ice. "Sebastian and Joaquin are in second and third. Kim fell as badly as you did."

"Maybe she hit the same spot on the ice."

Trevor shook his head. "They sent the Zamboni over it twice more after you fell."

"Wonderful. Maybe I'll avoid a repeat performance."

Trevor looked amused.

"Any last encouragement?" Thad asked.

"Skate your best and don't make your shoulder any worse."

"Will do."

Thad's name was announced over the arena's speakers, and he skated to the center of the ice. His shoulder still hurt, and he hoped he wasn't visibly wincing. When his music started, Thad grit his teeth and began skating. His legs felt tight and every movement was a chore. His first jump, a triple Lutz, sent sparks of pain through his shoulder as he dug his toe pick into the ice. Thad winced again as he landed and was amazed that he managed to stay upright. *I have to get through this program.*

Thad's skating got faster as he warmed up, but each jump made him yelp in pain. *I'm so glad the judges can't hear that over the music.* A minute later, he managed to lift his arms just enough to make his last spin worthwhile, and then his program was over. *Thank God.* Relief cascaded through Thad as he lifted his left arm to wave to the crowd.

When Thad got off the ice, Trevor was waiting for him. "I can't believe you skated that well."

Thad winced as he put his skate guards on. "We'll find out tomorrow if that was a good idea or not."

Trevor looked amused as they both sat in the "kiss and cry" area. Then he handed Thad another package of ice. "I'm still worried."

Thad nodded. "I'm sure I'll feel worse later."

They were both quiet until his marks came up: 6.0, 6.0, 6.0, 6.0 5.9, 5.9, 5.9, 6.0, 6.0.

"Wow," Thad gasped.

"Seriously," Trevor said. "I didn't think you were that good."

Thad made a face at him, and they both laughed. Then Thad stood and acknowledged the crowd's cheers—using his left hand again. *There's no way I'm risking moving my right arm.*

"How are you feeling?" Emily asked as soon as Thad and Trevor met her backstage.

"Uuuhhh," Thad said. "I just hope I didn't do something that'll kill the rest of my season."

"He says that now," Trevor said, rolling his eyes.

Emily smiled. "At least you came in first."

Thad managed a smile in return. "How'd you do?"

"First!"

"Yes!" Thad wished he could high five her, but his shoulder hurt too much.

"You only won by half a point!" Jenni hollered from a few feet over.

"She still won!" Thad hollered back without thinking.

Emily burst out laughing.

"You didn't even deserve it!" Jenni said. She glared at Emily.

Trevor stepped in between them. "Enough," he said.

Jenni gave all of them a mean look and stomped off.

When she was gone, Mia dropped her arm around Emily's shoulders. "I'll take a picture of you with your gold medal around your neck and send it to all the papers."

Emily laughed again. "Serves her right."

When the medal ceremony was over, Trevor eyed Thad. "Your shoulder is still hurting, isn't it?"

Thad nodded before he could stop himself. *I didn't want to say anything, but I can't help it.*

Trevor dug into his bag and pulled out a bottle of water.

Without thinking about it, Thad put out his right hand to take it, winced, pulled it back, and put out his left hand instead. "What's this for? I have my own water."

Trevor pulled out a small bottle of white pills from his bag and held one out to Thad.

"Painkillers." Thad put the bottle of water on a nearby table and took the pill. "I hope this works quickly."

"It will." Trevor ducked into the trainers' room and came back out with another package of ice.

"Thanks." Thad applied the ice to his shoulder. A second later, he felt the cold through his shirt. "Aaahh, that feels good."

"I still can't believe you skated at all with an injury like that, much less that you skated as well as you did." Trevor checked his watch. "Our press conference starts in fifteen minutes. Make sure you can sit up straight."

Thad nodded and watched his coach disappear up the hall. Then he jumped as raised voices sounded around him. "I can't believe you made me do this!" a woman's voice yelled, and it was right nearby.

That sounds like Kim, Thad thought. He hid against a wall and stuck just enough of his head around the corner to see who Kim was shouting at.

Elizabeth McGrath stood a few feet from her daughter, and Thad was struck by how much they looked alike, especially up close. Elizabeth was the same height as Kim, with the same large blue eyes and bright blond hair. She was rounder, though—much rounder—and lines creased her face.

"You knew this would happen!" Kim yelled. "You knew I wasn't ready for competition yet and you made me enter anyway. Look what happened! Are you happy now?"

Elizabeth frowned. "If this is what you look like on the ice, maybe you needed this competition to get you shaped up!"

Kim let out a wordless scream of frustration and stomped off.

Thad waited for Elizabeth to disappear in the other direction before he hurried after Kim. "Kim, wait!" he called. He stepped down a little too hard and winced as pain shot through his shoulder. *Dammit,* he thought as Kim turned around.

"I need some air," Kim said, so Thad followed her outside and squinted into the bright fluorescent lights just above them. Once the door slammed behind them, Kim took a deep breath as a cool breeze washed over them. Then she eyed Thad and his ice pack.

Thad hid the ice behind his back, using his left hand and hoping that his right shoulder wouldn't hurt more for the gesture.

"Don't bother," Kim said. "If I hadn't seen it, I'd be throwing a bunch of ice at you." She shook her head. "I can't believe you skated."

Thad reminded himself not to shrug. "I have a couple of programs I've been working on. I needed to see how they looked."

Kim shook her head. "I don't have that courage. I would have been off the ice in a second. But maybe that would have been a better outcome than my skating."

"Don't worry about it. This meet doesn't count as much as the Grand Prix events at the end of the year."

"And yet all the big skaters are here." Kim made a face.

"Maybe everyone else sees it as a warmup, too."

Kim rolled her eyes. "Whatever. I'll just be glad when I'm on my flight home and I can forget about this whole disaster."

Thad looked at her for a moment.

"What?"

"You don't seem to have a such a great relationship with your mother."

"Thanks for the obvious."

"Is there any way for her to step back from you and your career for a while?"

Now it was Kim's turn to eye Thad for a moment in silence. "What, like go do something else with her life?"

"Yeah. In a different city."

"Don't I wish." Kim rolled her eyes again.

"You skated well at Nationals and Worlds," Thad added. "I'd hate to see that derailed over your fights with your mother."

"This from the guy with a perfect family life."

"What does that mean?" Confusion bolted through Thad faster than the pain in his shoulder.

"Oh, come on, Thad. Your family is at all of your competitions. *And* Trevor and Anne are like a set of parents I never had."

"Things aren't perfect."

Kim sent him a look that said she didn't believe him.

"You didn't see the mountain of debt my parents accumulated to pay for my skating, for one thing."

"Yeah I did—it's the same mountain my parents have. Skating is crazy expensive and it's made *them* crazy."

I'll bet they were crazy before that, too, Thad thought as he pictured Elizabeth. "Still, it's not worth throwing away your talent for."

"It's not just the money, it's the fighting, the screaming." Kim clenched her fists, and her face wrinkled in frustration.

"That's what I was saying—maybe you and your mom need a break from each other."

"That would be nice," Kim mumbled. Then she shrugged. "Whatever." She went back into the arena.

Trevor appeared in the doorway once she was gone, and Thad knew his coach had been waiting just inside. "Come on," Trevor said. "We have to do that press conference. Then we can leave."

"Ugh." Thad followed Trevor inside.

"I agree, but we're obligated. If you don't want to do them, you should stop winning." They both laughed, even as Thad winced. "I'm glad we don't have another competition for a while," Trevor added. "You need to heal."

Thad nodded. "I know. Not what I wanted in the first meet of the season."

Trevor shot him a sympathetic look as they walked into the press conference.

Thad took his seat at the dais, in between Grigoriy and Sebastian. Joaquin was nowhere to be seen, and Thad didn't blame him. *I'd be back at the hotel already too if I didn't have to be here.* To his surprise, however, his body had started to relax, and in a second, he knew he was feeling the effects of the pill Trevor had given him. *What a relief. I just hope I don't look too out of it.*

Then the questions rang out. "How is your shoulder?" one reporter called.

"How do you feel about your performance?" a second one asked.

Thad took a breath and leaned toward the microphone. "My shoulder hurts, no doubt about it. When I fell, it popped right out. I'm glad I could skate at all, let alone give a solid performance."

Grigoriy shook his head and grabbed his microphone.

Uh oh, Thad thought.

"We all know Thad won because the judges felt sorry for him," Grigoriy said. "He was stiff and he never should have won."

Sebastian leaned forward and looked at Grigoriy. "This from the guy who stepped out on a couple of his jumps. Maybe you shouldn't have come in second."

Relief flowed through Thad, even as Grigoriy glared at Sebastian.

"I'm serious," Sebastian continued. "Thad was in first after the short program. It takes some serious stones to skate with an injury like that. He could have easily walked away, but he didn't. That's a true competitor."

Thad smiled. "Thanks."

Grigoriy shook his head and stared angrily into the crowd of reporters.

When the press conference was over, Trevor carried Thad's belongings out to the car. Thad looked over at Sebastian as he, too, left the arena. "Thanks for standing up for me."

"Oh, don't worry, I even meant it." They both laughed. "Ignore Grigoriy. He's just angry you aren't a sissy."

"No, I think he's just angry. Period."

Sebastian thought about it for a second. "That could be true, too." He nodded at Thad's shoulder. "I hope you heal fast." Then he took off.

"Let's get out of here," Trevor said. "I'm driving. Sit behind me so you can use your left hand on the seat belt."

"You think of everything, don't you?" Thad teased.

"That's my job."

Three days later, Thad was back on the ice, but stiffly. "You look like you're afraid of moving," Trevor said when he joined him at the center of the rink. "I thought I told you to keep up with the painkillers and the ice."

Thad swung his left arm. "Ice, ice, all around."

"And not a drop to use on your shoulder," Trevor answered. They both laughed. "You only know that poem because of James."

"Him and my tenth-grade English teacher, who promised the first day of class that we'd have the first fifteen lines of it memorized by a certain point in the semester." Thad thought of the school's copy of *The Rime of the Ancient Mariner*, ripped and marked up and probably as old as the seafarer himself.

"I remember when you brought that book home, and when you got a special leather-bound copy of it for your father for Christmas."

Thad nodded. "Dad said he'd heard lines of it recited his whole life but had never owned a copy or read it the whole way through." Even now, Thad remembered the rough cover of that book as he had wrapped it in garish Christmas wrapping paper. A smile played on his lips.

"Come on," Trevor said. "Let's get off the ice. The afternoon folks need it."

By the time Thad removed his skates, Trevor had returned with a package of ice that he helped Thad apply to his shoulder. "How does that feel?"

"Better."

"Good."

Thad was both stretching and trying to keep the ice on his shoulder when Emily sat down next to him and began putting her own skates on. "How's your shoulder?"

"It hurts. Even if I've been downgraded to Advil."

Emily looked amused. "Maybe for the best, even if I'd probably use the heavier stuff at night so I could sleep."

"I was planning on doing that."

"Good. You need to heal." Emily hauled herself to her feet and took off toward the ice, where Mia was already waiting for her.

Thad watched her go with amusement before he swallowed three of the Advil from the small bottle he was holding. When his stretching was over, he, too, got to his feet and was glad that his shoulder did not hurt as much as it had in Sacramento. *Injuries,* he thought. *I've been mostly lucky until now, but this was a bad one.*

The next day, Thad was glad when practice was over. Once more the TV in the stands was on, and Thad recognized the ice rink he saw on the screen. *That's where Sebastian and Grigoriy skate. Why does someone keep turning it to this station?* He glanced around for the remote as he stretched until he gave up and focused on the TV itself.

Onscreen, Grigoriy was skating fast, and before Thad could catch his breath, his rival had tossed off two quadruple Loops in a row. Thad sucked in a breath. Then the screen went dark, and he jumped.

"Media ban still applies," Trevor said, and he was holding the errant remote.

Brianna was right next to him. "Your practice today looked a little better. I think we'll be good to go full speed again once your shoulder has healed."

Thad bit his lip. "Should I start trying for a quad?"

"You could," Trevor answered. "Can't hurt to try."

Thad sighed. "I'd rather be spinning."

Trevor smiled. "I, too, would hate to see the quad become the only thing that matters in skating."

"Who keeps turning the TV to the one station that's always following Sebastian and Grigoriy's rink, anyway?" Thad's frustration rose within him.

Trevor shrugged. "Must be one of the hockey players."

Thad laughed.

Nearly an hour later, he dragged himself out of the arena. Every muscle in his body complained. A dull ache throbbed in his shoulder, and he groaned. He opened the front door of his car with his left hand and collapsed sideways into the driver's seat, his right side facing the steering wheel and his legs still sticking out into the parking lot. "Uuhhhh," he groaned.

It took him a minute of sitting before he felt like moving again, and even then it was barely enough to turn himself around so that he was facing his windshield. *I am so tired. I'm going home and I'm taking a nap.* That thought alone was enough to get his keys in his ignition and the car door closed.

Cheesy pop music flowed through the car, and Thad jerked his hand away from the ignition, as if it were hot. Then he winced. *Oh, my damn shoulder.* He heaved a breath. *It's better, but it still hurts.*

Then he stared at the buttons on his car's dashboard. *I thought I turned the radio off. What is this stuff, anyway?* It took him a moment of racking his brain before he thought of the blond, teenage band behind the cheery music coming from his speakers. *Oh yeah. Hanson.* His thumb hit the button to change the station.

A second later, a few notes of classical music flowed through the car as Thad put his seat belt on. *There we go. I need music for at least a few new programs. Both for Nationals next year and for the Olympics, even if the second is just wishful thinking right now.*

The piece he was listening to ended as Thad pulled out of the parking lot. Then the announcer came on. "That was Handel's *Water Music*." His calm voice and cool enunciation reached Thad's ears.

"He sounds so upper class," Thad said, speaking aloud without meaning to. "I'll bet anything he went to Harvard." Then he chuckled. *Harvard. Like I didn't move out of Gloucester sixteen years ago.*

He started paying attention to the radio again just in time to hear the announcer say that the next piece was from Vivaldi's canon of sacred music. *Vivaldi's sacred music? All I know is the* Four Seasons, *and I don't want to skate to that.* He was just thinking of changing the station when the music soared through his car. Violins reached his ears for several seconds before a pure soprano, high and perfect, made its way into his brain.

Thad caught his breath. He did not understand the words or even know what language they were in, but none of that mattered. All he could picture was the heavens, with stars and meteors. Images of galaxies and space flowed through his mind in the same motion as the music. *Wow.*

Thad's breath came in gasps. He pulled over to the side of the road as the music ended and ignored the cars that whizzed past him, honking. He grabbed a pen and paper from his glove compartment. As the announcer came back on, Thad scribbled words for all he was worth. It was only when the next piece of music came on—something by Wagner whose name he had missed—that he looked up.

Thad's eyes stared at the streets around him for a minute before he remembered that he was in Denver. Then he realized that he had driven past the exit to get to his house. *Damn,* he thought, but he was not upset. Instead, a euphoria he had not felt in a while floated through him. Another minute went by before he looked down at the pen and paper in his hands. "*Nulla in mundo pax sincera,*" he had written. He took a deep breath.

Then he started driving again, remembering just in time to check his mirrors before he pulled out into traffic. *I have to get a copy of that. I need to set a program to it, no matter what.*

Chapter 10

The next day, when practice was over, Thad went back out to his car with much more purpose. His shoulder still ached, but he didn't care. Within minutes, he was at the large Tower Records downtown. *I've always loved this place,* he thought as he headed upstairs to the classical section and looked around. He was locating Vivaldi's name from among the alphabetized section of composers' names when a store employee, whose nametag said Vincent, approached him. "Can I help you?" Vincent asked.

"Yeah, I'm looking for some of Vivaldi's sacred music." Thad hoped his ignorance didn't show as the warm soprano he had heard the previous day welled up within his brain.

Vincent smiled. "We have an extensive selection of Vivaldi's music, including his sacred work—but then, he wrote a lot of that. Do you have anything specific you're looking for?"

Thad nodded and reached into his pocket for the piece of paper he had written on. "Yeah, it's a piece called *Nulla in mundo pax sincera*. I heard it on the radio yesterday."

"Were you listening to Colorado Public Radio?"

"I was. How did you know?"

"I heard the same piece—we have that version in particular, with those singers. It's a slightly older version, but we just got several copies in the other day." Vincent turned and started going through the CDs in front of him.

Thad blinked. "I'm impressed you know it."

"Garrett Reed and I have similar tastes." Vincent named the radio announcer as his eyes remained on the CDs. "He's been in here a few times, looking for music." He pulled out a two-CD jewel case. "Here, this is the one I was thinking of."

Thad took it and found himself looking at green and white artwork.

"Are you looking for music for new long or short programs?"

Thad looked up, his eyebrows raised.

"Oh, come on, Thad. A two-time Worlds medalist and a three-time National Champion? The whole city knows you train here."

Thad smiled. "I don't know if it's the whole city, but yeah, after hearing this yesterday, I was thinking of setting something to it."

"Then let me suggest a few other pieces as well. Maybe something will inspire you."

"Thank you."

"You're welcome. I've always liked your skating."

Amusement and surprise swirled within Thad as Vincent went back to the CDs in front of them.

"Here," Vincent said a minute later as he handed Thad one CD and then two more. "Those are my favorites. I listen to them more than I should."

"No such thing."

Now it was Vincent's turn to smile. "Don't hesitate to come back if you need more."

"I won't."

That Saturday night, Thad was ready by the time Emily rang his doorbell. He grinned as he pulled the door open. Emily smiled back at him as she stepped over the threshold. "Thanks for coming," Thad said, even as he glanced down the hallway.

"Don't worry, Trevor didn't follow me this time."

"Did you take the long way to shake him off?"

Emily laughed. "No, I saw him head out with Mia as I was leaving the rink. He isn't following me."

"What a relief," Thad said as they went into the kitchen.

"Ooh, that smells good."

"Now it's my turn to be a good host."

"What are you cooking?"

"You smell the potatoes right now, but I'm also making haddock. It was one of the few other things my dad fished for besides cod." Thad tossed the last of the bay leaves over the fish and put it into the oven.

Emily shook her head. "I've never even been out on a boat."

Thad made a face. "You're not missing much."

Emily laughed again.

"I mean it. I never got completely seasick, but I never enjoyed it, either. I'd rather be on the ice."

"Did you not even go to the beach in the summers?"

"Oh, we did that plenty." Thad waved a hand at her. "I liked doing that, sticking my feet in the water. Scott and I swam plenty and made sandcastles and did all the usual beach stuff. When I wasn't at the rink." He took a deep breath. "We lived right near the water, and walking to the beach was a free thing to do."

Emily nodded. "I hear you on that one. How are you cooking the fish?"

"As simply as possible—it's encrusted with parmesan, Old Bay Seasoning, lemon, and some other spices. I put the potatoes in a while ago. They take longer."

"That sounds good."

"It's one of my favorite recipes." Thad opened the oven again, and its heat hit his face like a wave. He waited until he could see again before poking at the potatoes. When he had closed the oven, he looked back at Emily. "It's one of my mother's recipes. She was great at cooking fish a million different ways, especially the cod. It tasted like we were eating something different every night, and a lot of her recipes cooked in twenty minutes or less."

"That's awesome. My dad often cooked when my mom was taking me to and from skating. I wish he'd been as creative."

Thad looked away. "Of course, there were plenty of nights where we were eating the same cod casserole for a third night in a row, but..."

"It's still food."

"That it is." Thad gestured toward the nearest door. "Come on, I'll show you the living room. I need to check on the fireplace anyway."

"I can't believe it's gotten this chilly," Emily said. "My thermometer said 58 when I left the house."

"Yeah, it's unseasonably cold. But it gives me the chance to use the fireplace." Sure enough, the wood was burning low, and Thad put an extra log on.

"This is pretty."

"It's one of my favorite features about the place."

Emily inhaled deeply. "I love the smell of a wood fire."

Thad smiled. "Me too."

A few minutes later, they landed back in the kitchen. Thad checked on the food and then went to set the table. "What do you want to drink? I have sparkling water, milk, orange juice..."

"I'll take the sparkling water."

Thad pulled two glasses from the cabinet and poured some of the sparkling water for both of them. Napkins, forks, and knives came next. His flurry of activity continued as he grabbed the serving utensils and larger knives to cut the fish with. Then he encased his hands in potholders and went to the oven. A second later, the earthy smell of the roasted potatoes filled his nose as he transferred them to the table. The haddock came out a moment later, and Thad slammed the oven closed. Then he looked at Emily. "Ready to eat?"

"Oh, yeah." Emily lowered herself into a seat in front of one of Thad's place settings. "This looks amazing."

"Hopefully it tastes good too."

"Oh, it will."

Thad was glad when the fish was, in fact, good. "What a relief."

Emily shook her head at him, but she was smiling. "Have more confidence in yourself."

When the meal was over and the dishes were clean, they ended up back in the living room, staring at the last of the fire's dying embers. After a minute, Emily looked around the room again. Her eye fell on an open magazine on the small table next to her chair. "Oh, is this an issue of *Sports Illustrated*?"

"Know the magazine well, do you?" Thad answered drily. "I've never seen anyone be able to identify a magazine from the middle."

"It has a unique layout. Besides, I read this article—it's about figure skating. It's not like them to cover skating."

Thad swallowed as Emily lifted the magazine into her lap.

"Oh, this is the article that calls you an automaton. I didn't remember that." Emily looked back at Thad. "Even if I do remember them comparing you to Sebastian Adler."

"Unfavorably." Thad rolled his eyes.

Emily stared at him for a second before leaping up, ripping the article out of the magazine, and throwing the pages into the fireplace. The rest of the magazine landed on top of the errant pages a minute later.

Thad leapt to his feet. "What are you doing? Are you crazy?"

The magazine caught fire. The offending article went first, and when its flames leapt toward the top of the fireplace, the rest of the magazine caught too. Immediately, the room felt warmer.

Emily stayed in between Thad and the fireplace. "Let it go. The press will never be right about you unless they're singing your praises."

Thad tilted his head so that he could see around Emily's shoulder. The magazine was almost gone now, and the sudden flames were starting to flicker and die. The remnants of the magazine crumpled and curled as the fire ate the last of it.

To Thad's surprise, tears welled in his eyes and pain leapt at his chest in the same motion as the flames.

"I mean it, Thad," Emily said. "You're a great skater and you have fan clubs all around the country. There are people who have travelled to see you skate at competitions, not just watched you on TV."

"How do you know that?" To his horror, some of Thad's tears overflowed, and he swiped at them with the back of his hand.

"I was sitting behind some of them at Worlds. There was a whole group of them, sitting a few rows in front of us, and they were all excited to see you skate. I was with your family, and your parents decided not to tell them who we were."

"They would have recognized you if they'd seen you."

"Maybe." Emily shrugged. "That's not the point. Let go of the negativity. The press just needs an article to write—that's how they keep their jobs and stay relevant. You're better than that, and you've touched so many lives."

Thad swallowed hard. *Is it possible she's right?*

Emily reached up and stroked Thad's cheek.

Thad's face burned and his heart began to race. He met her gaze as he clasped her hand in his. Her warm eyes were like magnets, drawing him in. Thad's feelings of despair began to flow out of his body like water. He pulled her into a hug, tight against his chest. "I'm so glad you're here for me when I need it."

Emily smiled. "And I always will be."

At the end of August, Thad flew back to Gloucester for another week off. "Wheee!" Scott yelped as he picked him up from Logan Airport. "A whole week to do something other than skate!"

Thad laughed as the humid Boston air washed over him. "I'm looking forward to the golf course already."

"I'll go with you this weekend. I have to work the whole week you're here, though."

"Working stiff."

"There are times I envy your non-normal schedule."

Thad smiled. "Don't worry, Dad has a day or two off during the week. He said he's up for some golfing while you're not around."

"Dad manages to keep busy for a guy who's retired."

"He's only retired from the commercial fishing."

"And he only says that because he doesn't go out before dawn every morning." Scott shook his head. "He still gives cruises to the tourists and takes groups out fishing."

"Good for him." Thad tugged on his seatbelt. "It keeps him busy and earns him money."

Scott nodded. "Mom said he works at the library a couple of nights a week too."

Thad stared out the window and watched the white puffy clouds move across the sky. "Yeah, I heard. Helping them catalogue their fishing books and acquiring more."

"He was doing that at first. He's been doing more historical work recently about Gloucester's past."

"That sounds interesting." Thad caught a glimpse of the water.

"I think he's enjoying it."

"You sound surprised."

"I guess I am. I never thought he'd enjoy the more intellectual work like that."

Thad looked back at his brother. "You think you're the only one with brains in this family?"

"Oh yeah, how could I not? I'm the only one with a degree beyond high school. And I have two of them."

"That could change if I ever stop skating, Mr. Marine Biologist."

"You'll never stop skating, Thad, we both know that."

Thad was quiet for a second. Then he started laughing.

Scott began laughing too, and by the time they arrived in their parents' driveway, they were both struggling to breathe.

Thad had to force himself to inhale. "It is so good to be home."

The next day, the green of the golf course went on forever when Thad arrived with Scott and James in tow. "Yesss!!" Thad said when he saw how empty it was. Only two other groups were visible, and they were much further down on the course.

"I'm glad you're happy," James said.

"Yeah, you're the only one who's good at this game," Scott added.

"You guys haven't been playing while I'm gone?" Thad asked. "I thought you, at least, would do your best to beat me." He jokingly swung his club at Scott.

"No way," Scott said. "It's only fun when you're around. Too much waiting around otherwise, not enough action."

"It is a gentleman's game," Thad agreed.

"Definitely not for Scott, then," James teased.

"Are you calling me a low life?"

"Yes," Thad said, pretending to hide his answer behind his hand as they got to the first hole.

"Shut up!" Scott cried, but both brothers were laughing again.

"You never would have appreciated golf as a child," James told his older son. "You were all hockey and basketball. All running, without a moment's rest."

"Even now, it's not my first choice," Scott admitted. "I can only enjoy it when you guys are with me."

Thad smiled as he eyed the white ball in front of him. Then he swung. The ball disappeared into the sunlight for a minute before landing seventy yards down.

James shook his head. "I can never believe how good you are at a second sport. You could have gone into golf instead of skating."

"No way. I like golf, but it'll always be a hobby. Skating is where it's at for me."

It was not until he and James were driving back to James and Rosie's house that Thad thought more about that line. *I still love skating,* he realized. *I've got to make it to the Olympics—and medal when I get there. I'll never be happy with myself if I don't.*

"What time are you due at the rink?" James asked Thad the next morning.

"Not until two."

"Oh, you have the whole morning free. Do you want to go out on the water? I'm not taking out a group until noon."

"Sure," Thad answered. *Mostly to spend the time with Mom and Dad. I'm not any better with boats than when I was a kid.*

Sure enough, they had barely gotten away from the dock when Thad began to feel a little queasy. He put one hand on the railing and stared back at the shore, hoping that its straight line would make him feel better.

Rosie joined him at the railing. "You still haven't gotten used to it, have you?"

Thad shook his head.

Rosie looked amused. "It's taken me years to get comfortable on your father's boats, but I've always liked the water."

"I still prefer the ice," Thad mumbled.

"And with good reason." Rosie smiled. Then she glanced to where James was steering the boat. "I'm just glad he's still doing something that makes him happy."

"Yup." Thad stared out over the water. He was glad when it got close enough to noon that James turned the boat back around and headed for the shore. He was even happier when he was standing on the dock.

"Have a good time at the rink," James said as a group of tourists approached.

"I will."

By the time he arrived there, carrying his skates, Thad already felt like he was gliding. *And I'm still on solid ground.* A smile lit up his face as he saw a number of kids of various ages heading inside. Several parents followed, and Thad thought back to when Rosie would drive him and other kids to the ice. *That feels like forever ago.*

Thad made his way across the parking lot. He reached the door to the rink just behind a group of kids. One of the mothers turned to look at him as she held the door open for him. Then she smiled. "I heard you were coming to teach lessons today."

"Here I am," Thad replied. *She recognizes me. Maybe there is a benefit to all that media attention.*

Inside, Thad met with Courtney Cook, the woman who ran the rink's skating lessons. "We've never had someone that's as famous as you come to teach a lesson," she said. "You are definitely going to inspire these kids."

Thad smiled back. "I'm only as good as where I came from. I know what it's like to grow up in a small town without access to resources. This rink has grown a lot since I was a kid and I'm happy to help continue that."

"Half of it is from the tourists who are here in the summer. It's the only indoor rink in this area. We get more business in the summer than the winter."

Thad shrugged. "Whatever it takes to stay open."

"Now that I agree with. Come on, let's get to the ice."

Thad needed no urging to follow her, but he waited at the side of the rink as she gathered the students together. *These must be the youngest students they have,* Thad thought as he guessed that the kids ranged in age from three or four years old to eight or nine. Of the close to thirty kids on the ice, there were only two boys. *Typical,* Thad thought as Courtney quieted the kids down.

"Last week I told you all we would have someone special here today," Courtney said. "This skater is a two-time Olympian, has been National Champion three times, and Worlds medalist three times as well. But best of all, he grew up right here in Gloucester and skated at this very rink when he was a kid. Please help me welcome Thad Moulton."

Thad heard clapping from the stands, and for the first time, he realized that a number of parents had gathered. But it was the kids whose expressions tugged at his chest. They were all smiling, and a few were wearing grins that took up their whole faces. Thad grinned back as he skated to the center of the ice.

"How is everyone today?" he asked.

"Good," the kids all yelled at the same time.

"Great. First, we're going to start by warming up. Everyone grab a friend's hand and we're going to skate around the ice a few times." Thad reached out to the girl nearest to him and was rewarded with a strong grip in return. He waited until the kids were all holding on to each other before leading them in four laps around the rink.

Then he began showing them different edges, both for jumps and different types of spins and footwork. Three of the oldest kids were already working on double toe loops, so Thad gave them pointers and demonstrated a couple of jumps. "Great work!" he cried when one of the girls landed one after only a few minutes of instruction.

Then one of the boys in the class danced up to Thad, a big grin on his face. He skated smoothly around Thad twice and then began a few steps of fancy footwork. Thad grinned in reply and answered with a few steps of his own. The boy copied them, and Thad did a few more. The boy followed him without hesitation. Within seconds they were swirling around the ice.

The other kids moved out of their way as Courtney and the parents around her began clapping. Soon all the kids were cheering. By the time Thad made it back to the group, he was laughing as hard as the little boy was. "Having fun?" he asked.

"Yeah!" the little boy shouted back.

When the lesson was over, Thad made his way into the stands. The parents took pictures of him, both alone and with their children. It was more than an hour later before the rink started to empty out.

"That was great!" Courtney said. "Those kids had so much fun!"

"It's wonderful to be here." Thad grabbed his coat and unzipped one of its small pockets. A second later, he was handing Courtney a check. "This is for the skating lessons that the rink gives. If there are kids who are having trouble affording the lessons, I want this to go toward helping them first."

Courtney glanced down at the check and sucked in a breath. "This is very generous."

"I grew up with hardly anything. My parents had trouble affording lessons too. The community came together to help fund my skating when my parents couldn't pay anymore—it's why I've gotten as far as I have." Thad took a breath. "I want to help other kids who are in the same position."

Courtney nodded and put the check in her pocket. "Saying thank you doesn't even begin to express it. Your being here today has already changed these kids' lives."

Thad smiled. "That one little boy knows his footwork."

Courtney laughed. "Kyle. He's a firecracker, isn't he?"

"I hope he stays that way. We boys are in the minority in figure skating."

"Yeah, that hasn't changed much since you skated here as a kid." Courtney's eyes flickered past Thad.

Thad turned around. His father was hesitating at the edge of the stands, as if he did not want to be seen. "Hi, Dad." Thad's eyebrows came together. "How long have you been waiting?"

"Not too long," James answered.

It's longer than he's saying, I'm sure of it. "Well, we're just about done here."

Courtney took a few steps forward. "I'm so glad your son came out today. This has been something we'll all remember for a long time."

A slight smile made James' lips twitch upward. "Yes, Thad has that effect on people."

Thad raised his eyebrows as Courtney said her goodbyes and headed back to her office. "I've never heard you say that."

"You don't see the number of people around here who ask if I'm related to you."

Thad smiled as he and James left the rink. Outside, the summer sun was making its way toward the horizon, and Thad inhaled a long breath that smelled of the nearby water. "It's nice to be here."

James nodded as they got into his car. "How much money did you give them?"

"Ten thousand dollars."

"That's a lot."

"Skating is expensive."

"I know." James rolled his eyes in Thad's direction as they pulled out of the parking lot.

"I meant what I told Courtney. My career would have ended a decade ago except for the community's help. Some of those kids there today have potential, but it isn't easy."

James nodded. "Don't I know it."

Both of them were silent as they wound through the familiar streets of Gloucester. Then James turned the car onto the street where Thad had grown up. "Thanks for picking me up," Thad said as they turned into the driveway.

"Sure, I wouldn't have missed getting you. I don't see you enough as it is."

Chapter 11

T wo days later, Thad felt the chill of the ice as he left the locker room at McNichols Arena. He rounded the corner, picturing his blades gliding across the ice—and he caught sight of Trevor and Mia together in the stands. The two coaches were holding hands, and Trevor's free arm was around Mia's shoulders.

Thad's heart rate spiked, and his face got warm. "Trevor, what's going on?" He was shocked when the words came out smoothly.

Both coaches jerked toward him at the same time, and Mia pulled away from Trevor. Trevor glanced at her. Then he looked back at Thad and stood up. "Nothing's going on. Come on, let's get onto the ice."

Who is he kidding? Thad thought as he looked over at Mia. But Mia stared out over the ice. Her jaw was clenched, and Thad knew he would not get anything out of her.

"How was your time in Gloucester?" Trevor asked.

"Fine," Thad said curtly. He sat down on the bench closest to the ice and began putting his skates on.

Trevor watched him for a moment before pulling on his own skates. The two men skated to the center of the ice in silence. Thad glanced back up into the stands. Mia had already disappeared, and Thad wondered where Emily was.

"After you warm up and stretch, I want to do a run through of the long program we've been planning to *The Untouchables*," Trevor said.

Thad nodded and began doing laps around the ice, slowly at first and then faster. Everything felt loose and easy, and Thad was surprised. *Maybe having a few days off was a good thing.*

When he left the ice to stretch, Mia was still nowhere to be found. Thad took a minute to check the schedule that was hanging on the boards. *Emily isn't due on the ice for another two hours, and the rest of Mia's students don't come in until this afternoon. What else was she doing here, except to be with Trevor? She should have been sleeping in.*

When he was finished stretching, Thad got back on the ice and made his way to the center of the rink. He had barely been holding his starting pose for a few seconds when the opening strains of his music soared through the arena. Thad raised his arms and pushed off across the ice. His arms felt loose and long, and his legs worked on their own.

The music picked up its pace, and Thad moved along with it, through three triple jumps and two doubles. Each note vibrated through his body, and peace flowed through his brain. *This is so nice,* he thought as he pulled himself into a spin. He went faster and faster until he was finished. Three more jumps followed, and Thad was smiling by the time the music ended.

"Nice job," Trevor said as Thad came off the ice. "Now, what I want to work on next is..."

Thad spent more time on the ice, and when his workout was over, Trevor talked more than usual. Thad listened with half an ear. *Trying to fill the space, Trevor?* he thought as images of Trevor and Mia walking off together in the airport before their flights to Worlds leapt into his mind. *This has been going on for a while.*

Thad clenched his teeth but could not stop the ache that was rising in his stomach. *This will not end well,* he thought, and his anxiety rose within him like a tornado.

Still, it took Thad several days to work up the courage to talk to Emily about their coaches. He waited in the stands until she had finished practice. Then he glanced around the arena and was glad when Trevor and Mia were out of earshot. *I don't see Trevor anywhere,* he realized.

"Trevor might have left already," Emily said, bringing Thad back to the present. "I saw him heading for the door."

Thad nodded. "Perhaps that's best." He lowered his voice. "I saw him and Mia together when I first got to the ice a few days ago. I wondered if maybe they were seeing each other."

Now it was Emily's turn to look around the arena for her coach. "I was wondering that too." Her voice was also lower than normal. "They do seem to be spending a lot of time together—more than I would expect just by being our coaches. And I've thought for a while that they seemed more... friendly than necessary."

Thad made a face. "I can't help but think of Anne, though."

"Yeah." Emily drew out the word. "I can't say I'd ever want to say anything to her, though. And I'd want more proof."

"Proof? Like, catching them in the act, even more than what I saw the other day?"

"Yeah, like that. Though I don't know that I'd say anything to Anne. Ever."

"I lived with them, though. It's different." Thad thought of the warmth of Trevor and Anne's house and sadness tugged at his chest.

"It is different for you, I agree."

Both skaters looked around the arena again. Trevor was still gone, and Mia was on the ice with two of her other students.

Thad swallowed. "But Trevor followed us and has been watching us, and he's the one having an affair? It isn't right."

"I'd still want more proof before coming to any conclusions," Emily answered. "Both Trevor and Mia deserve that much, at least."

"You're right," Thad said, if only to end the conversation. *Not that I have any idea what that looks like.*

The next day, Thad was just arriving at the rink for an afternoon practice when he saw Emily up ahead of him. "Emily, wait up!"

She turned around and smiled when she saw him. "Hey, Thad." She held the door to the arena open for him. "Getting in an extra practice session?"

"Why else would I be here?" Thad turned toward the locker rooms.

Emily took a deep breath.

Thad wondered if she was nervous. He stopped and waited.

"So there's a production of *Les Miserables* coming to Denver. It's playing at the Denver Center for the Performing Arts. I was wondering if you wanted to go with me?"

"Les Mis? That's a musical, isn't it?"

"Yeah. My family and I tried to see it on Broadway a few years ago when we were in New York, but the shows were sold out."

"You really want to go, don't you?"

"Oh, I'm going. I don't care if it isn't as good as Broadway. It's still an amazing show."

Thad nodded. "It's gotten great reviews everywhere. I'm happy to go with you if you want."

Emily grinned. "Awesome, I'll get tickets!"

Thad smiled at her enthusiasm. Only looking around for their coaches dampened his own happiness. He didn't see either Trevor or Mia, however. *They wouldn't do anything stupid,* Thad thought as he went to the locker room. He was changing his clothing before he thought of Emily's invitation again. *That's going to be fun. I'm looking forward to it already.*

Trevor ended Thad's practice that day by saying, "on Saturday, I'm going to a dinner that the mayor is hosting, about sports in Denver. He's hoping to attract more events, more advertising."

"I saw something in the paper about that. And the mayor—that's high level."

"Yeah, black tie event. I can't wait." Trevor's words were sarcastic, but he was smiling. "I want to put in a good word about more funding for skating."

Thad rolled his eyes. "It'll mean more funding for hockey. That's the only kind of skating the mayor knows about."

"Not if I have anything to say about it."

"Good luck. By the way, Anne invited me for dinner on Friday."

"Yeah, she told me. Make sure you're on time." Trevor was still smiling.

"I will be." *When does he ever have to remind me?* Resentment, unbidden, rose in Thad's chest.

That Friday, Thad arrived at Trevor and Anne's house looking forward to the evening. It was almost dark by the time he arrived, and Thad found himself looking at the clock on his dashboard. *Fall already,* he thought. *But it is September.* He had barely gotten inside when Caleb bounced into the room, grinning. "Hi, Thad!" he yelped.

Thad smiled back and ruffled his hair. "I hear your training's going well."

Caleb's head bobbed up and down. "Yeah! I'm hoping to place at one of the junior events in the next couple of years!"

"I hope so too—that would be great, wouldn't it?"

A little while later, Anne looked over at Trevor as they sat down to dinner. "What time is your event with the mayor tomorrow night?"

"It starts at 8, but I was planning on being there a little earlier. There are a lot of reporters and big donors that are supposed to be there." Trevor looked over at Thad. "I'm glad Sunday is a day off from the rink. These damn things run until two or three in the morning."

"I won't wait up for you," Anne teased.

"Good idea," Trevor answered seriously. "I took a room at the resort for the night—I don't want to drive home that late."

"Resort?" Thad repeated. "Why did I think it was at the Oxford? Isn't that downtown?"

Trevor shook his head. "It was there last year. This year it's at Breckenridge. It can take a couple of hours to get there during the day, far enough that I don't want to be driving home in the middle of the night."

"Why would the mayor hold an event so far outside the city?" Thad asked.

"Because he's spending a few days there on vacation." Trevor smiled. "Sometimes I think he has a better job than I do."

Despite Trevor's smile, Thad thought he detected something else in his coach's gaze too—uncertainty? Anger at being challenged? Thad wasn't sure. He swallowed and looked at his plate. *I know that event is at the Oxford because I saw an article about it in the paper yesterday—the mayor wanted to hold it there because it's one of the city's oldest hotels,* he thought. *Trevor is lying. Maybe he's afraid of being caught, and that's what I see in his face.*

Thad thought about the time his coach had been spending with Mia, and his face burned. He pushed his food around his plate without being able to eat it. When he looked back at Anne, though, she was smiling.

"Well, I hope you get to speak with the mayor and everyone else," she said. "It would be wonderful if figure skating were recognized for a change."

The next day, Trevor said, "you're on your own for this afternoon's practice. I have to get my stuff together and head out to Breckenridge."

Thad nodded. "That sounds good. I'm planning on working on the music for my short program. Brianna and I are setting something to *Carmina Burana.*"

"Ooh, good idea."

When practice was over, Thad watched his coach leave in a hurry and shook his head. *I wonder if Anne knows or suspects anything.*

Then Emily skated over. "He leaving for the dinner with the mayor?"

"Yeah."

"Mia's going too. She left already."

"I'd be willing to bet they're going together."

"On some levels, that makes sense. They're two of the top coaches in the area, and they both have skaters who are going places." Emily smiled.

"And on other levels?" Thad asked wearily.

"Mia said she was staying overnight at the hotel because the thing runs so late. It would be nice if I could do that sometimes without her yelling at me."

"Trevor said he was staying overnight too—only he told Anne it was in Breckenridge."

"Oh boy." Emily frowned.

"I know, a direct lie. I don't know if I can live with that." Thad looked around the arena and was glad when he only saw Joaquin on the ice. The rest of the skaters and parents were on the other side of the arena, too far away to hear the conversation.

Emily took a deep breath. "I don't know. There are so many levels on which I just want to leave all that alone and focus on my skating. Nationals and Olympics aren't that far away—I just want to leave everything else alone until those competitions are over."

"Yeah, I hear you. I just don't know if I can do that."

Emily reached out and took his hand. "Let it go. There's nothing you can do about their behavior. Focus on your skating."

"It's a bit hypocritical of them, though, don't you think? Trevor keeping an eye on us while he's the one having an affair?"

"Oh, I don't think any of it is right. All I'm saying is, it's not our problem. Our problem is Nationals and Olympics."

Thad sighed. "But our lives are so intertwined with our coaches that separating what they're doing from our skating is sort of impossible."

Emily dropped his hand and looked out across the ice. "Maybe we need to do that anyway. I know I've worked too hard to get to where I am to let them undermine it now."

On Monday morning, Thad crossed the parking lot at McNichols Arena for his usual six a.m. practice session. The rising sun cast pink streaks across the sky, and Thad inhaled the cool air around him. *It's beautiful out,* he thought.

A light went on nearby, and Thad's head jerked in that direction. A man was getting out of his car, and the car's interior light burned into Thad's retinas in the semi-darkness. It went off as the man slammed his car door, but then it was sound that reverberated across the previously silent parking lot. Thad winced.

The man hurried toward him, and Thad tensed. "You're Thad Moulton, aren't you?"

Thad winced again as the man's high, whiney voice reached his ears. "Who're you?" he answered, even as he kept walking.

"Eric Tucker, with the *Denver Post*. I've covered figure skating for years now."

"So you already know who I am." Thad's annoyance reached hurricane level.

Eric ignored his tone. "Is it true that your coach is having an affair with Mia Spencer?"

Thad froze. "What?"

"So it's true then?"

"I didn't say that. Where are you getting your information from?"

"Both of them were at the mayor's event on Saturday night, and they shared a room when it was over. They looked pretty cuddly at breakfast the next morning, too."

"Go away." Thad began walking back toward the arena.

Eric stepped in front of him. "Does Trevor's wife know about this? Did you?"

"I have nothing to say, except that I'm now late for practice, thanks to you." Thad glared at Eric, and the reporter stepped back. "Some of us have a job to do."

"That includes me!" Eric said indignantly, but he did move a few more inches away from Thad.

Thad shoved past him and went inside. He was glad for the silence of the arena, and for the coolness of the ice. He made his way to the locker room and shoved his duffel bag into the nearest locker. He put his skates on the floor and changed into his workout gear. Then he sat on the bench in front of the lockers, leaned back against the lockers themselves, and closed his eyes.

It was a few minutes later before he had collected himself enough to go out on the ice. Trevor was already in the stands, but he said nothing as Thad warmed up. *He has to know something's going on,* Thad thought. When warmups were over, Thad made his way off the ice to stretch out. Trevor gave him some time before he came over with instructions for the day's workout.

Now's my chance, Thad thought. *If I don't say something now, we'll be overrun with reporters, and it'll be ugly.* He took a deep breath. "There was a reporter from the *Denver Post* waiting for me in the parking lot when I got here."

"What?" Trevor's voice was sharp.

"Only person in the parking lot besides me."

"What did he want?"

"To know about you and Mia."

Trevor burst out with a series of expletives.

Thad cringed. "So he was right, then?" He hadn't finished speaking when a group of people appeared at the edge of the seats. Eric was in front.

Trevor's head jerked back toward Thad. "You are not to say anything about this to anyone, you hear me?" His voice was dangerously low.

Thad stood up. "Sounds like I'd better get back on the ice." He had barely glided away when the reporters started shouting questions at Trevor.

"How long have you and Mia been together?" someone yelled.

"Does your wife know?" someone else asked, and Thad thought he recognized Eric's voice.

Thad winced and skated faster. *I'll go through my short program, even without the music,* he decided. He ran through the program once and then again. He practiced his triple jumps and footwork before realizing that Trevor had disappeared and that the reporters were now lined up around the ice, taking pictures of him instead. *Great,* he thought sarcastically. *I'm glad I landed all my jumps.*

The reporters surrounded him as he got off the ice. "Thad, you look great on the ice," said a woman Thad did not recognize. "Your jumps are clean and your footwork is flawless."

"Thanks," Thad answered automatically. *What does she really want?*

"Did you know Trevor and Mia were seeing each other?"

"No comment." Thad tried to move forward and was held in place by the crush of reporters.

"How does this affect your chances in competition?" Eric asked. "You have a few big ones coming up next year, don't you?"

"*No comment,*" Thad repeated forcefully. He shoved his way through the mass of people, cameras, and microphones in front of him and hoped he didn't trip over his skates. He was relieved when he made his way back to the locker room, even as he hoped the reporters did not follow him in there.

"Noisy out there, isn't it?"

It took the words a minute to register in Thad's ears. When he looked over, several members of the Avalanche were looking at him as they got changed. Jack Wallace was nearest to him, and it took Thad another second to realize that it was Jack who had spoken.

"Yes, it is." Thad's eyelids felt like they were glued open, and he hoped his shock didn't show.

"Don't worry, those reporters won't stay around for long." Jack grabbed his hockey stick and made a dash for the door. The rest of the team followed him, heading for their own practice.

Thad managed a smirk as he shook his head in the now-quiet locker room. *I hope they get the media out of here. Maybe their sticks will be more useful than my words.*

When he had finished stretching out and changing back into his street clothes, Thad grabbed his duffel bag, took a deep breath, and headed for the back door. Everything around him remained quiet, and Thad was relieved. Outside, he made a dash for his car. He pictured Trevor and Anne's house as he started the ignition. *I'll bet anything Trevor's there now,* he thought.

Clouds gathered as he drove, black and ominous. *There's a storm coming, no doubt about it.* It was quiet outside Trevor's house, though, and Thad almost dared to hope. *Maybe the locusts haven't arrived yet.* Still, he parked in front of the house next door, just in case.

Anne's car was in the Galloways' driveway. Trevor's was not, and Thad wondered where his coach could be. He left his bag in his back seat and jogged up the front steps. Then he jammed his finger into Trevor and Anne's doorbell. A second later, the bell's chimes rang through the house.

Anne pulled the door open a minute later. She was still wearing her coat and gloves. "Thad, what's going on?"

"Is Trevor here?"

"No, I thought he was with you at the rink." Anne stepped back to allow Thad to come into the house. "I just got back from work. What's going on?"

Thad closed the door behind him. "Is Caleb here?"

"No, he's at school for the afternoon. What's going on?" Anne pulled her gloves off.

"Anne, there were reporters at the rink. One was waiting for me in the parking lot when I got there at six this morning!"

"What did they want?" Anne looked bewildered.

"The mayor's event on Saturday wasn't at Breckenridge like Trevor said it was—it was at the Oxford. Trevor and Mia both stayed there overnight."

"Mia Spencer? The coach? What did she..." Anne looked at the floor, then back at Thad.

"I'm sorry. I was hoping Trevor was here to tell you himself before it hit the news."

"Are you saying what I think you're saying?" Anne shrieked.

Suddenly, Thad's mouth was very dry. He managed a nod.

"That stupid pig!" Anne threw her gloves across the room. "I should have known!"

Thad shook his head and wished he could say something, but his words died within him. Two cars pulled up in front of the house. One had a *Denver Post* logo on it, the other a CBS insignia. "Crap," he mumbled.

Anne went to the window. Already, Eric and two other reporters were approaching the house. Anne's face hardened as two more cars pulled up across the street. "Go out the back door," she ordered. "Get out of here without them seeing you."

"What?" Thad yelped. "You want to deal with them without Trevor here?"

"He's probably with that little bitch. I should have known something was happening." Anne shook her head. "I don't want you involved with this at all."

"Too late," Thad mumbled.

The doorbell rang, and Anne cursed. Then she pointed at the back door. "Get out before they see you! I'll deal with this!"

"Anne—"

"I mean it! Go! I'll do this my way."

Thad saw the determination on her face and headed for the back door. He put his hand on the doorknob but waited long enough to hear Anne open the front door and start speaking. "I don't know why you're here or what you want!" Her voice was loud and firm.

Multiple yelling voices answered her, and Thad heard both Trevor's name and Mia's. Then someone asked, "will this affect Thad Moulton's chance at the Olympics? Will he leave for another coach?"

"The Olympics are only a few months away," someone else called. "Why would your husband hurt his best chances at a medal?"

"This is a private matter between me and my husband," Anne answered. "How we handle it, and how Thad handles his future, will be discussed in private."

Another cacophony of voices answered her.

"I'm sorry, I do not have a statement to make at this time." Anne's voice was calm and controlled, even if it was louder than normal.

Thad closed his eyes. It didn't stop his tears from spilling out and falling down his face. He yanked the back door open and ran from the house. His breath came in gasps as he crept through the bushes separating the Galloways' property from their neighbors. He moved faster once his feet hit manicured lawn again, and soon he was diving into his car. He jammed his seat belt across his body and thrust his key into the ignition. Then he slammed his foot onto the accelerator, ignoring the one-way sign on the street and the fact that he was going in the opposite direction. *I have to get out of here.*

Thad's mind raced as fast as his car as he flew down the street. It was not until he was on I-70 that he realized that he had no idea where he was going. *Damn,* he thought. He pictured Trevor and Mia, and thought of Anne facing all those reporters alone. Then he was unable to swallow around the lump that rose in his throat.

Up above him, the black clouds that had been gathering opened up, and Thad found himself ensconced in a wall of rain. *Fantastic,* he thought sarcastically as he struggled to see out the windshield. His mind continued to seethe even as the miles of beautiful scenery passed by. *I wish I could see more.* Thad shook his head at himself. *That would only help if I could see into the future. What if those reporters are right and this kills my chance at the Olympics? I can't wait another four years.*

The rain let up enough near Idaho Springs that Thad was comfortable getting out of the car to get gas. Then he continued in the same direction rather than going back to Denver. *I don't want to be home,* he realized.

It was not until signs appeared for Vail, more than two hours after he had left Denver, that Thad finally felt like stopping. Memories of competitions in Vail flooded through his mind, many from when he, Trevor, and Anne had first moved to Colorado. *That feels like forever ago,* Thad thought, but one hotel stood out in his mind, *and thank God for that. I need a place to stay.*

A few minutes later, Thad pulled into the parking lot of the Sonnenalp Hotel and hoped no one recognized him. *Though I guess that'll depend on how much the news is reporting on Trevor and Mia.* Thad rolled his eyes as he got out the car and grabbed his duffel bag. *I can't believe any of this.* Inside, Thad approached the front desk and was relieved when they had a room available.

A few minutes later, he dragged himself to his room and was glad for the quiet. He filled up his water bottle at the faucet in the bathroom. It was not until he had emptied the bottle again that he realized how thirsty he was. *Damn,* he thought as he refilled the bottle once more.

When he made his way back into the room, the sparsity of his duffel bag on the bed, with no other belongings, hit him. He sank onto the bed, and his spirits sank even further with the motion. It took all of his energy to get up and pick up the phone. His fingers dialed his parents' number without any command from his brain.

"Thad, is everything alright?" Rosie asked a minute later.

"Not really," Thad answered as he heard James pick up one of the other phones in the house.

"What's going on?" Rosie asked. "It's unlike you to call this early in the day."

Thad struggled to take a deep breath and cursed inwardly when it came out shuddering. "Trevor has been having an affair with Emily's coach. It's been going on for a while and they got caught. The press is all over it—they even went to Anne's house and hassled her!"

Rosie took a breath. "Did you know this was happening?"

"I suspected. Anne was totally in the dark, though." Thad clenched his teeth and willed his tears not to overflow again.

"Where are you now?" Rosie asked. "Are you at the rink?"

"No, I had practice this morning before everything blew up. I went for a drive to get out of the way once the reporters descended." Thad stood up and paced around as far as the phone's cord would let him.

"Where are you, then?"

Thad sighed. "At a hotel in Vail. I just got into the car and drove. I don't... I didn't feel like going home. I don't know what to do anymore." He sank back onto the bed.

"Well, we haven't heard anything about it on the news here, if that makes you feel better."

"Not really. I'm sure the east coast just hasn't caught on yet."

"Well, take some time to process it all, but you need to get back to your training at some point."

"Is that all you can tell me?" Thad had to control himself from throwing the phone across the room.

"It's not something you don't know already. The timing of this couldn't be much worse, except to be even closer to the Olympics."

Thad's anger flared. "That's all anyone is thinking about these days!"

"Including you, I'd wager," James said.

"Oh, finally, you say something, Dad!" Thad burst out. "This whole thing is killing me! I can't believe Trevor would act like this, and now it's all the press will focus on! So much for my skating being good or anything else! It's always been like this, and I'm sick of it!"

His parents were silent for a moment. *They don't know what to say,* Thad realized.

"I think it would be a shame to let this derail your Olympic dream. You're so close," Rosie said. "You've been in fine form recently, and you have a good shot at medaling. That's the only thing that should matter to you now."

"It *is* the only thing that matters to me."

"No, Trevor's behavior bothers you, as it should," James answered.

"Thanks, Dad." Thad rolled his eyes and swiped at his nose. It was only when his hand came away wet that he reached for the box of tissues on the nightstand.

"I would be more worried if it didn't bother you," James said. "You are human, and this is exploding in your face. The question now is how to move forward with your training with a clear mind."

"Brianna has been good for you since you and Trevor brought her on," Rosie said. "Do you think switching coaches would help?"

"Like firing Trevor completely?" Thad took a breath. "I've been skating with him my whole life."

"I know that," Rosie answered. "But he's obviously not a good influence right now."

"Yeah, you need someone who's steady at the helm," James added.

"And I think Brianna is," Rosie said.

Thad took another deep breath and thought of his focus after the missed jump and injury in Sacramento. "Yeah, she is."

"Well, think about it," James said. "You need to get rid of every distraction right now."

"Hang in there, Thad," Rosie added. "You've been through some rough patches in the past and you've always come out stronger for them. This will be no different."

"I wish I had your confidence."

"You will. You'll get there, I promise."

Thad was exhausted by the time he hung up the phone. *I'm also hungry,* he realized. *What are my options?* He went to the window, pulled back the curtain, and looked out. A view of the mountains in the gathering evening calmed him slightly. *This is beautiful, at least.*

He spent another moment staring out before twisting his head in the other direction. Twinkling lights up the street told him that there were plenty of restaurants there, but none of that appealed to him. *I don't feel like going somewhere, sitting and ordering. Besides, what if someone recognizes me? I can't handle dealing with people right now.*

Thad spent a few more minutes staring out over the mountains. Then he turned around and saw how dark the room had become. He closed the curtains and turned on the nearest lamp. Then his eyes fell on the hotel's room service menu. *That's perfect. I just hope they have something good.*

Thad's stomach was growling by the time his hamburger and French fries arrived half an hour later. He thanked the man delivering it but was glad when he left. Then he tossed himself into the room's desk chair and started eating. It was not until he turned to put ketchup on his fries that a smile almost broke through his gloom. *They gave me a lot of extra ketchup.* Memories of dumping ketchup on absolutely everything as a kid turned his smirk into a full smile. *Maybe the people working here know who I am after all.*

Thad felt a lot calmer when his plate was empty and his stomach was full. *This is Trevor's fault, and it's also his problem to deal with,* he decided. *I still want an Olympic medal, even if I have to do it without him.* He thought of Rosie's suggestion that he work with Brianna exclusively. *She's right. I need Trevor out of the way, probably until the Olympics, but at least until all of this crap blows over.*

Chapter 12

T had left Vail early the next morning. *If I get back to Denver early enough, I can still get some time on the ice,* he thought. He caught sight of the occasional yellow and red leaves as he drove. *Time is waning. The Olympics will be here before I know it.* He was glad when the drive home went faster than his fleeing the day before. He glanced into the rearview mirror and saw his duffel bag and skates in the back seat. *I'll just go to the rink rather than going home first.*

Thad focused on the road again as he changed lanes. Then he thought of Brianna and the conversation with his parents. He stared out the windshield, first at the long highway in front of him, then at the few other cars around him. When he thought of Trevor again, he cringed. *I can't keep working with him.*

Thad arrived back in Denver an hour later. The rink's parking lot was crowded, much more so than he was used to seeing at six in the morning. *What were you expecting, dummy?* he asked himself. *It's almost ten o'clock now.* He parked, steeled himself, and went inside.

A few of the usual groups were there—kids for lessons, but also some of the more advanced skaters. Thad caught sight of both Joaquin and Emily on the ice and went to put his skates on. It was not until he was tightening his laces that he realized how many reporters were in the stands, and how many cameras were now focused on him. Thad swallowed and kept a neutral expression on his face. Then he looked for Trevor.

His coach was at the boards, giving instructions to some of his younger students. Thad searched the ice for Caleb and didn't see him. To his shock, Mia was nearby, giving Emily some tips. *You'd think they'd at least play at not being together.* Then Thad realized that most of the parents in the arena were watching Trevor and Mia, and none of them looked happy.

This is wonderful, Thad thought sarcastically as he stepped onto the ice. He took a deep breath and focused on himself. Then he went through his warmups as usual. It was not until he returned to the side of the rink to stretch that Trevor spoke to him.

"Nice of you to show up. You missed your regular session."

"I'm here now."

Trevor glanced at the reporters around them. When he looked back at Thad, he was all business. "I want to work on your long program and your spins today."

Thad nodded and took off. *We'll have to have the conversation about Brianna when there aren't so many people around.* He was glad when Joaquin met him in the center of the ice.

"I'm now glad Trevor never took me on as a client," Joaquin said.

"Count your blessings, right?" Thad quipped.

Joaquin lowered his voice. "You know, Laura and I were discussing everything last night—maybe it's worth it for you to work with Brianna instead of Trevor. I've always thought he was a difficult guy, and all this comes at a bad time."

Thad looked down at the ice. "Yeah, I was thinking that too."

"Thad!" Trevor called from the side of the rink. "Get moving."

The barest of amused looks crossed Joaquin's face. He gave Thad a nod before skating off.

Thad swallowed and glided across the ice. Then he moved into the first steps of his long program. He could barely hear his music above all the other noise in the arena, but somehow it was enough. He went through the program once and then worked on the jumps that had not been clean.

Trevor nodded as he came off the ice. "A couple of falls are fine at this stage of the game. I wouldn't worry about it now."

"I'm not worried," Thad answered, and was surprised when he was telling the truth. He stretched out and went to the locker room. He was walking toward the door of the arena when he saw Emily on the ice. He paused for a second to watch her. She came out of a spin that looked slow before she turned in his direction.

Thad was sure he saw sadness in her eyes, even from halfway across the ice. *Should I talk to her?* he wondered. *This can't be easy on her, either.* But Emily continued skating, so Thad turned and left. Outside, he was glad to be out of the arena—until he saw Trevor in the parking lot, waiting for him. His teeth clenched.

"Have you seen Anne?" Trevor asked, despite the number of reporters that were coming toward them.

"Not since yesterday."

"Did you tell her what was going on?"

"I didn't have to. A dozen reporters showed up at your house while I was there."

Trevor winced, and Thad was glad he was finally showing some compunction. "She wasn't there when I got home last night."

"I don't blame her." Thad glared at Trevor as he felt the heat of the afternoon sun on his back.

Trevor swallowed and glanced at the reporters that were a couple of feet away. "What would you have had me do, Thad, walk away from Mia?"

"That would have been smart."

Trevor shook his head. "You don't get it. Your parents have a happy marriage, so you think everyone else is going to be like that. But it's not possible for everyone."

"You could still have handled it better."

"Life isn't always clean, Thad." Trevor's anger pulsed through his voice like a low bass under the rest of the music.

Yeah, I'm beginning to see that, Thad thought, but he could not get his tongue to work. He saw Trevor's struggle in his clenched jaw and pleading eyes.

"We'll discuss this later," Trevor said.

"Or not," Thad mumbled. He turned to go back to his car.

Trevor grabbed his arm. Thad jerked away from him. Trevor glanced at the reporters before looking back at Thad. "Don't go running off. We still have to train for Nationals and the Olympics."

No, only I have to, Thad thought. But instead of saying anything, he turned away again and headed for his car. This time, Trevor let him go, and Thad made it all the way to his car before realizing that Trevor was just standing there, watching him go. The reporters around him continued staring too—and taking pictures. *Great,* Thad thought.

Sadness welled up within him as he put on his seatbelt and put his keys in the ignition. *I wish I didn't have to fire him. But I can't continue like this anymore.*

The next morning, Thad picked up the newspaper from the hallway as he left to go to the rink. He made a face at an article about Trevor and Mia that was on the first page, at the very bottom of the paper. *Unbelievable,* he thought. *Front page? Why couldn't they have relegated it to the sports page like they did every time they reported negatively about me? Or buried it on page five of the city section?*

Because everyone will want to know about it, that's why. Thad answered his own question as he tossed the paper into the passenger seat of his car and lowered himself into the driver's seat. He spent the ride to the rink picturing the ice and his short program. When the parking lot was filled with reporters again, he found himself becoming annoyed. *Don't these guys have a life?* He pulled his duffel bag from the back seat and walked toward the arena.

It took less than a minute for reporters to surround him. "Thad, are you going to continue working with Trevor?" a few of them asked.

"Do you think changing coaches this close to the Olympics could be detrimental?" one more asked.

"Go away," Thad answered. "I'm here to train, not to answer questions." He went inside and slammed the door behind him. He was glad when Brianna was on the ice alone. "Would you be willing to work with me instead of Trevor?" he murmured into the silence.

Brianna nodded. "I think that's a smart path forward."

"Then let's do it." Certainty landed in Thad's stomach, and relief flowed through the rest of his body. *I'm glad that's settled.*

Late that morning, Thad got off the ice with Brianna trailing him. Trevor was nowhere to be found. "He knows what's coming," Thad mumbled. "We'll have to go to his house."

"You okay with that?" Brianna asked.

Thad nodded. "I have to deal with this. The longer I stay in limbo, the longer it's a problem."

Brianna cleared her throat. "Okay. Stretch out and cool down and we'll head over there."

She's nervous, Thad realized. *I'm not anymore. I need to move forward. I need to make the Olympic podium.*

An hour later, he pulled out of the arena's parking lot with Brianna following him in her red Nissan. He drove to Trevor's house, feeling like his eyes were seeing everything around him while his mind remained blank. His hand even found his turn signal on its own. *I could do this drive in my sleep.*

Trevor's car was in the driveway, but the house was quiet. *Is he home?* Thad wondered as he rang the doorbell. Next to him, Brianna bent over to look into one of the front windows. "Anything?" Thad asked.

Brianna shook her head.

Thad heard a step just inside the house, and his head jerked back to the front door. A second later, Trevor pulled open the door. "Thad, what..." He stopped speaking when he saw Brianna.

"Can we come inside?" Thad asked.

Trevor looked back and forth between him and Brianna, and for a moment Thad thought he would say no. But Trevor stepped back, so Thad went inside. Brianna followed him, even as Trevor sent a mean look in her direction.

The house was quieter than Thad had been expecting. *It feels different in here,* he thought. Then a realization hit him like a sledgehammer. *It's because Anne isn't here. It doesn't feel like home anymore.*

"Look, Trevor, I've decided to hire Brianna as my coach instead of you," Thad began.

"You have to be kidding me!" Trevor burst out. "We've been together since you were ten!"

"And now it's time to move on." Thad's words came out quietly, and he was shocked by how calm he felt.

"This close to the Olympics?" Trevor yelled. "Are you out of your mind?"

"No, that's exactly why I'm doing it. I only continued skating after Worlds because I wanted to redeem myself on Olympic ice—have you forgotten about that?"

Trevor looked away.

"That's what I thought."

Trevor shook his head. "Do you want to turn out like Josh Hall, Dylan Carter, or Brandon Adams? I could name a dozen skaters who changed coaches right before the Olympics, only to crash and burn!"

"Most of those skaters had other problems and you know it!" Brianna answered. "It wasn't because they changed coaches."

"They needed stability and they weren't getting it!" Trevor snapped back.

"I've had nothing but stability and you're the one who's changing it, Trevor," Thad said. "And even with that stability, I've never done well at the Olympics. Something needs to change."

Brianna nodded. "We have two world class athletes here who are only a few months away from competing at two of the biggest competitions of their sport, and you brought the media circus down on them."

Trevor rolled his eyes. "Joaquin isn't at that level."

"You've never given him a chance," Thad answered. "It's another reason I need a change."

Trevor glared at him. "Can't change your mind once you've decided something, huh, Thad?"

"Scott said the same thing." Thad wished he could smile, but all he felt was the sadness crushing his chest. "I wish it didn't have to come to this, Trevor."

"It doesn't." Trevor swallowed. "You can always reconsider."

Thad shook his head. "I need to do this. I'm sorry, Trevor." He bit his lip and hoped the pain would banish the lump that was rising in his throat. It didn't, and he had to choke out his next words. "It's over, Trevor. I'm sorry."

"Not as sorry as I am." Trevor stared back at Thad, and his eyes were glassy.

Thad turned to leave before his pain overwhelmed him. He was out the door before it closed behind him. Only the sound of Brianna's footsteps told him that she was behind him while Trevor stayed in the house. A second later, the house's front door slammed shut. *Good,* Thad thought as he raced back toward his car.

Brianna caught up to him long enough to grab his arm. "I think you're doing the right thing, even if it doesn't look like that now."

Thad's throat closed up. All he could do was nod.

"I'll see you at the rink bright and early tomorrow. In the meantime, go and do something to clear your head—a long drive, a long hike, whatever it is."

Thad got into his car, drove away, and was glad when Trevor's house disappeared behind him. He got all of three blocks before pulling over. Then he put his head on the steering wheel and sobbed. *Sixteen years of my life down the drain. I hope the Olympics make up for that.*

After dinner the next night, Thad found himself pacing around his living room, feeling agitated but unsure of what to do with himself. Images of Emily skating her slow spin, and the hurt in her eyes, flashed through his mind. Before he could stop himself, he was reaching for the phone. He felt the night's chilly breeze through the window as he dialed and shuddered.

"Hi, Thad," Emily said a moment later.

Thad heard the hesitation in her voice. *Maybe she doesn't want to hear from me,* he thought. *Maybe calling was a bad idea.* "How are you doing? It's been a rough time recently, hasn't it?"

"For real." Emily paused for a minute. "You know, after I medaled at Nationals and Worlds, more reporters were following me. Mia said to expect that, so I thought maybe a few of them would show up at the rink sometimes."

"This is more than a few of them, and it's all the time."

"Yeah, they're there all day!" Emily exclaimed. "And they're not even there for me."

"I know. The focus is completely wrong."

Emily shook her head. "I expect that kind of hoopla at competitions. This is different. This is..." Her voice trailed off.

"I know," Thad jumped in. "I've never liked dealing with the press, but at least I know what they're going to ask at competitions. Here everything's just out of left field."

"Yeah, the rink used to be my quiet place to get everything right in my skating. It didn't matter if I fell or messed up. Now everyone's watching. I'm scared of what pictures of me might end up in the papers."

"Me too. But maybe that's one good thing about them focusing on our coaches—maybe they'll report on our falls less."

"I wish I had your optimism, Thad. I think those reporters are looking for us to screw up under the pressure, so they can report on it. I just hope it doesn't hurt our chances in competition."

"Yeah, that worries me too. I'm just trying to do my best on the ice now, even in practice." Thad looked over to where his blinds were moving in the breeze. All he could see beyond them was the night's darkness.

"That's a good idea," Emily said, and Thad thought she was smiling.

"Still, we shouldn't have been put in this position at all."

"Now, that I agree with."

"What are you going to do about it? Find a new coach?"

Emily hesitated on the other end. "I don't think so," she said after a minute. "I really have been skating better with Mia. And I don't have anyone else waiting in the wings, like you did with Brianna."

"Brianna wasn't waiting in the wings. I wasn't thinking of switching over to her at all until this whole thing happened with Trevor and Mia."

"Still, she's been there for you. I don't have anyone like that."

"You could look around. I'm sure there are other coaches who would be happy to work with you."

"That doesn't mean they'd be a good fit, Thad, especially this close to the Olympics."

Thad nodded, even if he wished the sadness in his chest would go away. "Yeah, the timing on all this is brutal."

That conversation swirled through Thad's head for a couple of days before he decided to talk to Emily about it again. He practiced off the ice as he waited for Emily's ice time to end. One dryland rotation jump followed another—two triples and then a double. *Wow, that feels good. Brianna has had me doing more of these than Trevor ever did, and I think they're helping*. He did several more before making his way back to the ice. Emily was finishing her workout, and Thad was glad. *I really need to talk to her.*

Still, he waited until Mia, who had been on the ice with Emily, made her way to another part of the arena. Mia did not even make eye contact with Thad, and he was relieved. *She reminds me of Trevor. I wish they both would go away.*

"Uh oh, I know that look," Emily said when she saw Thad. "You're unhappy about something."

Thad sent another look at Mia's back.

"How about we talk about this once we're outside?" Emily whispered. She glanced around at the other skaters that were nearby, then at the parents of the youngest kids who were waiting for ice time. "I don't want everyone to hear us."

Thad nodded, despite the frustration that was rising within him. *Mia and Trevor have gotten us plenty of attention already. I don't want to add anything else to the arena's gossip cauldron.* He joined Emily as she cooled down and stretched out. Then they both headed out into the fall's crisp air.

"You're unhappy that I've decided to keep Mia as a coach." Emily spoke in a normal voice now.

"How'd you guess?"

"I know you pretty well by now, Thad."

"Well, she and Trevor have done so much damage to our reputations and brought a lot of unwanted attention on us, at exactly the wrong time." Thad kicked at a pebble in the parking lot and succeeded in sending it flying.

"I only agree with the second part of that. No one thinks less of us as skaters because of what's going on with our coaches."

"Plenty of people have questioned our focus because of it." Thad felt like his eyes were shooting bullets at Emily. "I've already fired Trevor. I was hoping you would do the same to Mia."

Emily took a deep breath as she looked everywhere but at Thad. "I still agree with what I said on the phone the other night. I've been skating so much better with Mia. You've been with Trevor forever and were still looking for ways to improve your skating. It's different."

"Is it?" Thad's anger raged within him. "I can't look at Mia without thinking of Trevor."

Emily looked at him directly in the eye now. "Then you need to fix that. You've already switched coaches—if you're happy with Brianna, you need to let go of Trevor in every other way."

"This from the skater who's keeping the one strong tie to Trevor." Now it was Thad's turn to look all around the parking lot. "We have a lot at stake here, Emily."

"Don't you think I know that?" Emily's voice rose, and her anger brought Thad's eyes back to her face. "I know you've been to the Olympics already, but this could be my only shot!"

"It will be my last shot, I know that." Thad struggled to swallow.

Emily sighed, and now Thad thought she sounded more sad than angry. "None of this has been easy—not for either of us, but not for Mia either."

Thad shrugged. *I don't care how Mia's feeling. She brought this on herself.*

Emily filled the silence. "You know, when Mia moved here, her husband decided to stay in New York. They never had kids because Mia thought kids would interfere with her skating and coaching. That's a tough path too."

Thad looked back at her. The sadness in her eyes melted the anger from his body.

"She tried to make her marriage work long distance, but her husband started seeing someone else. They've been divorced for years now, and I think this is the first time she's started seeing anyone else."

"Yeah, seeing someone who was already married. Besides, she and Trevor did it in the least discreet way possible." Thad's anger burned in his body again, and he wished for the chill of the ice.

"And she's still a good coach. I'm staying with her." Emily turned toward her car.

"Emily, wait!"

"For what, Thad?" she called over her shoulder. Then she stopped, took a quick breath, and turned to face him. "I've been thinking about this a *lot,* and you can't change my mind. I have to do this. I have to make the Olympics, just like you, and changing coaches right now won't help me!" Tears glistened in her eyes. She turned around again, and this time, Thad let her go.

Emily got into her car and drove off. The parking lot was immediately emptier for her absence. Thad clenched his teeth and hoped his tears did not overflow. Then he went back to his own car. *First I lost Trevor, now I've lost Emily,* he thought. *I hope the Olympics are worth all of that.*

Chapter 13

T had spent the next several days avoiding Emily. His face burned and his heart pounded every time he even got a glimpse of her, but he could not bring himself to talk to her.

One night, the clock in his apartment had just clicked to 9:30 when Thad started yawning. *I'm not going to make it through this episode,* he thought as he watched the prosecutors of *Law and Order* start arguing their case. *Too bad. I'm enjoying it. I'll have to catch it on rerun.* He picked up the remote control to turn the TV off—just as a "breaking news" headline flashed across the bottom of the screen in red.

Thad leaned forward. "Figure Skater Grigoriy Arsenyev involved in car wreck in New York City," the headline read. "News at 10."

"Crap," Thad said aloud. "Now I have to stay up to see that." He stood up and paced around his apartment, hoping the movement would help him stay awake. Instead, he continued yawning. It was not until the news came on that Thad felt his anticipation wake him up. He paced around faster now, moving back and forth in front of the TV, and he was certain that his blood was moving through his veins somewhat faster as well.

Finally, a picture of Grigoriy appeared in the upper right-hand corner of the screen, and the news anchor began speaking. "Russian figure skater and World Champion Grigoriy Arsenyev has been arrested in New York City after crashing his car on the Belt Parkway," she said. The screen behind her cut to a picture of a highway with a crashed car off to the side. An ambulance and several police cars, all with flashing lights, surrounded it.

"Word has it that after submitting to a breathalyzer, Mr. Arsenyev was at twice the legal alcohol limit."

"Damn," Thad said as the cameras panned in closer. The cameras rested on a smashed car on the side of the road, but even at that angle, Thad recognized a late model Jaguar. *Wow, sweet ride. Maybe not anymore, though.*

"Police are taking Mr. Arsenyev to the hospital for observation, and word is still out on whether he'll remain in police custody after that. Mr. Arsenyev and his coach, Tatiana Lenkova, relocated to the United States for training, though he still skates for Russia…"

The reporter's voice disappeared as Thad shut off the TV. *Guess I'm not the only one having problems,* he thought as he got ready for bed. *I wonder how that will affect Grigoriy's skating.*

After three weeks of cool silence between him and Emily, Thad stepped off the ice to find Brianna glancing back and forth between the two of them. *Uh oh, I'm in for a lecture now,* he thought.

But Brianna was all business as Thad went through his cool down and stretching routine. "I think your stamina is improving," she said. "I want to continue with the regimen we've set up, including off the ice, and I want to continue running through your long and short programs in full."

Thad nodded. "That sounds good to me."

It was not until they were in the parking lot that Brianna said, "come with me. We need to talk about something else, and we need to do it away from here."

"What about my car?" Thad looked in the opposite direction from where Brianna was headed.

"I'll drop you off here when we're done."

Thad bit his lip just long enough for Brianna to get several steps away from him. Then he followed her. A few minutes later, they were sitting in the corner of a tiny, out of the way coffee shop, and Thad was glad it was almost empty. *I know what this is about.* He tugged the string on his teabag and watched as the tea brewed.

Brianna cleared her throat.

Thad dragged his eyes away from his cup.

"One of the reasons Trevor had me start working with you was to help you convey the joy you feel while skating," Brianna said. "And the last couple of weeks, you've been anything but happy."

Thad looked away and thought of Emily. He said nothing as the smell of coffee filled his nose. He raised his cup to his lips and got a mouthful of acrid tea. He reached for the sugar on the table and dumped two packets into his cup. *Two whole packets more than I normally use. I hope this conversation ends soon.*

"Would you feel better if you and Emily got back together?" Brianna asked.

"How is it that everyone knows about that?" Thad burst out. One of the baristas glanced over at him, and Thad cursed inwardly.

"I'm not everyone," Brianna answered. "The change in how you two have been acting isn't hard to notice." She paused, and Thad had trouble meeting her gaze. "So what happened between you two?"

"She decided to keep Mia as a coach, despite everything that's happened." Thad described the fight he and Emily had gotten into.

"She's allowed to make her own decisions, Thad."

"I know that. I just…"

"Just what?"

"I don't know, Brianna! It's been tough to put all of this behind me!" Thad's voice was still louder than he wanted it, and anger rose in his chest like a spike.

"It's been tough for Emily, too—and I don't think it's a good idea to throw the baby out with the bathwater."

"What's that supposed to mean?" Thad's confusion and frustration now competed for space in his chest. *Can't she just come out and say what she means? Why do I have to guess?*

"You and Emily could support each other through this. You shouldn't be running away from her. I want to see you smiling on the ice again."

Thad took a deep breath. "I'm not even sure how to fix it at this point."

Brianna smiled. "Don't worry, I'm capable of working magic there, too."

"Change of plans," Brianna said as Thad got off the ice two days later. "Tomorrow afternoon, we're getting outside and going hiking instead of being on the rink."

"That suits me," Thad answered. "A change in scenery might do me some good."

The following afternoon, he pulled into the trailhead of Red Rocks Park. To his surprise, only two other cars were parked there, and one of them was Brianna's. *The outdoors has always done me good.* He got out of the car and inhaled the fresh air. *In spite of all the time I spend at the rink. Or maybe because of it.* He took another deep breath and smelled the fallen leaves nearby, crisp and plentiful. "Ahhh," he said, speaking aloud without meaning to.

"I knew this would be good," Brianna said.

Thad's smile disappeared, though, when Emily and Mia got out of the other car nearby. Emily pressed her lips together when she saw his expression, and Thad thought he saw tears shining in her eyes. *Maybe I shouldn't be so hard on her.*

To his surprise, Mia approached him and Brianna first. Emily stood still for a minute before taking a deep breath and following her. "I'm sorry for everything that's been going on, Thad," Mia said, and her words surprised him even further. "I wouldn't have chosen the timing of any of this, and I hate how it has affected you and Emily."

Thad clenched his teeth and stared at the ground. Regret made his stomach sink.

"I never planned to get involved with Trevor when I moved here," Mia continued. "We were both married, and I respected Anne and everything she had done for Trevor, and for skating. But life has a way of happening, despite all our plans."

"Yes, I know that much." Thad thought of his previous Olympic outings, and of Nationals at the beginning of the year. To his surprise, the thought of his former trials did not sting as much as they always had. *Maybe I'm making progress with Brianna,* he thought. *Maybe I think better of my chances this season.* He took a deep breath and looked back at Mia. "Still, your actions have put both me and Emily in a bad position."

"I understand that, and it's not what I wanted." Mia looked at the ground for a minute, then back at Thad. "But the Olympics are coming up, and I know how much you and Emily want and deserve to be there. Life will always have its challenges, but part of that is putting them behind you and remaining in the moment enough to do well in competition."

"Yes, Brianna and I have been working on that." Thad sent a smirk in his coach's direction. After a minute of silence, Brianna tossed her head toward the trail, and Thad followed her. *No sense staying in the parking lot.*

Mia and Emily followed them. Mia matched Thad's strides and Emily stayed a few steps behind them. "Emily had more energy on the ice when you two were seeing each other," Mia added. "I don't want to get in the way of that."

You already did, Thad thought, and he was glad when his brain somehow commanded his tongue not to say that. "It's been tough," he said instead. "We're so close to Nationals and the Olympics that what's going on is a big distraction—a distraction that Emily and I don't need."

"I understand that," Mia said. "But I think you two are better together than at odds."

Thad glanced back at Emily as they continued walking and found her eyes on him. "I'm sorry," he told her.

"We have a common goal, Thad," Emily answered. "We should be working together to get there, not against each other."

Thad's face burned, even as he felt the chilly air on his cheeks. "You're right. I'm sorry for how I handled everything." He fell back to walk with her as Mia moved forward to talk to Brianna. Both coaches glanced back at them, but Thad pretended not to notice.

Emily reached out and took Thad's hand. "Retreating further into the bubble isn't always good."

Especially when the bubble looks like Mia and Trevor, Thad thought. Then he pictured his falls at his last two Olympics. "I know, and I've been trying to change how I handle everything."

Emily eyed him, and Thad squeezed her hand. "We can do this," she said. "The Olympics are only a few months away. We are so close to our goal."

The next night, Thad's phone rang. *I hope that's Emily,* he thought as he went to pick it up. He smiled when he heard her voice on the other end. "I was just thinking of you."

"I knew you'd want to hear my voice," Emily teased, and it sounded like she was smiling too.

"Oh, yeah, that's true." Thad laughed and wished they were in the same room together.

"Listen, we still have those tickets to Les Mis for this Saturday. I want to go."

"I do too. I haven't forgotten about the performance, don't worry."

"Good. When I bought those tickets, it felt like the performance was far in the future." Emily took a deep breath.

Thad was surprised to hear that breath shudder as it came out. "And you thought with the fight we got into that I wouldn't want to go."

"Not just the fight, the fact that we weren't talking to each other…"

"I know. I'm sorry for all of that. I want to go on Saturday, I really do. I never meant to get so far away from you." Thad bit his lip.

"Good." Emily took a steadier breath now. "Then I'll see you on Saturday."

"That you will."

On Saturday afternoon, Thad picked Emily up from her house. He had chosen to wear black pants and a dark blue, button-down shirt, but as Emily came outside, he hoped he had not dressed too simply. Her makeup and jewelry popped out at him, and her magenta dress emblazoned its color onto his eyeballs. "You look nice," he said as she got into the car.

"Thanks." A satisfied look graced her features as her perfume filled Thad's nose.

Thad pressed his foot to the accelerator so that he would not be required to say anything further. Emily did most of the talking until they arrived at the theater.

The parking lot was packed, and Thad had to search for a parking spot. "Wow, there are a lot of people here."

"I'm not surprised," Emily answered. "It's only playing for a week, and all the performances are sold out."

"I thought it would be quieter at a Saturday matinee."

"I didn't think of that. I got tickets to the afternoon performance because you have an early practice in the morning."

"One of the few times I'm not off on Sunday. Thanks for the reminder." Thad rolled his eyes as he found a parking spot and maneuvered into it.

"I knew you wouldn't want to be out too late."

"Thanks." Thad managed a smile. "You're always so considerate."

Inside, the place was teeming with energy, and Thad felt drawn in. *People are excited to be here,* he realized. Emily took his hand, and Thad looked over at her, surprised.

"Don't worry, I won't bite," she said.

"I hope not," Thad teased. Still, discomfort rose within him. *What if Trevor sees us again?* Then he chastised himself for even thinking that. *Damn it—there's nothing wrong with what we're doing. And he's not even my coach anymore.*

They stood in line at the box office for a few minutes, and when they had their tickets, they wandered through the crowd. Thad looked around and noticed people looking back at him, some openly, some surreptitiously. *They recognize us,* Thad thought.

Emily wandered into the theater's small store, and Thad followed her. "Do you want to get the soundtrack?" he asked.

"I have a copy already, from the original Broadway production. I've been thinking of setting a program or two to some of the music."

"Ah, no wonder you wanted to see this production. It all becomes clear now."

Emily smiled. "Keep an open mind. You don't just have to stick to movie soundtracks."

Thad thought of the Vivaldi music that had been flowing through his veins for the last couple of months. "Oh, I won't be."

Emily had a copy of the Denver production's soundtrack in a small bag when they left the store. "I couldn't help myself," she said with a shy smile.

"Don't worry, you're doing the right thing." Thad smiled back.

When they were in their seats, Thad looked around. They were sitting in the first row of the mezzanine, and the view was excellent. "I'm glad you got these seats. We're high enough up and far enough back that we have a great perspective."

"Yeah, without being in the last row." Emily laughed.

Thad nodded. "I've had plenty of those seats in my lifetime. It's nice to do something different."

A few minutes later, the lights went down and he leaned back in his seat. *I'm glad we're doing this.* A smile graced his face, even in the darkness.

Then the music jumped into the arena, and Thad found himself sucked into the story of the chain gang and Jean Valjean. As each character was introduced, Thad felt the tug of opposites— Valjean against Javert, pure Cosette against the darker Thenardiers. As the clouds of war gathered, Thad leaned forward in his seat. Onstage, Enjolras goaded Marius into making a decision between love and war, and the song's colors, red and black, swirled through Thad's head.

By the time the curtain fell to start the intermission, Thad was gripping his armrests. As the house lights came up, he was sure his hands were glued into position. It took him a minute to realize otherwise, and he hauled himself to his feet. "Wow."

"Yeah, that was amazing," Emily said, and she, too, sounded like she was struggling to get her words out.

They walked into the hallway to stretch their legs, and it was not until Thad was in the bathroom that he realized how much cooler it was outside the theater. *Or maybe it's just me that's overheated,* he thought as the words to the song "Red and Black" pulsated through him. *I've got to use that for a program.*

At their seats a few minutes later, Emily sat down and looked at Thad for a moment without speaking.

"What?" Thad asked.

"You know, your shirt matches your eyes."

"That's exactly what I think about when I get dressed."

Emily smiled at his sarcasm. "You should think about it. Dark blue looks good on you."

Thad shook his head, but he was laughing.

Then the house lights dimmed again, and they both faced forward. When the curtain came up, the music resounded in Thad's ears, and once more he became engrossed in the action in front of him. He ducked as shots rang out all around the barricades and seethed in frustration as the students lost to the French army. When the production was over, his heart was racing in his chest. "That was intense," he said as he and Emily left the theater.

"See, I knew you'd enjoy it. Do you want to borrow my soundtrack?" Emily held up the bag she was carrying. "You can tape it and give it back to me."

Thad thought about it until they found his car. Once more, the words of "Red and Black" rang in his ears. "That's a good idea," he decided as he put his key in the ignition. "I think I have some ideas for the music already."

Emily stared out the window as they inched toward the exit. "Ugh, I wish I didn't have to go home."

"I can leave you in the parking lot if you'd like." Thad couldn't stop his laughter.

Emily shook her head. "Not interested." But she was laughing too.

Thad kept his eyes on the cars in front of him as they started moving enough for him to use the accelerator rather than the brake. "Do you want to come back to my place? You can stay the night if you want."

Emily looked over at him. "You're okay with that?"

"As long as you're okay with a six a.m. practice tomorrow."

"Oh yeah, those are always wonderful." They both laughed again. "Yes, let's go back to your place."

"Great," Thad answered, and his heart pounded in his chest. *I am really looking forward to this.*

Chapter 14

I t took a few more days of working with Brianna without Trevor attending their practices for Thad to feel like he was calming down and
making progress again. Relief cooled his skin and slowed his heart rate.
Maybe I have a shot at making the Olympic podium after all, he thought.
Damn Trevor and his crap.

Trevor remained at the rink to coach his other students, however, and it
was not until Trevor cornered him in the locker room that Thad realized
just how angry his former coach was. "Even my younger skaters don't want
to work with me anymore!" Trevor yelled. "You are totally undermining
me!"

"Are you kidding?" Thad shot back. "You brought this on yourself!"

"There are still a million reporters out there, and you're working with a
new coach!"

"For the first time, ever." Thad's eyes shot bullets at Trevor. "Most elite
skaters change coaches at least a couple of times in their career, and a few
of them have been changing coaches every year or more!"

"No, only the ones who are impossible to work with do that, like Kim
McGrath and Evan Parker."

"Kim is doing well now. Evan was always a lost cause. But this isn't about
the other skaters, Trevor, or even about me. This is all about you!"

To Thad's surprise, Jack Wallace suddenly appeared next to them, and
Joaquin stuck his head around the corner from the nearest set of lockers.

"What the hell are you doing here?" Trevor demanded. "I thought the Avalanche had an away game."

Jack shook his head. "Tonight's game is here. We don't leave until tomorrow." He stared at Trevor without speaking until Trevor looked away. "We practice in this arena too, and all our home games are here. I'm sorry for whatever personal problems you're having, but you could have handled them differently. The fallout is crappy for all of us—the reporters are all over our arena too."

"You have no idea what it's like," Trevor mumbled.

Thad wondered what he meant, but Jack seemed to know.

"You're wrong about that," Jack said as a few of his teammates trickled into the locker room. "I had a crappy home life. My dad stepped out on my mom plenty, but he did his business where no one would find him."

"That was a different time, and your father wasn't famous. He didn't have reporters following him with cameras."

"All the more reason not to step out of line. Reporters are like sharks—they smell blood, and you've put a lot of it in the water. Besides, taking it out on your skaters will only make it worse." Jack looked over at Thad, then at Joaquin. "You have a couple of world class skaters here, and you act like *you're* at the top of the pyramid."

"What would you know about that?" Trevor challenged.

Jack shrugged, and Thad was impressed by how cool he was. "With a team sport, being great only gets you so far if you can't work with anyone. Holding your skaters back with your antics isn't going to do you any favors."

Trevor glared at Jack for a moment before storming out of the locker room.

Jack waited for him to leave before looking back and forth between Thad and Joaquin. "That went well."

Both Thad and Joaquin laughed. "He's always been stubborn," Thad said.

"Then you're doing the right thing, working with another coach," Jack answered.

Thad nodded. "Even if being right doesn't always mean it's easy."

"Don't worry about that, Thad. Stay the course. If you don't do well at the Olympics because of Trevor's crap, you'll never get a do-over."

Thad was glad for Jack's intervention, and yet his teeth were clenched so hard that his jaw hurt by the time he got home. His phone was ringing when he got into his apartment, and Thad spent a few seconds wondering whether to answer it. Then his sense of duty got the better of him, and he lifted the phone to his ear. "Hello?"

"Hi, Thad," Rosie said on the other end, and Thad was relieved to hear his mother's voice. "How has training with Brianna been going?"

"Pretty good, actually," Thad answered.

"You sound surprised," Rosie said with a laugh.

"I guess I am. I didn't know what to expect."

"How has Trevor been treating all that?" James asked.

"With a mean silence, until he came after me in the locker room today."

"Stay away from him, even if I never thought I'd say that before now," Rosie said. "You need to train for the Olympics."

"And Trevor brought this on himself," James added.

Thank God for that perspective, Thad thought.

"Where is Anne these days?" Rosie asked.

"She took Caleb back to his parents and arranged for a new coach for him. Then she went out to her parents' house in rural Nevada." Thad swallowed.

"That's quite a change," Rosie said.

"And I had to hear about it from some of the parents at the arena," Thad said. His chest ached.

"Sounds like this is the first time you're glad for figure skating gossip," Rosie joked.

Thad almost smiled.

"Still, I'm glad you think your skating's improving," James said. "That's all that matters right now. There will always be an asterisk next to Trevor's name as coach."

"That's harsh," Thad said.

"Maybe not," James answered. "I'm willing to bet Trevor's hoping that no one will remember this in a year or two, but the figure skating world is a pretty small, well connected one."

"I feel bad for Anne, though," Rosie said.

"Me too," Thad answered. "Her whole life revolved around Trevor and skating, and now this. I hope she lands on her feet." Thad glanced up at the clock and yelped when he realized how late it had become. "I'd better go. I invited Emily to dinner. She's been having a tough time with all of this too and I thought it would be a nice break for her."

"That's a fine idea," James said. "I wish we could all get together at some point."

"That may be after Nationals and Olympics."

"That's okay too."

The next afternoon, Thad inhaled deeply as he and Emily walked across City Park. The sun shone in his face and a calm serenity moved through his body. "Ahhh," he said.

"It's beautiful out," Emily agreed. "The fresh air is lovely, even if it is chilly."

Thad nodded as the breeze ruffled his hair. "How are you feeling about your programs?"

Emily smiled. "I heard the music of 'On My Own' in my dreams last night."

"Eponine's song of loneliness." Thad shot Emily a smile.

"Makes me glad I'll be using that program for both Nationals and Olympics." Emily's smile faltered for a moment, and she stared straight ahead.

"What's the matter?" Thad asked.

"That song really fits what's been happening with Trevor and Mia—there's a part of me that thinks Mia's more interested in Trevor than my skating. Despite everything I've said until now."

I'm so glad I switched coaches, Thad thought. He took a deep breath and hoped he could reassure Emily somehow. "From where I stand, it looks like Mia is still focused on you."

Emily nodded. "I know it looks that way, and I've been happy with the results my skating has been getting. As I also said."

"But?"

"I've been thinking about this a lot recently, and I think 'On My Own' is also a song of not being noticed."

"You think you don't get noticed for your skating? I think nothing could be farther from the truth."

"I know, it's just..." Emily shrugged. "Maybe I'm still used to being in Jenni's shadow."

"You aren't anymore, though—that's been changing for a while. If anything, I think she's the one who hasn't caught on to that."

"I agree, but she was top of the tops when we were juniors. She won everything by a mile for years."

"Still, that was a few years ago already." Thad's eyebrows came together as he tried to figure out what was bothering Emily.

"I know, but sometimes I think there's still this perception that she's better than me. The media still covers it that way a lot, and she has better name recognition than I do."

"These things can be hard to shake."

"Yeah, you've been dealing with it for some time now too. Most of your career, it feels like."

"Thanks for the reminder." Thad smiled and hoped it looked genuine, even as Emily's sadness felt like it was catching.

Emily reached out and took his hand.

Thad clenched his teeth and had to struggle not to pull away. He looked around and was glad that no one seemed to be looking back at them. He stared at the trees until he felt calmer.

"You're still uncomfortable holding hands in public," Emily said. "I can't believe it."

Thad cringed. "Ever since Trevor showed up at your place, staring at us, I've just been so self-conscious. It makes me feel like everyone's watching us—even more so with all the reporters that have been at the rink."

"It's not just that, Thad."

"What do you mean?" Thad frowned in confusion.

"The times I've been around your parents, I've always been struck by how formal they've seemed."

"You think my mom is formal?" Thad laughed. "She's always been the talker, the warm one that draws everyone in."

"Maybe it looks that way to you because your dad's so quiet and into his own space."

Thad looked around the park again for a moment, trying to decide what he thought of that. Then he nodded. "Yeah, my dad's a quiet guy. You have to know him well to know what he's thinking. It drove me crazy as a kid. But my parents love each other, they just aren't over the top about showing it."

"I don't know. My parents aren't like that. They hold hands and put their arms around each other. Yours don't."

Thad rubbed his chin with his free hand. "Our parents aren't the same people, Emily. Mine come from a conservative culture—I don't remember my grandparents, but from what I've heard about them, they would have frowned at my parents being all lovey-dovey. And it's not in my parents' personalities either. It would look weird to me for them to act that way."

"But you're that way because they are."

"Is that a bad thing?"

"If you're uncomfortable even holding my hand in public, it is."

Thad looked away and clenched his teeth again. "I don't know what to tell you. Like I said, it also comes from a place of knowing that we're always being watched, especially on the ice. There are newscasters with cameras and a million fans taking pictures. The only time I can forget about any of that is when I'm skating."

"But we're trying to have a life off the ice too, Thad. And this is part of it."

Thad swallowed, and his face turned red. "I know that. It just takes some getting used to."

The next night, Thad went home after practice and put his Vivaldi CD into his stereo. Then he eased his body into his lounge chair and listened. The pure, high notes surrounded him and lulled him into serenity. After a few minutes, the music felt like waves, and Thad was sure he was rocking in calm waters.

Suddenly, the phone rang, cutting into the music. Thad leapt a foot, and his heart jumped into his throat. *Damn,* he thought as his breath came in gasps. It was the third ring before he remembered to get out of his chair and walk to the phone. "Hello?"

"Hi, Thad, it's Emily. For a moment there, I wondered whether you were going to pick up."

"Yeah, well... I'm not used to getting calls. It took me awhile to figure out how to use the phone."

"Shut up!" But Emily was laughing.

"Besides, don't you get enough of me at the arena?" *I'm also surprised she's still willing to deal with me after our conversation at the park yesterday.*

"Of course I don't see you enough. Also, my parents are visiting in a couple of weeks and my mom wants to go to the Art Museum—they have a modern art exhibit that she's wanted to see forever." Emily took a breath. "I was wondering if you'd be interested in coming with us?"

"Oh." Surprise made Thad's eyebrows jump. "The museum. I don't think I've ever been there."

"What?" Emily yelped, and she sounded as surprised as Thad felt. "I've been there a bunch and I still don't think I've seen everything."

"You think the modern art is worth seeing?"

"Oh, definitely. Why wouldn't it be?"

"I can't say I understand it." Thad had to search his memory. "I didn't go to museums much growing up. I'm still not sure my parents are into art."

"Well, mine always have been. The invitation is open if you want to go."

"Yeah, that would be great." *I should go,* Thad thought.

"Great!" Emily said. "We can figure what time in the next day or two."

Thad spent the next couple of days trying a quadruple toe loop, and he found himself sprawled across the ice every time he tried. "Ow," he yelped the fourth afternoon in a row, when he took yet another tumble. He spent a second on the ice—just long enough to feel the cold through his pants. Then he hauled himself back up into a standing position.

He had to skate around the rink several times before his knee and leg stopped throbbing. *That's going to be a bruise for sure.* He launched himself into one double toe loop, then another. It took a few more jumps for him to regain his equilibrium. By the time he got off the ice, there were still reporters in the arena, and Thad wished they would point their cameras somewhere else. He was glad to get away from their prying eyes and into the silence of the locker room.

A minute later, Thad pulled open his locker and let out an audible groan that broke the room's quiet.

"Rough practice?" someone asked.

Thad looked up.

Joaquin was at a nearby locker, pulling workout gear from inside it.

"I didn't even see you," Thad said.

"I move as quietly on land as I do on the ice." Joaquin smiled.

Thad groaned again. Then he closed his eyes and leaned up against the lockers.

Joaquin finished changing before he spoke again. "When I first moved to Denver and was looking to work with Trevor, this is part of what motivated me."

Thad looked over and saw him holding out a small piece of paper. His eyebrows came together as he reached out and took it. A minute later, he was holding a picture of himself.

"Some journalist took that during the 1996 Nationals," Joaquin said.

"The last year I won." Thad held the picture back out to Joaquin.

Joaquin's hands remained down at his sides. "Look at that picture, Thad. It was taken right before your long program. You were in first place after your short program and you'd won Nationals twice before, and yet still the press was predicting you'd lose."

"I remember all of that." Still, Thad had to take a deep breath and steel himself before he could look back down at the picture he held. Then his head jerked in surprise as he saw the glare in his eyes—a fierce stare that he did not remember. "Wow."

Joaquin nodded. "I always thought your focus was amazing."

Thad swallowed. "I never saw the photographer who took this. Or anyone else in the arena until after I finished skating that night."

"That's what I mean. You have that focus, that concentration. Don't let those reporters out there bother you. Don't let Trevor and his crap bother you, either. We're both skating better with Brianna's help, and we've both always been better than the press gives us credit for."

"That's true." Thad took another breath. "We should both leave those reporters behind and charge into Nationals and the Olympics on our own terms."

The next Saturday afternoon, Thad was flipping through the TV section of the newspaper, trying to forget the fact that it was already October. Then one of the movie listings caught his eye. *Hmm, Gettysburg is on. I remember when that movie came out in '93. I wanted to see it in the theater, but I never made it.* For a moment, Thad racked his brains, trying to remember why, but nothing specific jumped out at him. *I just didn't make it. I had only been at the senior level for a few years and Trevor had me working at practice until all I wanted to do was sleep.*

Anger flared in Thad once more, and he had to get up and pace around his apartment until it stopped. *Firing Trevor was a good idea.* He took a few deep breaths and willed his heart rate to slow down. Then he went to wash the black newsprint off his hands.

That night, Thad made himself a bowl of popcorn and sat down to watch the first section of the movie. *They had to split it up over two nights,* he realized as he looked back at the listings. *I didn't realize it was four hours long. Oof.* But as the movie started, he was glad to be watching. It beat just being exhausted.

Thad put his bowl on the small table next to him and grabbed the remote. Once the volume was higher, he leaned back in his chair and watched, letting the music and the action wash over him. It was an hour later before he realized he had forgotten about his popcorn. *Movies always do that to me,* he thought as he reached for the bowl.

Still, he kept his eyes on the action in front of him as the music swelled. Something familiar rose within him. *I want to set a program to this music,* he realized as the first part of the movie ended. He shut the TV off and put his bowl in the sink. Then he paced around his apartment again.

Is skating to another movie soundtrack a good idea? he wondered. *The last time I skated to a soundtrack was* The Godfather *at Nationals and look how that turned out.* Thad shook his head at himself as he thought of the programs he had been setting to the music for *Goodfellas* and *The Untouchables. Maybe I haven't learned much from Nationals.*

For a moment, he went back to the window in his living room and stared out. *I like the theme that connects* Goodfellas *and* The Untouchables, he decided. *There's a lot to work with in* Gettysburg *too.* Even so, Thad's mind was still racing more than an hour later as he got ready for bed. *Don't decide anything now,* he told himself. *Watch the second part of the movie on Monday, maybe even get the soundtrack and decide from there.*

The following Friday afternoon, Thad managed to get to the edge of the ice during a moment when both Emily and Joaquin were there. "Hey, do you guys want to come over and watch a movie? I just bought a copy of *Gettysburg.*"

"Ooh, *Gettysburg,*" Brianna said from nearby. "I'll bet you could set a program to that music."

Thad nodded. "I was thinking of doing that." He looked back at Emily and Joaquin, who were pulling their skates off.

Emily glanced over at Mia, and Thad was sure she was thinking of the time that Trevor had been outside her house, watching them. Then she looked back at Thad. "I'd be happy to hang out."

"Me too," Joaquin said.

That night, Thad made all of them a dinner of salmon and asparagus before they settled into the comfortable chairs in his living room. "At least Trevor won't join us this time," Emily said.

"He still might," Thad answered, sending a pointed stare at the window. He loaded the video tape into his VHS player and hit the play button.

Emily laughed. "At least we're a few stories up. He won't see much."

"Maybe you should set a program to this music, though," Joaquin said a few minutes into the movie. "You do like soundtracks, and this music isn't bad for it."

Thad nodded. "It's one reason I was looking to watch the movie again—get some outside opinions."

"Everything is about work with you, isn't it?" Emily groaned.

"Not everything," Thad joked. "I wouldn't bother having you over if it were."

"Thanks a lot." Emily threw a piece of popcorn in his direction.

Thad ducked, and the popcorn landed on his floor. "Ugh, now I have to clean up after you." He pulled himself out of his seat.

Emily made a face at him.

Thad made a show of tossing the errant popcorn into the trash.

Joaquin laughed. "You guys are great together. Maybe you two should show this side of yourselves to the public more."

"No way," Thad answered. "I do need to have a private life somehow." But he was smiling. *At least we're away from the cameras and the reporters. And I'm happy to be with Emily.*

Chapter 15

T had spent the next few days thinking about Emily's parents' upcoming visit. "Where are they flying in from?" he asked. "Do they still live in Pulaski?"

Emily shook her head. "No, we moved to Nashville when I was eleven and they still live there."

"Oh." Thad thought of his poor performance at Nationals and of his flight through the streets afterwards. *I didn't even think much of Emily or her performance there*. "So Nationals was like a homecoming for you."

"Oh, yeah." A big grin lit up Emily's face. "It was awesome. I got off the plane and there were big signs at the airport—'Go Emily!'" She waved her arms around and danced a few steps.

Thad looked amused. "That's a big change from Pulaski. Nashville's a decently-sized city."

"Yeah, there weren't really a lot of skating opportunities in Pulaski."

"What a shock."

Emily snickered. "My mom got sick of driving forever to get me to a decent rink. Nashville had a lot more opportunities."

"What do your parents do for a living?"

"You're just full of questions today," Emily teased.

"This from the girl who wants me to meet them," Thad teased back.

"Alright, alright. My mom worked at the University of Tennessee Southern when we lived in Pulaski, though she quit once we moved so that she could focus on my skating, and my sister's. My dad worked at Johnson Controls when I was little."

Thad's eyebrows came together in confusion.

"They're an auto company—they specialize in car seating. But they're called something else now. My dad got a job with Toyota once we moved to Nashville. He's one of their regional executives."

"That's a big deal."

Emily nodded. "Now that Ryan, Chelsea and I are out of the house, my mom works at an art gallery."

"Ah, no wonder she wants to go to the museum here."

"Yeah, I wasn't surprised to hear that."

"Emily!" Mia called. "Get on the ice!"

"Gotta go." Emily took off toward the ice.

Thad's face crinkled in amusement as he watched her. When he was done stretching, he stood up and headed off to the locker rooms.

That Sunday morning, Thad luxuriated in bed for a while. *Only day all week I don't have to be at the rink.* Then he remembered his outing with Emily and her parents, and his stomach quivered with anxiety. *What?* he asked himself. *You've been seeing Emily for months.*

Yeah, but now she thinks you're important enough to meet her parents, another part of him answered. He groaned as he sat up. *Perhaps it's appropriate. She's met Mom and Dad a couple of times.*

At ten o'clock, he headed to the museum. *I hope this is good. Art isn't my thing.* He parked in the museum's lot and looked for Emily as he approached the museum's entrance. He spotted her immediately—her blond hair made her stand out from everyone else who was heading toward the museum.

"Emily!" he called when he got closer. She turned in his direction. *She was looking for me, I know it.*

"Thad!" Emily said. She held out her arms for a hug.

Thad hoped his surprise didn't show. *I wasn't expecting that,* he thought, but he hugged her back anyway.

Then Emily gestured at the people hovering just behind her. "This is my dad, Ryan, my mom, Brooke, and my brother, Tyler. Everyone, this is Thad."

Oh, her brother's here, too. Thad remembered the time he had seen Tyler at the rink. *I thought it was just going to be her parents.* "It's nice to meet you," he said.

Brooke nodded. "We've followed your career for years now." Next to her, Ryan and Tyler eyed Thad with interest.

Or wariness, I can't tell which, Thad thought. "Thanks," he said.

Emily looked back and forth between him and her family. "Why don't we go in?"

Thad looked over at Emily as they made their way up the steps. "Your sister didn't come?"

"Nah, she's still training, and you know how that goes."

"I sure do." Thad looked over at Tyler and found that he was still eyeing him. "How much older than Emily are you?"

"Three years."

"And Chelsea is six years younger than me," Emily added.

"Yeah, I remember you saying she'd make it to senior Nationals in the next year or two." He looked back at Brooke and Ryan. *Emily looks like her mother.*

"We're looking forward to seeing how Chelsea does at the senior level," Brooke said. "Even if watching one of them compete at a time is stressful enough."

"Luckily, only I have a real shot at a medal," Emily joked.

"I'll tell Chelsea you said that," Tyler teased.

"I'm sure you will." Emily smiled.

"I've been looking forward to this art exhibit forever," Brooke said as they made their way to the modern art wing.

"Emily told me," Thad said, and wondered, as an afterthought, if Emily had told her family that he couldn't remember having been to a museum. *I hope they don't think less of me for it.*

"I studied art history in college and keep hoping my kids will do the same," Brooke continued. "It's too late for Tyler, of course, but maybe Emily and Chelsea will go back to school after their skating careers are over."

"I do have a couple of years before that happens," Emily said.

"Of course, honey," Brooke answered.

Her tone made Thad wonder if she was being serious or sarcastic. "Don't rush her. She shouldn't give up her skating quite yet."

Emily smiled at him and took his hand. Her skin was warm against his, and Thad's heart rate quickened. He smiled back at her.

"Of course not," Brooke said. "She has a few more titles left in her."

"We could say the same of you too, Thad," Ryan said.

"Thanks, I hope so," Thad managed.

A few minutes later, he and Emily dropped behind Brooke, Ryan, and Tyler as they walked through the museum. Thad was glad for Emily's presence as he examined the paintings and sculptures in front of them. *I don't understand this stuff one bit.*

Up ahead of them, Brooke was talking animatedly, and Thad turned his ears in her direction. It was nearly an hour later when he realized that he had gotten caught up more in Brooke's explanation of what he was seeing than in the paintings themselves.

"I studied some of these artists in school," Brooke explained. "But it never felt like enough. I always wanted to see more, do more."

"You're seeing it now, Mom," Emily said.

"I know that, honey." Brooke smiled.

Exhaustion crept up on Thad as they all left the museum in the middle of the afternoon. The fresh air felt good, but it was not quite enough to wake him up. He suppressed his yawns as they crossed the parking lot, but he was glad to say his goodbyes and get into his car. His yawns overwhelmed him as he watched Emily and her family get into a car he didn't recognize. *That must be what Ryan and Brooke rented at the airport,* he thought as he turned his key in the ignition. Then another huge yawn disfigured his face. *Damn. I should have gotten some tea at the museum's café or something.*

Thad pulled out of the parking lot and pointed his car toward his home. His eyes threatened to close the moment he stopped at a red light, and he opened the window. This time, the cool breeze made a difference, and Thad made it all the way home. Inside, he made a beeline for his bed. *Time for a nap. That was fun, but I'm wiped.*

At practice two days later, Brianna got Thad's attention after he had finished a series of spins. "So what draws you to the music we've been working on? For *Carmina Burana* and *Gettysburg* in particular, I mean."

"*Gettysburg* is a good movie. I finally got to see it on TV after I missed it in theaters."

"So you're skating to the music because you missed seeing the movie in the theater?"

"No, of course not. I..." Thad looked away as Brianna's eyes dug into him. He looked all around the rink and wished he could see outside.

"What is it about the music that speaks to you?"

"The movie is really an epic—grandiose, with big themes."

"That's the movie. I asked about the music."

Thad heaved an annoyed breath. "It speaks of conflict, big and small. It's dramatic and good to skate to."

Brianna folded her arms across her chest and stared at Thad.

"What?" Thad looked around. He and Brianna were still standing by themselves in the middle of the ice. "What do you want from me?"

"To convey what you think of the music to the audience— and the judges—through your skating. Right now, you're not even sure why you're skating to this music."

Thad swallowed and looked toward the top seats in the arena.

"You need to convey your emotion to the fans who are sitting in those top seats." Brianna pointed to where Thad was looking. "If you were alive in 1863 and got drafted to fight at Gettysburg, what would you think?"

Thad's heart rate quickened. "I understand why both sides were fighting. The South wanted to keep its way of life. The North wanted to abolish slavery and keep the country together. And yet..." Thad took a deep breath. The cool of the ice felt like a breeze on his neck and hands, and the arena around him was silent.

"And yet?"

"War is such a terrible waste of life. The Civil War killed more Americans than in all other wars." Thad swallowed, and his throat was dry. "I hate to think I'd desert if I got drafted, but I do feel for those men from Maine who were forced into Chamberlain's regiment at the beginning of the movie—exhausted, having watched so many men around them get killed."

Finally, Brianna began to nod, even as an amused look graced her face. "So, an anti-war program skated to a war movie's soundtrack."

"I never thought of it like that." Thad began skating toward the side of the rink. "I need to stretch out."

Brianna followed him. "And *Carmina Burana*?"

"That one's easy. The music is dramatic and it's about fortune and how fickle it is. No one knows *that* better than me."

Brianna smiled. "I think people will relate to that, given the ups and downs you've faced in your career. And it certainly is a dynamic piece."

Thad looked at her wearily as he removed his skates.

"Were you expecting this to be easy?"

Thad groaned and sought out the one patch of sunlight coming in through the windows. Then he plunked himself down in the middle of it and began stretching out.

"You should be trying to tell a story on the ice, Thad. You obviously feel the music and have reasons for choosing the programs you do. I just want to know why. At the very least, we need to tie it to each of the elements you perform."

"And at best, I become a master storyteller on the ice."

"That would be ideal."

The throng of reporters began to thin out as autumn progressed and the aspen trees turned a fiery yellow. Thad left the rink after his morning practice one day and was greeted by a number of changing leaves. He smiled, and the smile widened as he remembered his flight to Vail. *I'll bet that ride is gorgeous now.*

The idea stayed with him overnight, and his dreams were filled with the highway, surrounded by trees that looked like they were on fire. By the time he arrived at the rink the next morning, he had another idea. He finished his morning practice and waited for the coaches to go to lunch. Mia and Trevor left together, and Brianna left by herself a few minutes later.

Then Thad went over to Emily and Joaquin. "Brianna gave me a day off this coming Friday, and I heard you guys had a break then too. Do you want to take a drive and see the leaves?"

Emily perked up. "Yeah, I'd love to."

Joaquin smiled. "Sure, I'm happy to do something other than stay home."

Friday found the three of them in Thad's car with Emily in the front passenger seat and Joaquin spread out in back. They were quiet as Thad drove through the streets of Denver and on to the highway. Thad allowed the leaves around them to burn into his retinas before he spoke. "It'll be nice to get out and go hiking. We'll see more from the trails than the highway."

"And the fresh air is lovely this time of year," Joaquin said.

"It's pretty great all year round," Emily said.

"I don't know, last winter I got sick of it after a couple of weeks," Joaquin answered.

"A couple of weeks?" Thad said with a laugh. "Winter here is a whole lot longer than that."

"I'm a California guy, remember? Mild all year round is my jam."

Once they were out of the car and on the hiking trails, Thad inhaled a deep, long breath. "This is wonderful."

"Nice to get a break, isn't it?" Joaquin said.

"Oh, yeah," Thad and Emily said at the same time.

"This is all beautiful," Emily added.

"It is nice to get away from the rink sometimes," Joaquin said. "Most of the time, I've needed the ice to get away from the rest of my life, but sometimes I've needed to get away from the rink to remind myself of the bigger world out there."

"What did you do for leisure when you lived in California?" Thad asked.

"I went to the beach. It was a long bus ride away, but it was worth it."

Thad nodded. "My dad always found the water cleansing."

"I have to agree with him."

It was not until they had reached a clearing and were enjoying the long view that Emily and Joaquin pulled snacks from their bags as Thad pulled out a bottle of water. "Ah, I brought popcorn and you brought carrots," Joaquin said.

"You've always been a bad influence," Thad teased.

Emily laughed.

"I'm not that bad," Joaquin said, winding his arm back as if he were about to throw some popcorn at his fellow skaters.

"Hey, no littering!" Emily yelped.

"Yeah, no sense wasting good popcorn," Thad added.

All three skaters burst out laughing.

A minute later, Thad shook his head as he managed to breathe again. "This was such a good thing to do."

The next Monday, Thad made a point of approaching Trevor for the first time since their confrontation in the locker room. "Have you heard from Anne recently?" he asked as his old coach got off the ice after teaching several younger skaters.

Trevor shook his head. "Just the divorce papers she filed a while back. We only speak through our lawyers now."

"That sounds wonderful."

Trevor shrugged. "What were you expecting, Thad? Things haven't exactly been good between us."

"Thanks for the update." Thad rolled his eyes. "But I'd like to talk to her, at least."

"Then call her."

"Do you have her number?"

"She's still at her parents' house."

"Do you have their number? Because I sure don't." *What is this, pulling teeth? What's wrong with him?*

"I should have lost it when Anne moved there." Trevor made a face.

"But it sounds like you didn't. Why don't you give it to me?"

Trevor glared at Thad for a minute. Then he reached into his backpack and pulled out a day planner. He flipped through a few pages, one at a time and more slowly as he went.

Thad struggled to control his frustration as he took off his skates. *Was he always this much of an ass?*

Finally, Trevor found what he was looking for, picked up a pen and grabbed a smaller pad of paper from his bag. He wrote down a bunch of numbers, ripped out the page and handed it to Thad.

"Thanks," Thad said, once more controlling himself from yelling. He hurried out the building so that he did not start a fight. *I'm so glad I switched coaches.*

That afternoon, Thad was flipping through the paper's arts section when his heart jumped in his chest. "Vivaldi–Sacred Works," an ad read.

Thad grabbed the paper and lifted it up. The words "*Nulla in mundo pax sincera*" leapt out at him. *Oh my God, the Denver Philharmonic is giving a concert of these pieces. I have to go.* He reached for the phone and dialed the number in front of him. Ten minutes later, he had a ticket to a Sunday afternoon performance—and his heart was beating as fast as if he were on the ice, skating fast. *This is going to be amazing.*

He was still buzzing with anticipation when he arrived at the arena the next morning. To his surprise, Emily was already inside. "Mia switched my practice," she said.

"Did I even ask?" Thad teased.

"You were about to. You looked surprised. Oh, and I have something for you." Emily reached into her backpack and pulled out a newspaper clipping.

Thad took it, and a familiar ad met his eyes. "Oh, yeah, the Vivaldi concert. I already got tickets." He beamed.

Emily laughed. "I'd go with you, but I'm going back to Nashville for a few days around then."

"That's too bad. I was wondering if you wanted to go."

"I do. I would if I were here."

Then Joaquin came over. He stood still and looked at Thad and Emily for a minute.

"Are you going to tell me about the Vivaldi concert too?" Thad asked. He held up the newspaper clipping that Emily had given him. "I already know."

"Then you know more than I do," Joaquin said. "I don't get the newspaper."

"The Denver Philharmonic is giving a concert that includes the music for my new program."

"And you should go," Brianna said from nearby.

Thad jumped and was glad when Emily and Joaquin looked startled too. "Did you get tickets also?" Thad asked.

"No, but you should go."

"Oh, I'm going."

"Good." Brianna looked around at the three skaters. "What are you waiting for? Did you come to practice or hang out?"

Thad took the hint and headed toward the locker room. Joaquin followed him as Emily headed for the women's locker room. *It's too bad she can't make it,* he thought as he felt the dry paper with the ad between his fingers. *I really want her to hear this music somewhere other than the rink.* He got into his workout clothes faster in anticipation of skating through that short program. *I want the whole world to hear this piece,* he thought. *It's amazing.*

Then his heart beat faster at the prospect of skating to that music on Olympic ice. *The whole world will hear it if you do that. Make sure that happens.*

The next afternoon, Brianna smiled at Thad as he got off the ice. "I think your *Goodfellas* and *Untouchables* programs are ready for competition."

Thad smiled back. "I do too."

"I like the differences in the music between them. I think your Gettysburg program is coming along nicely too. That should be finished soon if you want to use it at later Grand Prix competitions."

Thad took a deep breath as he thought about it. "I started on that program intending to use it for Nationals. I'm still leaning in that direction."

Brianna nodded. "That's fine." She paused for a moment. "So I'll be going with you and Joaquin to Detroit for Skate America. I think we'll have a full house for that."

"The Grand Prix events? We always do. The entire American team will be there and most of the top international skaters too."

"That includes Grigoriy Arsenyev."

Thad groaned, but he was also smiling. "At least we'll get to see what I can do against him, especially after that meet in Sacramento."

"Yeah, no falling this time. No injuries, either."

Thad nodded seriously. "I didn't mean to fall then, and I can afford it even less now. I'm keeping an eye on that Zamboni—gonna make sure it smooths every patch of ice."

"Good strategy. Make sure the driver is sick of you by the end of the competition."

"Oh, he will be." Thad smiled again. *I like my programs too,* he realized as he left the arena. *I may even be looking forward to this competition.*

Chapter 16

Two days later, Thad pressed his phone to his ear and waited as it rang on the other end. *I hope Anne's there,* he thought. *And that her mom doesn't answer—that woman talks nonstop.* He was relieved when Anne's familiar voice sounded on the other end. "Hi Anne, it's Thad."

"Thad, you know you don't have to keep calling me," Anne answered.

"I know I don't *have* to—I'm calling because I want to." *I lived with her and Trevor for years—has she forgotten that already?* Thad's eyebrows came together in a frown.

"Well, thanks for that. Some days, I can't tell whether I just want to forget the last half of my life or whether to use it to decide how to move forward."

"Well, what have you been doing with yourself?" Thad rubbed his free hand across his smooth kitchen countertop.

"Taking classes at the local university."

"Oh, that's..." Thad struggled to come up with an adjective. "That seems productive. I'm not sure it's something I would have thought of."

"Well, I only finished a year of college before Trevor and I got married, so I never got my degree."

"You were only nineteen when you married? I mean, I feel like I knew that, but..." Thad squirmed. "My parents were married when they were nineteen and twenty, though."

"Yeah, it wasn't that unusual a generation ago. Besides, Trevor is seven years older than me and was just finishing his skating career. It made sense to follow him."

"And now?" Thad pressed. *I need to know that she's okay.*

"Well, I guess I've been involved with the skating world for so long now that I'm not sure what to do with myself outside of it."

"And you think going back to school will help with that?"

"Maybe. At least there are deans and other advisors that have more wisdom than I do. And my parents spoke to the Registrar—they've lived out here forever and are on a fixed income. I don't have a huge amount of money either, so the university agreed to give me in-state tuition as if I'd been living here as long as my parents."

"That's great!"

"Yeah, the school has been wonderful. I've gotten some financial aid too and am working on campus, so I'm earning money, too."

"Sounds like you have a full life." *I'm impressed,* Thad thought. *I wouldn't blame her for just sitting around the house being depressed.*

"Yeah, I..." Anne's voice trailed off for a minute. "I think it's for the best. I certainly worked a lot of hours supporting Trevor and the skating program. Now it's time for me to put those hours into myself."

"That's smart." Thad stared around his apartment, trying to figure out what to say next. "What classes are you taking?"

"A lot of the basic ones that freshmen take—a writing class, an intro math class, a Spanish class and a history class."

"That's a decent mix."

"It's wide-ranging on purpose, Thad. I don't know who I am anymore or what I want to do. I need to keep all my options open."

A wave of sadness washed over Thad. "I'm sorry this happened to you."

"It's not your fault," Anne said emphatically. "And being back at school has been good for me. I'm surrounded by supportive professors and other students who are also trying to figure their lives out. Something positive will come of all this, I'm sure of it."

Three days later, an array of bare trees greeted Thad's eyes as his flight approached the Detroit airport. The few remaining leaves on the trees contained only the barest hints of color. Most were brown, and Thad missed Denver's aspens. Outside the airport, he shivered in the late October air. In his hotel's lobby, there was already a crowd and a commotion, and Thad frowned.

"What is all this?" Joaquin asked. He was only about a foot away from Thad, and his confused expression matched the feelings welling up in Thad, too.

"Yikes, the IOC," Brianna said softly from behind them.

Thad glanced back at her, then at some of the people in front of him. Only then did he recognize a couple of officials from the International Olympic Committee. He caught a flash of black bags as they swept out of the hotel.

Brianna herded Thad, Joaquin, Emily, and Mia toward the elevators, but Thad had already caught sight of Grigoriy and Tatiana heading toward the back door of the hotel. *The IOC must have caught Grigoriy for drug testing,* Thad thought as his feet began carrying him out of the lobby. To his surprise, Sebastian was already waiting for the elevators.

"My flight got in about an hour ago," Sebastian said when he saw Thad looking at him. He tossed his head toward the lobby. "Looks like the IOC caught up with Grigoriy. It's about time, too."

"What do you mean?" Thad asked, even as he remembered the newscast on Grigoriy's drinking and car accident.

The elevator doors opened and he, Sebastian, Joaquin, and Emily got in. The doors closed a second later, and Thad realized that their coaches hadn't gotten in. *Maybe they'll catch the next one,* he thought as he pressed the button for the tenth floor.

Sebastian pressed the button for the twelfth floor as he continued speaking. "Grigoriy likes his Russian nightclubs. There have been rumors forever that they serve more than vodka, but somehow Grigoriy is never available for testing when the IOC shows up."

"I'm amazed he can get past the vodka," Joaquin said. "I've been to a few of those clubs in Brighton Beach myself and they don't serve water in any of them."

Sebastian laughed.

Joaquin shook his head. "I've always walked out of there feeling poisoned. I'd be scared of anything else they serve."

Now Thad was smirking. "I'm amazed you could still compete like that."

"I couldn't," Joaquin admitted. "There's a reason I haven't done it in a while."

"Wish I could say the same for Grigoriy," Sebastian said. "I've been hearing rumors about the stuff he's been on since he moved to New York, but he makes it to the competitions and he always skates well."

Thad shook his head as he got off the elevator. "Maybe that'll change this time."

"Don't hold your breath," Sebastian said, rolling his eyes as the elevator doors closed again.

When Thad arrived at the arena the next morning for warmups, Grigoriy was already there, talking to reporters. He pumped his fist in the air as he spoke, and his voice was loud and confident. "The IOC has been after me for months. They got me yesterday and their tests showed nothing. I have nothing to hide! Their tests are a sham!"

"Yuck," Thad mumbled as he walked toward the locker rooms.

"Seriously," Brianna said. "Even if I thought those tests would be positive."

"You think he's on something?"

"I wouldn't be surprised. He's the favorite right now and thinks he can get away with anything."

"Then why would the tests have come up clean?"

"Maybe he stopped just long enough ago that they didn't pick up anything."

"Great."

Grigoriy was still grinning as he stepped onto the ice for warmups, and Thad wished he could break the guy's nose.

"Maybe we should trip him," Joaquin mumbled.

Thad laughed. "I would if I weren't so worried about dislocating my shoulder again."

"Yeah, that was a nasty one," Joaquin said seriously. He glanced back at Grigoriy. "I just wish we could get this guy already."

Thad didn't smile again until the bold strains of the music from *Goodfellas* came up for his short program. *This has been a fun piece to skate to.* A slight bobble on two of his jumps put him in third place behind Sebastian and Grigoriy, however, and he was a little disappointed.

"Don't worry, I think you skated fine," Brianna said.

"I was hoping for a little *more* fine."

"You can still bring that to the long program. Besides, both Grigoriy and Sebastian skated flawlessly. I'm not surprised they're ahead of you."

"Thanks a lot." Thad rolled his eyes.

Brianna shrugged. "I'm not saying anything you don't know already," she said as they left the arena. "Even if I continue to be amazed by how well Grigoriy continues to skate."

"Maybe it'll catch up to him eventually. Maybe even in time for the Olympics."

"One can only hope."

The following night, Thad watched Emily skate a beautiful short program that put her in second place behind Sakura Fujita of Japan. Kim McGrath was third, and Jenni was fifth, behind Marion Dubois of France. "Oooh, Jenni's pissed," Brianna whispered as Jenni stomped off after her scores were announced.

"Yeah, that's obvious," Thad said.

"Maybe if she'd skate better, she'd place better," Brianna said, making Thad smile.

Then his mind turned back to his long program. *I still have a chance at beating Grigoriy,* he thought as he and Brianna left the arena. *And I still want to.*

The next night, the wind howled off the water as Brianna drove Thad and Joaquin back to the arena for the long program. At warmups, Thad's muscles felt loose and his jumps came easily. *I can do this,* he told himself, especially as Grigoriy fell on a triple Lutz.

Sebastian groaned as they got off the ice. "I hope he does that during his program." He tossed his head back toward Grigoriy.

Thad smiled. "I don't usually wish evil on other skaters."

"Except this time, right?" Sebastian chuckled.

Thad's smile remained on his face as he threw one last glance back at Grigoriy. By the time he took to the ice, Thad knew that both Sebastian and Joaquin had had minor stumbles, and that Sebastian was slightly ahead of Joaquin. *My turn now,* Thad thought as he took to the ice in an old-fashioned three-piece suit.

Then the tense music of *The Untouchables* swirled through the arena, and Thad jumped into action as Elliot Ness, chasing Al Capone. The quick tempo propelled him toward his first jumps. When his two doubles and a triple Lutz in quick succession were all behind him, Thad smiled. A swift spin followed, and then a triple toe loop–triple Lutz combination.

A slower part of the music made Thad think of the movie's scene on a bridge, with Elliot Ness downcast after a failed raid. *I can relate to that.* He had just caught his breath when the tempo quickened again. After two clean triple axels, Thad was smiling in time to the audience's clapping. His feet moved of their own accord, through a footwork sequence that took him all the way across the ice. After another clean triple Lutz, Thad moved into his final spin, and his long program was over. He caught his breath and acknowledged the crowd's roar. *That was a good program,* he thought as he skated to the side of the ice. *I couldn't have hoped for more.*

"Nice job," Brianna said as Thad's marks, a mixture of 5.9s and 6.0s, came up.

"Thanks." Thad grinned. "I'm pretty happy."

"You should be."

Thad gave the crowd one last wave as they made their way out of the "kiss and cry" area.

"Even if I think the judges left enough room for Grigoriy to take the gold," Brianna added once they were away from the crowd and the cameras.

"Thanks," Thad said again, only now he was rolling his eyes.

Brianna shrugged. "He was ahead of you after the short program as it is."

Thad clenched his teeth as he removed his skates and stretched out. Much as tried otherwise, his eyes kept going back to the TV a few feet away, and his stomach sank every time Grigoriy landed a jump.

Then Sebastian and Joaquin came over. Joaquin bit his lip as he watched Grigoriy land yet another spectacular triple axel.

"Damn him," Sebastian said. "He really does like to party. I was hoping that at least some of the drug rumors were true."

"Maybe they are and he's just lucky for now," Joaquin said as Grigoriy finished his long program without so much as a step out of line. "He's always been a cocky bastard. I'm sure he thinks he can get away with it forever."

"We do have a number of international competitions coming up," Sebastian said. "Maybe we'll all get lucky and he'll be a mess by the time the Olympics are here."

Thad wished he could smile, but Grigoriy's marks were flashing across the screen now. They were identical to his own for the long program, and only the small difference in their short programs put Grigoriy in first place. "Damn it," he muttered.

Sebastian clapped him on the back. "Don't give up. Your long program was awesome and you're not far behind him."

Thad nodded as he kept his eyes on the screen. *Sebastian is third, but Joaquin is all the way in fifth, after Beau Tremblay of Canada.*

At the medal ceremony, Grigoriy smirked at Thad. "Maybe playing gangsters isn't your best look."

"Elliott Ness was the good guy," Thad answered before he could stop himself.

"But he was always overshadowed by the bad guy."

Grigoriy's grin made Thad want to punch him. He bit his lip to stop the torrent of curses raging within him. Still, when the medal ceremony was over, he felt the weight of his silver medal around his neck. *Sebastian was right—this is pretty good,* he thought as his fingers curled around the medal.

Then Grigoriy leaned over again. "Better get used to silver and bronze. Because you're never going to see gold."

"Shut up," Sebastian answered as he stepped off the podium.

Thad smirked and wished he could muster that attitude. "Don't be so sure of yourself," he told Grigoriy. "Another competition, another set of programs..." He shrugged. "It won't take much."

Grigoriy shook his head, and his cocky grin covered his face. "You'll never beat me."

The next night, Thad sat in the stands to watch Emily's long program. Jenni took the ice just before Emily. She looked happy, smiling the whole way through, even as she stepped out on one jump and two-footed the landing of another. When the program was finished, Jenni pumped her fist in the air to celebrate.

"Did she skate a different program than what we just watched?" Joaquin asked, making Thad erupt with laughter. "I wouldn't be as happy as she is with those mistakes."

Thad looked over at the judges. "Let's see what they say." A minute later, a series of 5.8s and 5.9s came up, and Thad shook his head. "That's still pretty good for a less than perfect program."

"For real," Joaquin mumbled. "I think Jenni benefits from a system that we're on the wrong end of a lot—I feel like I get marked low most of the time, especially when I don't make any mistakes."

Thad nodded in agreement. "Jenni was a really amazing skater on the junior circuit. Sometimes I feel like her reputation has carried over and she doesn't have to work for her scores anymore."

Emily's name was announced, and she skated to the center of the rink.

Thad cheered along with the rest of the crowd—until he glanced down at Emily's skates. Then he sucked in a breath.

"What's wrong?" Joaquin asked.

"She's not wearing her regular skates. She had to switch to her backup pair!"

"How can you tell? They look the same."

Thad shook his head. "The laces are different. That's why Jenni looked so happy. She stole Emily's skates, just like at that one junior competition!"

"I can't believe she would get away with something like that," Joaquin said as Emily's music started.

"She did before, and Emily could barely skate." Thad clenched his teeth. "Come on, Emily, kick her ass!"

Joaquin leaned over and looked at Mia, who was at the boards. "Ooh, she looks pissed."

Thad's gaze landed on Mia for a split second. "Yeah, she does. I'll bet anything it's because of Emily's skates." He sucked in a breath as Emily landed two clean triple Lutzes.

"Well, she's already skating better than Jenni did."

Thad nodded, and his mouth was very dry. "I hope she pulls this off." It was not until Emily's music ended after a very clean program that he stood and cheered.

"Well, if that wasn't good enough to beat Jenni, nothing is."

"For real." Thad waited until Emily's marks came up, then let out a howl when they were a mix of 6.0s and 5.9s. "She won!"

"And about time, too," Joaquin said. "Jenni must know her time is up."

Thad could barely keep a straight face during the medal ceremony. Jenni looked so annoyed that Thad wanted to laugh and never stop. *Serves her right.*

It was quiet for most of the ride to the Detroit airport the next morning. Then Mia spoke. "I'm thinking of filing a complaint against Jenni for stealing Emily's skates. I wonder if the USOC will finally listen."

Emily shrugged. "They may not. She's been such a golden girl forever."

"No, you're the golden girl now," Thad said. "Where's your medal?"

Emily smiled. "It's in here." She tapped her backpack.

In front of them, Mia still looked unhappy. "You shouldn't have to bring a second pair of skates to every competition just because you know she'll steal your primary pair."

Brianna nodded. "I agree. Jenni's behavior is atrocious, and she should pay for it. This has been going on for years now. It's not just a one-time thing."

Thad looked over at Emily. "Did you find your regular skates?"

Emily nodded. "They disappeared when I went to the bathroom right before the competition but somehow they were back in front of my locker after the medal ceremony."

"Convenient." Thad shook his head.

"I can't just stand by and watch this," Mia said. "I need to do something about it." She stared out the front windshield.

Finally doing something to protect your skater, Thad thought. *I'm not sure it'll change anything about the last few months, but I suppose it's better than nothing.* He looked out the window for a moment, trying to decide what to say. Then he looked back at Emily. "I'm proud of you. You gave two great performances, and you deserve that gold, especially given Jenni's behavior."

Emily grinned. "Thanks."

Chapter 17

Thad and Emily shared a cab to the Denver airport right before Christmas. The city's festive decorations hung all around them, but Thad felt disconnected from all of it. "Well, I'm happy to be going home, at least," Emily said as Thad's silence lengthened. "Even if Mia is sending me home with a bunch of workouts."

Thad nodded. *It'll be good to see Mom and Dad and Scott,* he thought, but he still could not bring himself to say anything. Signs for the airport began to appear before he got his tongue to work. "It's a tough balance, this close to Nationals and the Olympics. You don't want to burn out, but you do want to be ready."

"At least I'm starting to feel ready. I really want to skate at the Olympics! It's almost too bad it's still a couple of months away."

"All in due time," Thad said as they arrived at the airport.

It was not until they were approaching the security line's metal detectors that Emily asked, "so what happened with Anne? I stopped seeing her around completely once Trevor and Mia got together. I feel like she fell off the face of the earth."

"I've been speaking to her. I couldn't just let her disappear."

"Yeah, you lived with them for years."

Thad nodded. "Longer than with my parents! Anne was like a second mother to me. I couldn't just let that go, despite Trevor's attitude."

"I wouldn't expect you to." Emily adjusted the strap on her backpack. "How's she doing? None of this can be easy for her."

"It hasn't been, but I think the change in scenery has been good for her. She said the reporters haven't able to find her there."

Emily smirked. "Nevada is quite a change from Denver, though."

"Yeah..." Thad's voice trailed off for a second. "And she only moved here because Trevor made that choice for his coaching career. Skating subsumed their whole lives." Thad frowned as he handed his identification to the security personnel in front of him. He and Emily were silent again until they had gotten past the metal detectors and retrieved their backpacks. Then Thad looked at Emily and wished he were better with words.

"Well, maybe the time away will be good for all of us," Emily said.

"I'll still miss you," Thad joked, even as some other emotion that he could not name cascaded through him. *I'm not entirely joking,* he realized.

Emily smiled. "I'll miss you too, but it's only a few days." She gave him a whack on the shoulder. "You need to buck up, too. Your focus and your work ethic have always been amazing. Let that be in your favor now."

Thad smiled. "Thanks." He looked at his watch. "Alright, we'd better get to our gates. Have a good time in Nashville."

"I will. Wish your family a Merry Christmas for me."

"Will do." Thad surprised himself by opening his arms.

Emily gave him a long hug before they parted. Then Thad watched her go until she disappeared into the crowd of travelers.

After another minute of watching until he was sure he could not see her anymore, Thad turned and went searching for his gate. He threw himself into a seat in front of the window and stared out. He watched planes pull away from their gates before looking back into the airport. The holiday cheer of excited passengers mixed with the green wreaths, red ribbons, and decorative bells that hung around the airport.

Thad sighed. *I wish I could relax,* he thought. He pulled his CD player out of his bookbag and shoved his headphones over his ears. A minute later, the sounds of Neil Schon's guitar wailed into his ears from the first song on Journey's *Escape* album. Thad stared out the window in front of him again. This time, his eyes focused on the snow-covered mountains in the distance. *That's pretty, at least.*

He continued staring at the mountains until Steve Perry hit a high note. That, finally, made him smile. Then his breathing slowed down. By the time he boarded his flight to Boston, his heart rate had come down too. *I just need to relax. Nationals and then the Olympics are only a few weeks away. I can do well there.*

The familiar streets of Gloucester, decked out with Christmas lights, quieted the last of Thad's raging thoughts. The cold air reached the two patches of uncovered skin on his face as he got out of James' and Rosie's car at his childhood home. As usual, the wind was off the water, and Thad smelled the salt before his nose froze. He closed the car door behind him and pulled his suitcase from the trunk. Strings of Christmas lights surrounded each of the house's windows and swung along the roofline. "Are you still climbing up on a ladder to string those?" Thad asked his father.

"Of course I am," James answered. "I'll probably be doing it until I'm dead. At least this year I kept the ladder in the basement, so it wasn't iced over."

"Oh, God." Thad remembered the year James had left the ladder outside overnight, turning it wet and then frozen when a winter storm had swept through.

"What, surprised I'm learning from my mistakes?"

"Yes," Rosie answered as she headed toward the back door of the house.

Thad burst out laughing. He grabbed his bookbag and suitcase and followed Rosie into the house. James brought up the rear, shaking his head with mock indignation.

Inside, the Christmas tree was in the living room, and its colorful lights blinked on and off. Different colors of tinsel caught the light as James turned on a lamp, and the whole room felt warm and alive.

"Good to be home?" Rosie asked.

Thad nodded. "Yeah."

"I was hoping you'd take the time to relax," James said. "You've got some big events coming up."

"I know," Thad answered. "And I don't want to think about it right now."

"Fair enough."

Thad headed for the stairs, hauling his suitcase with him. He was halfway up before he heard his mother speak again. "He's as reticent as you are."

She's talking to Dad, Thad decided. He kept walking.

"Not everyone can chew someone's ear off, Rosie," James replied.

Thad pictured his father shrugging, and he laughed. At the top of the stairs, he made a sharp right turn into the bedroom he and Scott had shared as kids. He ducked to avoid the ceiling, before he realized that he could, in fact, stand up straight without hitting his head. He put his bookbag on one of the single beds in the room and looked around. *I can't believe Scott and I used to share this tiny room.* But as he thought back to his childhood, he realized he only had a few memories of sleeping there.

Sadness tugged at his stomach as he thought of Trevor and Anne and how warm their house had seemed. *That, too, is long gone.* Thad pulled his water bottle from his bookbag and downed the last couple of ounces. Then he went to the small bathroom at the end of the hall to refill it. When his thirst was satiated, he went back downstairs to find his parents.

Rosie spent the next day cooking, and Thad did his best to help her. He spent most of his efforts getting spices and other ingredients from the shelves Rosie could not reach. "You're making enough food for an army, Mom," he said when he had cleaned one shelf in particular of every spice and canned good it contained. "How many people are you expecting for dinner? I thought it was just us and Scott, and his girlfriend."

"Yeah, Scott told us Christina was coming a few weeks ago, but that's it."

"So what are we going to do with all this food?"

"Eat it, even if it takes a couple of weeks."

Thad thought of how long his mother had been able to stretch leftovers when he had been a child. He shook his head. *I'm glad things are different now, but this is way too much food.*

Scott and Christina arrived just before three in the afternoon, and Scott wrapped Thad in a bear hug. "Always good to see you."

Thad's grin reached his ears. "Likewise." He looked over at Christina.

"Thad, this is my girlfriend, Christina Martin. Christina, this is my brother, Thad."

"I've been looking forward to meeting you for a while," Christina said as she looked Thad over.

"Yeah, it's the only reason she's dating me," Scott joked.

Christina gave him a whack on the shoulder. "Not true!"

But Thad and Scott were already laughing.

"Are you from around here, Christina?" Thad asked.

"I grew up in the Boston suburbs, and I live in the city now."

"How come you aren't spending the holiday with your own family?"

"Because we're better than they are," Scott cracked.

Christina smirked. "My brother moved out to California a few years ago, and my sister now lives in New York City. Traveling for Christmas has gotten expensive and crazy, and my flights get cancelled half the time because of the weather."

"Your brother and sister don't come back to Boston?" Thad asked. "I would have thought that was normal if you and your parents are still here."

"You should put Thad on the phone with all of them," Scott teased. "That'll set them right."

Thad smirked. *I hope I'm not being too inappropriate,* he thought. He was relieved when Christina laughed.

"Everyone came back here for several years," Christina said. "But they started getting annoyed with the expense and hassle. I mean, for Oliver, I get it because he's all the way out in California."

"Ava was just being obnoxious, though, right?" Scott teased. "New York is only a train ride away."

"And you're worried about me scaring her off!" Thad said. But they were both laughing again.

Christina shook her head. "This year, my dad won a trip to Bermuda as part of a raffle his job held, so he and Mom are there now."

"Wow!" Thad said. "That's fun!"

"Yeah, they're having a grand old time. I'd almost be surprised if they come back."

"Maybe they should retire down there," Scott said.

"I thought that too!" Christina answered. "My dad's been talking of retiring, but I think he has a few working years left, at least."

Scott dropped his arm around Christina's shoulders as the family went to the long table in the dining room. A twinge of jealousy squirmed in Thad's stomach as he sat across from them. *That must be what a normal life is like—normal job, normal relationship.* Then he thought of Emily and of the time they had been spending together. *Could I have that with her?* He bit his lip. *All I can think about right now are Nationals and the Olympics.*

Thad jumped as something hit his shoulder. He looked down. A piece of celery sat in his lap. He made a face as he picked it up and dropped it onto the table. "Yuck."

"Pay attention!" Scott admonished. "Mom is talking to you!"

Thad looked over at Rosie. "Sorry, what did you say?"

"Do you want the turkey's dark meat or white meat?" Rosie asked.

"White meat. And some of the ham."

"Oh yeah, that's already on your plate."

Thad smiled. "Know me well, do?"

"Sometimes I think so." Rosie smiled back.

"Do you want seltzer or wine?" James asked. "Even if I think I know the answer to that, too."

Thad nodded. "Seltzer."

"I figured." James poured the clear liquid into his son's wine glass.

"What were you thinking about, that you couldn't even hear questions about the food?" Scott asked.

Thad shrugged. "Nothing."

"I doubt that, but it's Christmas, so I'm going to let it go." Scott handed his plate to Rosie for a hefty dose of food. When he had his plate back, he looked at Christina and began asking questions about her parents' trip to Bermuda.

He won't ask again what I was thinking, Thad thought, and relief flowed through him. *No one needs to know that.*

Chapter 18

The holiday time with his family passed more quickly than Thad wanted, and sooner than he was ready, he found himself back at Logan Airport. "I'm sorry you have to go so soon," Rosie said. "You weren't even here for a week."

"Nationals are just after New Year's," Thad answered. "If they were in February like normal, maybe I would have stayed longer."

"No, Nationals are more important," James said. "We're looking forward to seeing you compete."

Thad nodded, but his throat closed up, preventing him from saying anything. *I hope this competition goes well. At least I know it couldn't be worse than last year.* He was glad when his parents hugged him and he went inside the airport.

In Denver, Thad found Emily at the rink, smiling. "Mia went ahead and filed a complaint about Jenni's behavior with the USOC and U.S. Figure Skating," she said.

"Good for her. Did you hear anything back?"

Emily nodded. "They gave her a warning. If she does anything like that again, they'll force her to miss a competition or two."

"That should set her straight. I'm sure she won't want to miss Nationals or the Olympics."

"Oh, I was hoping she would do something that would put her out of both competitions."

Thad laughed. "Unfortunately, I don't think she's that stupid."

"No, I don't either."

"You'll just have to skate your best."

"Oh, I don't plan on doing anything else." Emily smiled and took off across the ice.

Thad spent the next couple of weeks putting the final touches on his long and short programs for Nationals, including skating completely through both programs in his costumes. Relief flowed through him when he got through both programs without a hitch.

"That looked great," Brianna said as he came off the ice.

"Yeah, I'm happy about that." A smile lit up Thad's face. "I wouldn't have wanted to mess up my costumes so close to Nationals."

Brianna shook her head at him, even as she looked amused. "I'm just glad you're not holding out on me and skating cautiously. Now's not the time to do that."

"I know, I skated all out for both those programs." Thad was being serious now.

Then, before he was ready, it was January 2. He and Brianna drove to the airport with Joaquin and Laura. Mia and Emily drove in a second car and arrived not long after them.

"Deep breaths," Joaquin said as Thad bit his lip.

"Are you talking to me or yourself?" Thad asked as they went into the airport.

"Yes," Joaquin answered.

Thad smirked as they checked their bags and made their way to the security checkpoint.

"Philadelphia, here were come," Emily said as they arrived at their gate and their flight was posted in red letters.

Thad's nervousness felt like a large clump of dirt in the pit of his stomach. He clenched his teeth and felt his jaw tighten. As they all boarded the plane, he forced his mouth open—his jaw was so tense that it had begun to hurt. *I've got to calm down.*

He reached for his CD player as the plane taxied to the runway. A few minutes later, Journey was blasting into his ears again as the plane took off, pinning him to his seat. When he could move again, he took his headphones off and looked over at Emily. "It's been a long road here, hasn't it?"

Emily nodded. "I'm glad for it in some ways, though. I don't think I'd be the skater I've become without it."

Thad smiled. "I always appreciate your positive attitude."

"Isn't that why you keep me around?" Emily was smiling now too.

Thad turned around and peered through the tiny opening in between their seats. Joaquin and Laura were sitting right behind them, and they were talking quietly. *They don't want us to hear what they're saying,* Thad thought, but, to his surprise, he was okay with that. *They've been through their own journey to get here.*

Thad turned and faced forward again. Trevor and Mia had seats together several rows behind them, and Brianna had a window seat close by, but Thad did not need to turn around to find them. *I would be amazed that Trevor is going to Nationals, except that two of his other skaters will be there. At least he's kept his distance and hasn't tried to talk to me.* Thad took a deep breath. *It's Brianna who will keep me grounded through all of this.*

The next night, Thad went to the arena to watch Emily's short program. *I want to see Kim skate too,* he realized. *And I'm hoping to watch Jenni fall on her ass, even if I will never say that out loud.* He scanned the crowd until he saw Ryan and Brooke. Tyler and Chelsea sat on Brooke's left, but the seat on Brooke's right was empty, so Thad sat there as his family grabbed a few empty seats across the aisle.

"Oh, hi, Thad," Brooke said, looking at him in surprise. "I didn't expect to see you here."

The rest of the family looked at him. So did a few spectators sitting behind them, and Thad wished he could hide. "Well, I'm competing too," he said, hoping it sounded like he was joking. "I thought everyone would expect me." He was relieved when he was rewarded with several smiles.

"I meant I wouldn't have expected to see you here in the stands," Brooke said. "Watching Emily makes me nervous enough."

Chelsea leaned over and nodded. "I get so nervous during competitions that I don't want to be anywhere near the arena when it's not my turn to skate. I was almost glad when I didn't make Nationals this year."

"And yet here you are anyway," Thad teased.

"I'm not competing," Chelsea answered in the same joking manner.

Thad looked down at the ice as he thought about it. "It feels different being here as a spectator. Everything will change for me tomorrow night."

Emily, Kim, and Jenni were in the last group of skaters, and sitting in the stands began to feel interminable. *This is how it feels waiting to skate,* Thad thought. *I never realized it feels that way from here too.* He took a deep breath as Emily's name was announced almost an hour later. Then he smiled as he watched her close her eyes for a long moment as she skated across the ice. *She's collecting herself. I think she'll skate well.*

Still, he found himself biting his nails as he watched Emily's short program. It was not until she was halfway through that he thought, *she's skating beautifully.* When the program was over, Brooke and Ryan leapt to their feet, yelling and screaming. So did Tyler and Chelsea.

Thad laughed as he stood and cheered with them. *I'm proud of her. That was great.* He cheered again when Emily's marks came up, high enough to put her in first place—*for now, anyway. Let's see what Jenni and Kim do.*

The crowd had not finished cheering for Emily when Jenni's name was announced. "Booo," Tyler said. He spoke quietly, but it was loud enough for his family—and Thad—to hear him.

Thad struggled to control his laughter as Ryan whacked his son on the back. "Sportsmanship," Ryan said.

Tyler shook his head as Jenni's music began, and Thad's laughter spilled out of him as he turned back to the ice. Within seconds, he was focusing intently. Jenni's first two jumps were clean, but her third one, a triple axel, was wobbly on the landing. When she two-footed her next two jumps, Thad knew her marks would be lower than Emily's. *She's not as good a skater as Emily has become. Their rivalry made sense when it started. It doesn't anymore.*

He turned and watched for Jenni's marks and was relieved when they were, in fact, lower than Emily's.

"Hooray!" Brooke cheered. "Emily will at least be in second."

Thad nodded as he looked back at her. "Now it just depends on what Kim does." *Even if I hope Kim is on.*

"For real," Ryan said. "She's been so inconsistent throughout her career that I never know what to expect from her."

When Kim's name was announced, she skated directly to the center of the ice and waited for her music. The fierce look in her eyes and the scowl in her eyebrows made Thad smile. *Go, Kim, go!* he thought.

She started moving as soon as the music came on, and when she hit her third triple jump in a row, Thad knew she would come in first.

"Her skating has improved too," Tyler said as they watched Kim connect her jumps with footwork and spins.

"Yes it has," Thad agreed. "I'm so glad she didn't just go off the rails."

"Not yet," Ryan joked. "She still has time."

"I'm hoping she keeps it together, at least through Nationals and the Olympics."

"Oh, me too. I always thought she could be amazing."

Thad stood up and cheered when Kim's program was over. He grinned when the rest of the arena did the same. "That was great!" he yelled. Next to him, Emily's whole family was nodding in agreement.

Thad stayed just long enough to make sure Kim's marks were high enough to put her in first place. Then he left and went back to the hotel.

Thad spent the next day breathing and trying to relax. When he got sick of being cooped up in his hotel room, he went for a walk along the Delaware River. Knots whirled around in his stomach as he remembered the previous year's competition. *You've come a long way since then—you've got this,* he tried to reassure himself. *Yeah, but a lot more has happened since then,* another part of him answered. *And there's more on the line than Worlds this year.*

It was quiet as Brianna drove Thad, Joaquin, and Emily to CoreStates Center that afternoon. Trevor and Mia followed in a separate car, and Thad was glad for that as he stared out the window. Before he was ready, Brianna turned onto South Broad Street, and the arena came into view.

Brianna parked in the arena's lot, and Thad inhaled deeply as he got out of the car. Emily and Joaquin were quiet as they got out of the car too, and Thad realized that he did not know what to say to them. *We're all in our own worlds,* he thought as none of them made eye contact. Then Trevor and Mia, who had parked nearby, came over, and together, the group walked into the arena.

Lights flashed, and it took Thad a moment to realize that they were flashbulbs from cameras. *Damn,* he thought. *The press is here in force. Maybe I'll get lucky and they'll focus on Trevor and Mia.*

"Thad, are you ready for this competition?" asked Marissa Jackson of the *Washington Post.*

"Yes, I am," Thad answered, even as he continued walking without breaking stride. "I'm looking forward to competing."

"Joaquin, your practices have looked great recently," said Shelby Thompson of the *New York Times.* "How do you feel?"

"I'm good," Joaquin answered with a smile. "I'm looking forward to this competition, too."

"Emily, do you have a chance of medaling?" Marissa asked.

"I think so," Emily answered. "Even if I have some strong competitors."

Then Trevor, Brianna, and Mia stepped in between their skaters and the media. "We'll take your questions," Trevor said. "This is a very important competition for our skaters. Please let them warm up and prepare."

Thad saw his opportunity and took off toward the locker room. Joaquin was on his heels. Within seconds, they were away from the crowd, and Thad started breathing again.

"Thank God," Joaquin said as they ducked into the quiet locker room.

"For real," Thad said. "Glad for Trevor for the first time in a while. We'll have to face the press after the competition, though."

"I'm okay with that," Joaquin answered as he put his bag down on one of the room's wooden benches. "It's getting slammed before the competition that bothers me."

Thad nodded in agreement. "It's hard to get into the zone when they're all over you like that."

Then Sebastian came into the locker room to change. The three men nodded at each other but said nothing more. The room became silent as each of them got into their costumes and made their way to the ice.

A large American flag, which Thad had noticed the previous night, still hung over the arena. Thad glanced at it as he stepped onto the ice. Then loud cheers met his ears, and he looked up at the stands. Different groups of people with more flags and banners with his name on them yelled to get his attention. He smiled but scanned the arena for his parents and Scott. His smile widened when he found them in the front row.

Other skaters joined him on the ice for warmups, and Thad saw Paul Monfils, who had medaled at the previous year's Nationals but had not gone to Worlds. *Hopefully there will be a different outcome this time,* Thad thought. *Paul still has a chance at medaling, but I need to be on the podium this year.*

He took a deep breath as he stroked the ice. He made his way through two full laps before his heart rate began to slow down. By the time he had finished a third lap around the ice, his body had begun to relax. *Ahhhh,* Thad thought, and felt some hope rise within him. Then he tried a few elements of his program. A double toe loop started everything, followed by a double axel and a triple toe loop. Thad skated another lap before landing a clean triple axel.

Then warmups were over. Brianna nodded as Thad got off the ice. "You looked good out there."

"Thanks."

"You're skating last tonight. Block out what everyone else is doing—I don't even want you watching on the monitors backstage. Focus on yourself. Stay calm, stay focused."

Thad nodded. "I have my CD player and a whole bunch of music."

"Great."

It was more than an hour later before Thad returned to the ice. He felt his blades start to glide and looked at Brianna for some last advice. "You've been improving all season," she said. "You can do this. Your run throughs have been perfect and you were great at warmups. Stay loose and break a leg."

Then Thad's name was called out, and the sound reverberated through the arena. Cheers soared around him as he skated to the center of the ice and held out his arms to the arena. Warmth flowed through him, and he smiled. *These people are here to see me skate*. His dark blue Union Army uniform fit snugly without being tight. *This is going to be good*. When it got quiet, Thad took his opening pose and waited for his music.

He moved as soon as the opening notes of *Gettysburg* reached his ears. The music got louder, and Thad leaned in as he glided across the ice. His pace picked up as the music's tempo got faster. Within seconds, he was launching into a triple toe loop. He smiled when he landed it cleanly. Then he was racing across the ice again. A triple axel–double toe loop combination followed, and relief soared within Thad as those, too, were clean.

The audience cheered, and their noise buoyed Thad. *Fight for what you believe in, but end this war, too*. His fancy footwork carried him back across the ice to the sound of drumbeats, and soon the audience was clapping

along with him. Thad's heart rate picked up as his most difficult combination neared, a triple axel–triple axel. He soared into the air for the first
jump. One, two, three rotations. Thad's foot touched the ice after the last
half-rotation. Then he threw himself into the second jump. Everything
around him spun, and he landed cleanly again.

Thad's smile widened across his face. He flew across the ice again to the
music of Chamberlain's charge. *Brutal but effective,* Thad thought as he
launched into a triple Salchow. In the crowd's roar, Thad knew he had a
clean program. He could just hear his music as he went into his final spin.
A minute later, he stopped moving as the last notes of *Gettysburg* came to
a stop.

His breath came in gasps, but he was still smiling. All around him, the
crowd was standing and cheering. Stuffed animals and a few flowers were
thrown onto the ice as Thad took his bows. He looked around the first row
for his family again and had to turn around to find them. He smiled and
waved at his parents and Scott in particular, and they cheered back at him.
After one last wave to the rest of the crowd, Thad made his way to the "kiss
and cry" area.

Brianna was waiting for him. "That was great! I want to see your marks."

"Don't we all?" Thad quipped as he sat down. He took a deep breath.
"How'd everyone else do?"

"Pretty well. Sebastian was in first before you skated. Paul was in second,
Joaquin in third."

"Paul came in ahead of Joaquin?" Thad tried not to frown as he caught
his breath. *Not what I was expecting.*

"By a couple of tenths of a point, and it could have gone the other way."

Thad looked around the arena and smiled at the still cheering crowd.
"This is great."

"You did really well, Thad."

Still, anxiety leapt in Thad's chest. Then his marks were called, and his
heart started racing. 6.0, 6.0, 6.0... "Whoa!" he yelped. The rest of the scores

kept coming, and none was lower than 5.9. "Yes!" he cried as he jumped to his feet.

"First place," Brianna said. "Congratulations."

"Thanks." Thad was still smiling as he made his way backstage.

Out of sight of the crowd, Thad joined the other skaters and was just congratulating Joaquin, Sebastian, and Paul when his family joined him.

"Thad!" Scott howled.

Rosie and James wrapped Thad in a big hug as Laura joined Joaquin and Sebastian's wife came over with their son. "Congratulations," James said.

"You did great!" Rosie added.

"Thanks," Thad said with a grin. "Now I just have to do it again in the long program."

That night, Thad fell into bed, exhausted. He slept long and hard and was glad when no alarm went off in the morning. Late in the afternoon, he watched the ladies' long program from Scott's hotel room as their parents joined them. "I wish I could watch it live like we did for the short program. But I need a break from the arena."

"And the pressure," James said with a knowing nod. "Don't worry, I'm sure Emily will understand."

"And her whole family is there to support her," Rosie added reassuringly.

Still, Thad found himself biting his nails again as the familiar music to "On My Own" came up. He only got in a few seconds of watching before Rosie took his hand and pulled it away from his mouth.

"Don't do that," she said.

"You're still five years old," Scott teased from across the room.

Thad shook his head, but the barest of smiles remained on his face as he continued watching Emily skate.

"The long programs are always the longest four and a half minutes, ever," Rosie said. "It's tough to watch, isn't it?"

Thad nodded. "They're tough to skate, too." He took a deep breath as Emily nailed her final combination of the night, a triple toe loop–double Lutz. Then his heart started to slow down. "She just has one more spin and she's good."

When Emily's program was over, she was smiling the largest grin Thad had ever seen on her, and the whole arena was cheering.

"Good for her!" Rosie said. "It's great to see her doing so well."

"She'll be ahead of Jenni," Scott said. "Jenni's long program was better than her short program, but both of Emily's programs were better."

"Yeah, Jenni didn't make any mistakes in her long program," Thad admitted.

"She's still a good skater, Thad," James said. "No matter how much you want it otherwise."

Thad smirked as he waited for Emily's scores to come up. "Yes!" he yelled as a number of sixes appeared on the screen. Then he held his breath as the rankings came up.

"Wow!" Scott said. "She's less than a point behind Kim!"

Thad smiled as he watched Emily cheer. "I'm still happy for Kim, though. She was amazing in both programs and deserves that gold."

Thad remained antsy all throughout the next day as he waited for his own long program. By the time he left for the arena, he was certain he was about to explode.

"Take it easy," Brianna murmured as they got to the rink. "I've never seen you so nervous."

"I have a lot on the line here," Thad answered. "Why do I even have to remind you of that?"

"You don't. Now, you skate next to last this time, but you're in a good position after the short program."

"Can't get better than first."

"And you do have a fair lead. Sebastian skates last, though, and he is within striking distance."

"Is he still planning a quad?"

"Oh, yeah." Brianna rolled her eyes. "He's been bragging about that all week."

"Do you think I should try one?"

Brianna shook her head. "You've only landed it in practice a couple of times now, and you've never practiced your long program with it. It's too much of a risk."

I have to agree with that, unfortunately, Thad thought as he went to change into his costume.

Out on the ice nearly a half hour later, Thad took stock of how his body felt. *My legs are a little tired,* he thought as he watched Sebastian launch into the air for a quad toe loop. He landed the jump cleanly, and Thad's stomach sank. *Do I have a shot at this title?* He took a deep breath. *It isn't just about another Nationals title, it's also about getting to the Olympics, and I only need to be on the podium to do that.*

Feeling slightly reassured, Thad finished his warmup, even if he did not leave the ice until the last call for the skaters to finish. Joaquin was just in front of Thad as they put their skate guards back on, and Thad saw the determination on his friend's face. *He wants this as badly as I do.*

Thad reached for his CD player, put his headphones on, and blocked everything else out. When it was almost time for him to skate, Brianna appeared backstage and jerked her head toward the ice. Thad was reassured by her presence and took a deep breath to calm the last of his nerves. At the very edge of the rink, he waited for the cheers for Paul Monfils to die down before he pulled his skate guards off. When Paul's marks were a mixture of 5.6s and 5.7s, Thad knew he had nothing to worry about. *It's just Joaquin and Sebastian in the running—after me, of course.*

When his name was announced, Thad's heart jumped in his chest. He skated to the middle of the ice and shook his arms out. *Keep it cool,* he told himself. The arena got quiet, and Thad took one last deep breath before his music started. As the strains of *Carmina Burana* vibrated in his ears, he whipped across the ice from one side to the other. Then he launched into his first triple jump, a Lutz that he landed cleanly. *Fortune,* he thought. *Swelling in my favor this time.*

The crowd cheered, but Thad was already focused on his next combination: a triple toe loop–triple axel. When he landed them cleanly, he smiled and looked up at the audience. Thousands of eyes were looking back at him, and he was glad for the slower part of the music as he flowed across the ice. By the time the music sped up, Thad was ready for his next jumps: a double axel–triple toe combination. Another triple axel followed several seconds later. The crowd cheered again as Thad wound through his footwork, dancing across the ice from one end to the other.

Then Thad's eyebrows came together as he flew into another triple axel. The ice spun around him as he landed it slightly less than cleanly—but at least he was still upright. *Good enough,* Thad thought as he readied himself for his last combination: a triple toe loop–triple Salchow. Those were both clean, and Thad smiled as the crowd's cheers reached his ears again.

After a final camel spin, Thad's long program was over, and the crowd's roar was deafening. *That was the best I could have done,* he thought as his smile reached both of his ears. He waved to the crowd a few more times before leaving the ice.

He was still trying to catch his breath as he put his skate guards on a minute later. Brianna sat next to him. "Nice job," she said. "It's too bad Sebastian still has to skate. If it weren't for that, I'd say the title was yours."

Thad nodded.

"I hope they give you the high marks that program deserves. If they leave any room for Sebastian, I'm going to be annoyed."

Thad smiled. Then his marks boomed out over the arena. "6.0, 6.0, 6.0, 6.0." Thad sucked in a breath. "5.9, 5.9, 5.9, 6.0, 6.0."

"Yes!" Thad yelped, jumping to his feet and throwing his fists into the air.

Brianna clapped him on the back as she stood up too. "That's going to be hard to beat."

Thad grinned as they made their way backstage. Sebastian's name was called out as Thad caught sight of Joaquin and Paul. After a second's hesitation, he made his way over to them.

"Congratulations," Joaquin said as Paul's eyes focused on the screen nearby, which showed Sebastian at the center of the ice.

"Thanks," Thad answered. "Just one more skater left now."

Joaquin nodded as he stood up. "I'm in second behind you. Let's see what Sebastian has to say for himself."

Thad forced himself to nod as anxiety raged through him again. *Relax, relax, there's nothing more you can do now.* Still, he bit his lip as Sebastian landed one beautiful triple jump after another. One triple Salchow and two triple axels later, Sebastian still showed no signs of slowing down.

"Damn, he's good," Paul mumbled.

"Yeah, when he's on, he's amazing," Joaquin said. "But he didn't get to Nationals or Worlds last year for nothing."

Great, Thad thought, rolling his eyes. He was glad when he managed to hold his tongue, especially to keep from cursing as Sebastian hit two more gorgeous triple Lutzes. Then his whole body tensed as Sebastian sped up, even faster than for his triple jumps. "He's gonna try the quad now." The words were out before he could stop them, and his eyes remained glued to the screen in front of him.

A second later, Sebastian launched into the air. His speed and height were incredible, and jealousy rose in Thad's chest. A second later, Sebastian hurtled back toward the ice—and went sprawling backward.

"Oof," Joaquin said.

"No kidding," Paul answered.

Thad sucked in a breath as Sebastian got up and continued skating. "That had to have hurt." He was impressed when Sebastian simply threw in another clean triple Lutz.

Next to him, Joaquin nodded. "Luckily for you, I think you'll keep your first place. Unluckily for me, I think even the quad attempt means I'll be third."

"You never know," Thad answered. "You skated a clean program, and your marks were pretty high."

Joaquin shrugged, and a neutral expression descended onto his features. *That's the look he gets when he's trying to hide what he's thinking,* Thad thought. *He's disappointed.* The cheers from the crowd above them told him that Sebastian's program was over. Sure enough, when he looked back at the screen in front of him, Sebastian was taking his bows. Thad took another deep breath as he tried to slow his racing heart.

Two minutes later, Sebastian's marks came up. "5.7, 5.8. 5.9, 5.8, 5.8, 5.8. 5.9, 5.9, 5.8."

Joaquin jerked in surprise. "I came in second."

"Told you," Thad mumbled.

Then Laura burst in. "Silver!"

A smile made its way onto Joaquin's face as Thad dropped his arm around his shoulders. "Congratulations," Thad said.

"Thanks," Joaquin answered as he went to hug his sister.

Thad's grin reached his ears again as he went back out to the ice. All around him, the crowd was cheering again. The cheers turned into a loud roar as Thad and Joaquin joined Sebastian on the podium for the medal ceremony. Thad caught sight of the American flag hanging in the rafters again as the gold medal was draped around his neck. Joaquin and Sebastian smiled also as they received their medals.

Then Sebastian looked at Thad. "Nice job. That was one hell of a long program."

"Thanks," Thad said.

When the medal ceremony was over, Thad found his family. Scott was cheering along with the crowd, but his parents opened their arms for hugs. Thad removed the medal from his neck and hung it around his mother's. Then he hugged both Rosie and James as his smile remained on his face.

By the time Thad arrived at the obligatory press conference with Joaquin and Sebastian, his fatigue was setting in. Next to them, Laura and Brianna looked excited. "The USOC just announced," Laura said. "The three of you are going to the Olympics."

"Yessss!" Joaquin said, raising his fists in the air.

Thad smiled back at him. "Hallelujah!"

"Now all I have to do is land my quad," Sebastian said, rolling his eyes as they all sat at the dais, facing the reporters in front of them.

"That would be something," Thad agreed.

"How does it feel to be going to the Olympics?" called out Erin Robinson of the *Salt Lake City Tribune*.

"It feels amazing," Joaquin answered.

Sebastian nodded. "Incredible."

Thad leaned forward and gestured at Sebastian and Joaquin. "I think these guys are going to have to carry me to the plane to get to Nagano, because none of this feels real yet."

"Thad, you've just won your fourth National title in eight years," Eric Tucker said. "That longevity is amazing. What advice would you offer other skaters?"

"Oh man, I wish I knew." All Thad could think about was Eric cornering him in the parking lot in Denver. He was glad when laughter filled the room. "Right now, I'm just happy to be here. This has been a long and difficult journey, and the Olympics are less than a month away. It's a lot to take in."

"You've had some distractions over the last several months," Erin said. "How did you keep your focus through all of this to win a gold medal tonight?"

Automatically, Thad glanced over to where Trevor sat at the back of the room. *Damn,* he thought when the rest of the reporters in the room looked at Trevor too. *Maybe he shouldn't have been here, anyway.* He swallowed. "I've been training at this level for years now, and focus has always been something I've worked on throughout it all. There will always be distractions. How you handle that shows who you are as an athlete."

"What do you think your chances are at the Olympics?" Marissa called out. "That's a question for all three of you."

Thad, Joaquin, and Sebastian looked at each other, then back at the reporters. "If I can stay steady and land my quad, I have a good shot at the podium," Sebastian answered.

"I, too, have been happy with how much I've improved over the last year," Joaquin said. "There were times I almost quit, but I kept going because I wanted to skate on Olympic ice. Right now I'll be happy with two clean programs. The rest of it will just have to fall where it does."

Thad swallowed as he tried to decide what to say. "I think U.S. Figure Skating is sending a solid team to the Olympics. Both on the men's side and the women's side. What happens on Olympic ice will always come down to seven minutes of skating, for each of us."

Chapter 19

The next morning, Thad was only too happy to sleep in and have breakfast at the hotel with his family. "What time is your train back to Boston?"

"Two o'clock," Scott said.

"I have a 3:30 flight back to Denver," Thad said.

"Doesn't that get you in pretty late?" Rosie asked.

"Six o'clock Denver time—not too bad."

"Haven't you adjusted to east coast time, though?" Scott teased.

Thad shrugged. "It's only a two-hour difference. I mean, I'm sure I'll be almost ready to go to sleep anyway, even at six o'clock, but..."

James nodded. "I'm sure you must be exhausted."

Thad suppressed a yawn. "I am. I think everything is catching up to me."

Rosie smiled. "At least you have some hardware to show for all your work."

Thad grinned. "And it's the best color hardware, too."

It was not until Thad was in the lobby saying goodbye to all of them that he saw Paul Monfils checking out of the hotel. "I didn't realize you were staying here, Paul."

"Oh, yeah, it was the closest hotel to the arena." Paul shrugged.

"Are you flying back to Seattle?" Rosie asked him.

"Yeah," Paul answered, and he looked surprised.

"What?" Thad said. "You're in the news as much as I am, and my family pays attention to skating. Of course they know you're from Seattle."

Paul smiled. "I just wish I had as good an outcome here as you did."

"I thought your skating was good. You could easily have come in third."

Paul shook his head. "Not with the way you guys skated, and anyway, I think U.S. Figure Skating wanted to send you three to the Olympics. It would have come out this way even if I'd skated better and one of you hadn't."

"I don't know about that."

"I do, and I'm okay with it." Paul was serious. "This is the end of the line for my amateur career, and I think that's fine. I already have an offer with Stars on Ice, and I'll make more money there in a year than I've made in my last five as an amateur."

"That's the way of these things."

Paul turned to look out the window as one of the hotel's shuttles pulled up outside. "Aright, that's my ride to the airport." He looked back at Thad. "Good luck at the Olympics. I mean it."

"Thanks, Paul." Thad watched Paul grab the handle of his suitcase and head out the door. Then he gave his parents and Scott a round of hugs as Emily and Mia joined them. "Have a good trip home."

"You too," Rosie said. "Get home safely, and we'll see you in Nagano."

The next day, Thad's head was still buzzing from the excitement, even in Denver. He spotted his gold medal across the room as soon as he woke up, and a smile he could not contain spread across his face. After breakfast, he ducked into his living room to make a call.

"Hi, Thad," Anne said on the other end. "I had a feeling it would be you. Congratulations on the gold—you were magnificent."

"Thanks." Thad was still grinning like an idiot. "I don't suppose you're up for flying to Nagano? I'd like to see you there."

Anne sounded like she was smiling when she spoke. "Cody Lewis called me about that already. He, too, was hoping I'd go."

"Ah, Cody, I know him."

"He trained with Trevor until he retired from skating."

"I remember. I saw him for a second at Nationals."

"Well, he's still choreographing. He did one of Sebastian's programs and has been working with Grigoriy Arsenyev for one of his Olympic programs, too."

"I won't hold that against him."

Anne laughed. "Well, Arsenyev is training in New York and Cody is trying to make a living, so..."

"Yeah, I know how it goes. Cody was the National Champion a couple of years in a row as I was winning at the junior level."

"He was the champion until you beat him at the senior level." Anne laughed again.

This time, Thad joined her. "Well, if you want to come to Nagano, I'm happy to speak to Cody to see if we can arrange it."

"That would be wonderful. You have been skating so well that I want to be in the audience when you win an Olympic medal."

"Your lips to God's ears."

They both laughed again. Then Anne took a deep breath. "It is so good to hear from you, Thad."

Two days later, Thad smiled at Emily as they and Joaquin walked into the Grand Hyatt for a joint interview. Brianna was on Thad's other side and Laura was right behind Joaquin. Mia was several steps behind them. Trevor was nowhere to be seen, but Thad only thought about it for a second. Emily looked as happy as he felt, and that was all that mattered to him.

In the lobby, the hotel's heat blasted onto them as the snow continued to fall outside. Several reporters from the *Denver Post* were waiting for them, and Thad noticed Eric among them. Once more he remembered being accosted outside the arena at the crack of dawn. *I'll bet anything Eric has different questions now,* he thought. *Reporters.*

A man that Thad did not recognize approached them. "Hi, everyone, I'm Craig Hall, the chief editor of the *Post*'s sports section." He gestured in one direction. "We have one of the conference rooms over there."

"The head of the sports section?" Joaquin said. "Shouldn't you be covering football or hockey?"

Thad laughed, and he was relieved when Craig looked amused.

"I usually do," Craig said. "But this is an Olympic year, and figure skating has been really popular the last several years."

"Yeah, thanks to Nancy Kerrigan and Tonya Harding," Eric piped up. "Made my job worthwhile all of a sudden."

Thad eyed him as everyone followed Craig out of the lobby.

"Hey, I was covering skating even before that," Eric said defensively. "I've been around a while."

"Yeah, but this is the first time that people are reading your articles," Joaquin teased.

This time, both Emily and Thad laughed.

Eric shook his head in frustration, but a small smile made its way onto his face.

A long table was at the front of the conference room. Thad went over and sat down, and Emily and Joaquin followed him. He looked out over the room and was surprised at how full it was. Brianna and Mia were sitting in the first row, as were Erin Robinson, Shelby Thompson, and a few other reporters. A couple of cameramen lined the walls, and several people Thad did not recognize filled the remaining seats.

The questions started with one for Thad and Joaquin. "You both are in quite a different position right now than you were a year ago," Eric said. "What do you make of that?"

"I've had ups and downs throughout my career," Thad answered. "Sometimes it was hard to keep going. But this time, I've made a point of retooling my programs and finding music that's meaningful to me. I've changed coaches, and my new coach is also a choreographer. I think all of that makes a difference."

"I would say the same," Joaquin added. "Both Thad and I have had to take a long look in the mirror and decide what's important to us. I think you're seeing the results of our renewed focus."

"Emily, you skated your long program to music from 'Les Mis,'" Shelby asked. "Are you planning on sticking with that for the Olympics?"

"I am," Emily said. "I like that program a lot, but there are a few changes I'll make for the Olympics."

"That's a sad piece, though. Don't you want to do something happier?"

Emily thought for a moment before answering. "It's not just sadness. There are many emotions packed into that song, and that range is what we go for as skaters. It gives us a lot to work with on the ice."

"How long have you been preparing that program?" another reporter called out.

"I started last year. Thad and I went to see 'Les Mis' when it came to Denver, and I'd already had that song in mind for a program when we went. This past year has been a rough one, and I often felt alone, like Eponine when she's singing this song."

Mia looked at the floor as Emily spoke, and Thad wondered if she was feeling the impact of everything that had happened.

"Has skating to this program helped you as a skater?" one reporter called.

"Yes, I'd say so," Emily answered. "I, too, have been fortunate that other coaches—as well as Thad and Joaquin—have stepped up to offer support. As a skater, especially at this level, it's important to have that network."

Thad smiled and took her hand. She smiled back at him.

Next to them, Joaquin swallowed and stared at the back of the room.

He's uncomfortable, Thad realized. But the questions kept coming, so he focused on the reporters again as the three of them took turns answering.

By the end of the press conference, Joaquin was his smiling, joking self again, so Thad decided not to say anything further, even as he thought of the conversation he had had with Emily in the park. *Maybe I'm not the only one who's uncomfortable with that stuff,* he thought. Still, he could not help but feel happy as he looked around the room. *I'm going to the Olympics next month, and I think I'm almost prepared for it.*

When Thad returned to the arena for practice the next day, Brianna was waiting for him. He took one look at the clothing bag she held and guessed its contents. "Are those my outfits for the Olympics?"

Brianna nodded and grinned. "Joaquin's will be ready in the next couple of days."

Thad opened the bag and took out the outfit on top, holding the clothing hanger instead of the outfit so that he would not destroy the pure white cloth.

"For your short program," Brianna said.

Thad had tears in his eyes just from looking at it. "Oh, this is beautiful."

"And an outfit you'll get dirty without even wearing," Joaquin joked.

"I have two duplicate outfits just in case that fit more like your workout clothes." Brianna nodded at the small suitcase next to her feet.

Thad handed her the white outfit for safekeeping and reached for the second set of clothing. A red shirt and black pants nearly leapt off the hanger. "This is perfect. I can't wait to practice again."

The next two weeks passed faster than Thad could blink. He arrived at the airport in Denver feeling like a heavy weight was pressing on his chest and shoulders. He struggled to inhale and almost choked instead. He closed his eyes, and Vivaldi's music soared through his head: *Nulla in mundo...* A second later, he could breathe again.

Emily grabbed his hand as they got out of Brianna's car. "I don't know if I can do this."

"Sure you can." *She needs my music.*

Behind them, Joaquin got out of the car and eyed their hands.

Thad swallowed and had to control himself from pulling away from Emily. "We've got a long flight to Nagano and a couple of hours before we even take off. I'll give you my CD player once we get past security."

Finally, Emily loosened her grip. "Do you have your music for your short program? That might do me some good."

Thad smiled. *She knows me well.* "I was thinking the same thing."

Together, the group walked into the airport, and Thad was glad to be moving forward. *These Olympics are happening even if we miss our flight. I need to get there and I need to skate.* They were past security when Thad reached into his bookbag and pulled out his CD player.

Emily smiled as she took it from him. "Even if I already feel better than I did outside."

"Then maybe you should leave the music with Thad," Joaquin teased from nearby. "That's his short program we're talking about."

Emily stuck out her tongue and put the headphones on. Then she pressed "Play."

Thad shot Joaquin an amused look and was glad when Laura did the same. He reached back into his bag and pulled out the biography on Vivaldi that he had been reading. *I'll need my CD player back from Emily at some point, but this will do for now.*

The book lasted him until they changed planes in New York. Then Emily handed him back his CD player, along with a few batteries.

"Did you charge her interest?" Joaquin cracked.

"Yeah, what is this?" Thad asked Emily as a mixture of amusement and confusion welled within him.

"I was listening to it the whole flight here. I'll bet I used up most of the batteries."

"How nice of you."

"You gave it to me. The extra batteries were the least I could do."

"And you're not worried about running out?"

Emily shook her head. "My mom sent me a care package before we left with a bunch of extras. I'll be fine sparing a couple."

"Aww, thank you."

But even with his book and his CD player, the flight into Narita International Airport was interminable. After eight hours, Thad was pacing the aisles, and after more than twelve hours, he was sure he was losing his mind. He couldn't believe it when they landed.

"I'm never doing that again," Joaquin mumbled as they stumbled off the plane.

"You're not planning on going home?" Thad asked.

"Shut up, Mr. Logical. I'll swim if I have to."

I can't even blame him, Thad thought. *I just hope I do well enough here that I don't have to keep skating for another four years.* Still, Thad's breath caught in his throat as he saw the Olympic flag across the airport. *This is still special. Work your hardest, but enjoy it too.*

The Olympic village was teeming with activity when they arrived. "This is a madhouse," Joaquin said.

Thad nodded. "On par with what I saw in the last Olympics." When they got their room assignments, he realized he was sharing a room with Joaquin.

"Oh, good," Joaquin said. "You're quiet and we're on the same competition schedule."

"I'm sure that's why they did it. When I was an alternate eight years ago, roommates were assigned randomly and people complained."

"That's crazy."

"Yeah, I was wondering what to expect this time. Half of me thought I'd end up with a loud hockey player."

Joaquin laughed, and they both went to unpack their belongings.

Thad fell into bed that night and got a solid ten hours of sleep. "Oof," he groaned when he pulled himself out of bed around eight o'clock the next morning. He checked the schedule near his bed. *Opening ceremonies start at 11. Glad I made it up for that.*

All around him, the excitement in the Olympic village was palpable. More athletes were arriving, and Thad was glad to see both Emily and Kim, along with Jack Wallace and several other hockey players. He recognized a forward from the New York Rangers and a left wing from the Boston Bruins. *The Olympic team pulled some real standouts.*

Emily smiled when she saw him. "Sebastian got here around the same time we did yesterday. I heard Jenni's around here somewhere, too, but I care less about that."

Thad laughed. "Are you marching at the opening ceremonies?"

"Oh, yeah, I wouldn't miss that for anything. I had to get the outfits Ralph Lauren made for us tailored, but I don't even care."

"Yeah, we all had to get those things fitted," Kim said, rolling her eyes. "They were made for hockey players, not figure skaters."

"Hey, you got a problem with hockey players?" Jack teased, giving her a shove.

"You know I don't!" Still, Kim took a step away from him. "But if I get injured before I get to compete, it's gonna be your fault!"

Jack took a mock swing at her.

Kim ducked. Then she took off down the hallway. "I'm getting dressed for the opening ceremonies before I get hurt!"

Thad and Emily looked at each other and burst out laughing.

Three hours later, they were all marching into the Olympic stadium in matching outfits and carrying small American flags. Jack had been chosen to carry the official American flag of the delegation, and he marched at the front of the large crowd of American athletes. Loud cheers rang out when they made their entrance into the stadium, and Thad grinned. Then he took a deep breath of the chilly air, and his nose tingled.

"This is amazing," Emily said.

"I know." Thad looked at the long line of athletes all around them. Cheering crowds in the stadium added to the cacophony. Excitement swirled within him, beating out the anxiety in his stomach for a moment. *I still wonder what my fate here will be, but at least I can enjoy how amazing this moment is.*

Thad looked around for Joaquin and saw both him and Sebastian a few steps up. Sebastian was craning his neck to see everything around them, and his face bore the same wonder that Thad felt. For a moment, Joaquin stared forward to the head of the American line, where the stars and stripes were waving proudly. Then he, too, looked around and waved to the crowd. *I'm glad they're both getting to enjoy this,* Thad thought.

It was more than an hour later before they were all seated in the stadium. Akihito, the emperor of Japan, opened the ceremony, and his dignity drew the eyes of every person in the stadium. Throughout the ceremony, Thad's body tingled as a chorus sang, bells gonged, and Japanese children welcomed them. *This is all amazing. After I placed fourth at the last Olympics, I never thought I'd be able to feel this joy again.*

Then Emily took his hand, bringing him back to the present. "Having fun?" she asked.

"Oh yeah, I'm so glad to be here." *A lot has changed in the last four years. I just hope these games end with me on the podium.*

Chapter 20

T he next four days felt like an agony of waiting for the short program. "Ugh," Joaquin said as he and Thad started pulling their belongings together to get to the rink. "If it were up to me, our events would have been first and the competition would be over already."

Thad managed a laugh, but it sounded hollow, even to him. "Me too."

They were silent as they got on the shuttle that would take them to the ice. Sebastian got on a minute later. He gave them a nod and sat near them, but he too was silent the entire ride over. They were just arriving when Thad realized that Grigoriy had not been on the bus with them. Relief flowed through him, cool and powerful, even as he wondered where his Russian rival was. *I still don't trust that guy.*

Inside, Brianna joined Thad as Laura gave Joaquin a hug and Sebastian joined his coach. "How are you feeling?" Brianna asked.

"Not too bad," Thad answered, even as butterflies of nervousness made his stomach flutter.

"Good. You're skating last tonight, which puts you in a good position."

Thad nodded as he removed his white outfit from its garment bag. Immediately, the smooth sounds and soaring soprano of Vivaldi's music soared through his head. He smiled.

Brianna nodded. "Keep that expression, keep your cool, and you'll do fine tonight."

Thad felt loose and flowing during the warmup. He breathed deeply and kept his eyes half closed so that he would not see what the other skaters were doing. *Stick to yourself,* he thought, even as he also thought of Emily. *You can do this.*

Still, waiting for his turn to skate seemed interminable once the warmup was over. Thad turned away from the TVs that broadcasted his competitors' short programs. He found a quiet corner, faced the wall, and put on his headphones. Once more, the languid, beautiful music of Vivaldi's sacred works flowed through him, and Thad felt as though he were floating toward heaven.

When Brianna came to get him, Thad rose and followed her. At the edge of the ice, he removed his skate guards and stepped onto the ice. *Olympic ice.* Thad felt his white clothing around him, tailored and perfect. *Make this program perfect too,* he told himself. Then his name was announced, and Thad's heart jumped into his throat.

Brianna clasped his hands. "You can do this. You're a wonderful skater and this is an amazing program."

Thad nodded and moved to the middle of the arena. His blades glided over the ice so smoothly he was sure he was floating. The cheers died down as he reached the center. Thad took his starting pose and took a deep breath.

The first notes of his music started, high and pure. Thad began moving without any command from his brain. His fingertips tingled, as if he were receiving the music through them. Calm flowed throughout the rest of the body, and when he went into his first triple toe loop–triple axel combination, he felt as though he were floating. He landed back on the ice as if he were weightless.

This was such a good choice of music, he thought as he picked up speed again. His next jumps—two more triple axels—came out smoothly too and Thad began to feel guided by some strong force. *Must be the music.* He clasped his arms to his chest as he went into a spin.

The crowd clapped and cheered as Thad came out of the spin and his intricate footwork carried him across the ice. Then he burst into a triple Salchow. A double axel followed, and the end of the program was in sight.

Thad smiled as he launched into his final triple Salchow. The crowd cheered at his last and best jump.

Thad was in his final spin before he realized that his short program was almost over. His spin stopped as suddenly as his music did, and for the first time that he could remember at a competition, he wished he could keep skating. *You'll have plenty of time to do that on Saturday,* he reminded himself as the crowd leapt to its feet and cheered.

The roar reached Thad's ears and brought him back to the present. His heart raced and his breath came in gasps. *Damn,* he thought. Still, a grin that he could not control reached from one ear to the other. He waved to the crowd and took a couple of bows. Then he skated back to where Brianna was waiting for him.

"That was amazing," Brianna said as she embraced him. "You looked flawless."

Thad just smiled as he caught his breath. The press of the crowd around him made him feel as though he were landing back on Earth. "Now if only my marks reflect that."

Brianna clapped him on the knee. "They will."

Thad leaned forward and looked toward the row of judges. "Come on, come on."

Brianna smiled at him.

Then Thad's marks came up, and his heart leapt in his throat. "5.9, 6.0, 6.0, 6.0, 6.0, 5.9, 5.9, 6.0, 5.9."

Thad's legs turned to jelly. "Oh, wow," he managed to stutter.

"Second place," Brianna said.

"Who's in first?" Thad's words caught in his throat.

"Grigoriy." Brianna rolled her eyes. "He got one 5.9 and the rest were sixes. He's only three tenths of a point ahead of you, though. This competition isn't over yet."

Thad smiled as he stood and waved to the audience, who roared in reply. Somehow, Thad found his family a few rows up and sent a large grin in their direction.

Scott gestured wildly. "Backstage?" he yelled. "We'll meet you there."

Thad nodded in reply. Then he followed Brianna, hoping that they would somehow get away from the crush of fans and reporters in front of him. Instead, they ended up right in the middle of cameras and microphones.

"Thad, how do you feel tonight?" Stephanie Chen asked.

"Ah, Stephanie, I was wondering if you'd be here," Thad answered, playing for time as he caught his breath.

"Here I am. How are you feeling after that magnificent short program?"

"Pretty good. It was a beautiful program—I had great music and a good choreographer. I couldn't ask for more than those marks, either."

"What about Saturday night? I hear you're skating to 'Les Mis.'"

"I am. Emily Burrows turned me onto that music after taking me to a production of 'Les Mis' in Denver. I should probably thank her."

"That's an intense piece to skate to on such a big stage."

"It is, but I wanted to take the fire of love and war to the ice. I'm excited about that program."

"You're less than a half point behind Grigoriy Arsenyev. Do you think you can beat him?"

"Anything can happen, Stephanie. You'll just have to tune in."

A minute later, Thad was glad the interview was over. He was still smiling when he got away from the crowd and found his family. Relief flowed through him as Rosie hugged him and Scott whacked him on the back.

"That was amazing!" Scott yelped.

James nodded and held his arms out to his younger son. "Good job."

"Thanks," Thad answered as he removed his skates and switched into his sneakers.

"Also, that outfit is divine," Rosie said.

"Kind of like my music," Thad joked.

"Literally," Scott answered. "I've never listened to sacred music before. I may have to start."

"If you do, start with Vivaldi. These songs have been haunting my dreams at night."

Brianna was standing nearby with Thad's duffel bag, and she handed it to Thad as he finished putting his sneakers on. "I'm proud of you, Thad. I also want to see a repeat performance on Saturday."

"Oh, I do too."

Scott dropped his arm around Thad's shoulders as Rosie slid her arm around his waist. "Come on, let's get out of here," Scott said, and the family headed for the door.

"Anne is coming to meet us too," Thad said as they got outside.

"Oh, how nice," Rosie said. "It'll be so good to see her again."

"We've called her a couple of times," James added.

"I didn't know that," Thad said.

"She was like a second mother to you," Rosie said. "We didn't want that to disappear down the drain with everything that happened with Trevor."

"It hasn't," Thad answered. "She should be here to celebrate this as much as you are."

The family caught up to Joaquin and Sebastian as the two other Americans left the arena, surrounded by their own families and coaches. After a round of congratulations, Joaquin and Sebastian dropped back to Thad's side.

Sebastian glanced toward his own family and coach before his voice came out in a whisper. "I know Grigoriy came in first, but did you see him skate at all?"

Thad shook his head. "No, I was skating after him, so I didn't watch anything. What happened? Did he not skate well?"

"No, his program was beautiful," Joaquin answered. "I knew you and he would be duking it out."

"But?" Thad asked, looking back and forth between the two of them.

"He looked really pale," Sebastian replied.

"I would have said gray," Joaquin said.

"You think he's sick?" Thad's heart drummed in his chest.

"Either that or the IOC should go after him again with their drug testing kits," Sebastian said.

"They will," Thad said. "They'll do the same for all of us."

"I know," Sebastian said. "But I was amazed Grigoriy skated as well as he did."

Thad bit his lip. "I wonder what that will mean for the long program."

"It means that nothing is set in stone until we're all done skating," Sebastian said. "Every last one of us."

Joaquin nodded. "I'm going to have tunnel vision until my four and a half minutes on the ice are over. This is my first time at the Olympics, and it's gonna be my last, too."

Thad smiled. "We all have a chance at the podium. Let's skate our hearts out."

When he got back to the Olympic village, the place was still bouncing with action. Thad shook his head. *How do these people compete if they don't sleep?* he wondered as he made his way back to his room. He passed Matt Mitchell, the Avalanche's goalie, who gave him a nod. Thad nodded back. A minute later, he saw Jack, and by then he was sure Jack was coming from his room. *He and Joaquin are definitely seeing each other,* he decided.

"Nice job out there tonight," Jack said.

"Thanks. Good luck against Norway tomorrow."

"Oh, we're going to blow them away." Jack was smiling as he continued down the hall.

Thad smiled too as he got back to his room. Inside, Joaquin was lying down with his eyes closed, and for a minute, Thad thought he was asleep. He closed the door quietly and crept into the room. Then Joaquin opened his eyes and sat up. Thad gave him a nod. "You skated well tonight."

"Not like you," Joaquin answered. "You're the talk of the town."

"And I'm still a few tenths of a point behind Grigoriy Arsenyev." Thad rolled his eyes. "No one will let me forget."

Joaquin shrugged. "We'll see if it stays that way."

Thad frowned. "What do you mean?"

"I'm with Sebastian on this one. I don't think Grigoriy looked well at all. Maybe he has the flu or something. Or his partying is finally catching up to him."

"I always wondered about that second possibility. His loss will be our gain."

"I hope so. I'm just behind Sebastian, and fourth place is a tough place to be."

Thad nodded. "Don't I know that. I finished fourth at the last Olympics. You don't hope someone will fall, but..."

"Yeah, you hope for it."

Both men laughed.

"If you keep skating the way you've been skating, you'll have something to show for it," Thad said.

"I hope so," Joaquin answered seriously. "This journey has been too long to walk away empty handed."

Chapter 21

The next morning, a newspaper was sitting just outside their door, and Joaquin stepped on it as they went out. He had to step further into the hall to be able to turn around and pick it up. "Oh, look at this." He held it up for Thad to see.

Thad's breath jerked inward as his eyes focused on the headlines. "Opening Ceremonies a Success, First Medals Awarded," the largest headline read. Below it, though, Thad saw a picture of himself and a smaller headline: "Moulton a Vision in White at Men's Short Program." Thad's heart rate quickened, even as he smiled.

Then Kim McGrath passed them. "One of the British skiers left that outside your door."

"Luckily for us," Thad said. "I can't start my day without a picture of myself."

Kim shook her head at him, but she was laughing.

Thad and Joaquin laughed too and headed off to find some breakfast.

Saturday came more quickly than Thad was expecting. He drummed his fingers on the side of the bus that took him and the other skaters back to the arena. Once more, no one said anything to each other, and now the tension ran through the air like water, soupy and thick. Once more, Thad noticed that Grigoriy was not on the shuttle. *His coach must be driving him,* he decided. *There's no other explanation.*

Backstage, Thad smiled at his costume. His red shirt and black pants set each other off perfectly, and Thad thought of being in the audience with Emily at the Performing Arts Center in Denver. He thought of the smoke rising on the stage and the passion of Enjolras and Marius, heading equally toward love and war. *That's what your program is about. Make it a good one.*

On the ice for warmups, Thad caught a glimpse of Grigoriy. His rival was moving slowly, and Thad wondered again if he was sick. He took a deep breath and looked away. Then he forgot all about Grigoriy as he prepared for a triple Lutz. When he landed it well, he knew he was ready for his long program. *I'm skating next to last. Only Grigoriy is after me. All of this will be over soon.*

Off the ice, Thad followed the same routine that had gotten him through the short program. He stayed away from the TVs and blocked out his competitors' skating. By the time Brianna came to get him, he was ready, and together, they walked toward the ice.

It was completely black in the tunnel away from the backstage area. Thad took a deep breath and closed his eyes one last time. The bright colors of the Olympic rings had already emblazoned themselves into his eyes, though, and the colors shone even against his closed eyelids. The roar of the arena's crowd also reached his ears, and Thad took another moment to focus. When everything around him was dark and quiet, he opened his eyes again and covered the last few yards to the ice.

He passed a mirror as he walked. For a second, he caught sight of his reflection, somehow willowy and taut at the same time. *Power and grace. Go for both.* Then Thad's name was called, and the crowd cheered. *This is it,* he thought. *No turning back now.* He stepped onto the ice and glided toward the center of the rink.

As he moved, he thought of the confrontation between himself and Jack Wallace, all that time ago on the Denver ice. *You won that competition, and you thought Jack was a formidable foe. You can do the same here.*

The crowd got quiet, and Thad thought of nothing but his program. In the silence, he struck his opening pose. Then his music sounded through the arena, forceful and strong. Thad whipped across the ice the same way, feeling the power in his muscles as he launched into his first triple Salchow. He landed cleanly, and the crowd roared.

Red, Thad thought. He launched into a triple axel and landed it well. *Black.* He spun through his favorite spin, fast and furious. *Love and war.* Two more huge triple jumps followed, and Thad felt the height he got on both of them. *Maybe someday I'll touch the ceiling.*

This competition is a war, he thought as his fancy footwork carried him across the ice a minute later. He pictured Enjolras, singing about the students' small lives being subverted to a higher cause. Then he launched into two double jumps and another triple Salchow. Halfway across the ice, he hit another triple axel without a problem.

By now, the crowd was roaring, but Thad only had ears for his music. *Les Miserables,* he thought. *From misery to ecstasy.* After two more triple axels, he was speeding into his final spin of the night—so fast that everything around him was a blur. He could neither think nor breathe until the spin was finished and he was standing still at the center of the ice.

All around him, the crowd leapt to its feet and cheered. It took Thad a second to realize that his music was over, and that he had just spent the longest four and a half minutes of his life in a glory of jumps and spins.

Then his body came back to him. All at once, Thad felt each of his muscles aching, felt the groan of his lungs as he gasped for air. *Oh, my God,* was all he could think. Roses and teddy bears landed around him as he took his bows and waved to the crowd. The ovation went on for longer than Thad was expecting, and he had to remind himself to leave the ice.

I need to see my scores, he thought as he grabbed a teddy bear and a couple of flowers. His legs carried him to the "kiss and cry" area, and he beamed at Brianna as he stepped off the ice.

"Unbelievable," Brianna said. "I think that was the most flawless program I've ever seen you skate, except for your short program. I'd be amazed if the judges take off for anything."

"Grigoriy still has to skate, though," Thad said as his breathing and heart rate began to return to normal. "They might leave some room in case they think he skates better."

"I'm not even sure how he could, unless he lands a quad."

"Think he will?"

"If he's ever going to land one, this would be the time to do it."

Great, Thad thought, but nothing could get in the way of his happiness.

Brianna looked over at the judges for the briefest of seconds. Then she nodded her chin at Thad. "What were you thinking about as you got to the center of the ice?"

"What do you mean?" Thad frowned, confused.

"You were *smiling.* I don't think I've ever seen you *smile* at such a big competition, with so much at stake."

"Was I really?" Thad laughed. "I didn't even realize it." He sucked in a long breath. "I was thinking of the time that Jack Wallace challenged me to that skating duel after Worlds."

Brianna laughed now too.

Then Thad's scores came up. A 5.9 came up first, and Thad's stomach dropped a mile. Around him, the crowd booed. Then the rest of his scores came up: 6.0, 6.0, 6.0, 5.9, 6.0, 6.0, 6.0, 6.0.

"Oh, my God," Thad choked. His legs shook, and Brianna had to help him to his feet again as the crowd cheered. Thad managed to wave to everyone around him. He tried to find his parents and Scott, but everything was spinning.

Brianna took his elbow and steered him away from the ice. "That was one way to end the evening."

Thad's face felt stiff from the shock. "Grigoriy is going to have to be perfect to beat me."

Brianna nodded. "Let's see what he does."

Away from the noisy crowd, Thad was glad for the relative quiet as his head continued to spin. He saw the rest of the skaters backstage and made his way toward Sebastian and Joaquin.

"That was amazing," Joaquin said. "Even if I'm saying that at my own expense."

"How'd you do?" Thad asked. He allowed himself a look at the TV and was rewarded with a view of Grigoriy stepping onto the ice as his name was called.

"He did great, and don't let him tell you otherwise," Sebastian answered, sending an evil grin at Joaquin.

"Yeah?" Thad asked, looking back at Joaquin.

"I'm happy," Joaquin answered, and Thad was relieved that he was genuinely smiling. "I didn't fall, my jumps were clean, my marks were pretty good."

"Where are you in the standings?" Thad asked.

"Third, behind you and Sebastian."

"Now it's up to Grigoriy," Sebastian said as the three skaters turned toward the TV.

Thad sucked in a breath as the camera panned in to Grigoriy's face. "Wow, he does look grey."

"Yeah, I almost crashed into him during warmups and I thought he looked awful," Joaquin said.

"Damn," Thad said as Grigoriy started skating. Then he glanced over at Sebastian. "How'd you skate, Sebastian?"

"I landed my quad without falling for the first time in competition." Sebastian's face lit up with a grin.

"And you're still behind me?" Thad asked. "How's that possible?"

"I two-footed the landing," Sebastian admitted. "And one of my triple jumps was a little messy too."

Thad nodded as his eyes went back to Grigoriy.

"I'm happy anyway," Sebastian said. "I skated better than I was expecting. I was so nervous before I went out that I was sure I was going to sprawl across the ice."

"Really?" Thad asked. "I never pictured you as a nervous guy."

"Oh, I'm a wreck before competition. I'm always glad when it's over."

"Me too," Thad and Joaquin said at the same time.

Then the three men were silent, watching their Russian competitor.

"Wow," Joaquin said as Grigoriy popped out of a triple axel.

Sebastian nodded. "I heard he was going to try for a quad, but he's skating too slowly for that."

Thad bit his lip, and anxiety hit him like a large wave.

"Well, Grigoriy's drinking has been hitting the news for a while now," Joaquin said.

"The drinking is the least of it," Sebastian answered. "He's always going out and partying. I'm amazed he's able to train. I really think those clean tests before Skate America were a fluke. Or luck."

In front of them, Grigoriy began to move faster across the ice.

"I'll bet this is it," Sebastian said. "If he tries the quad, it's gonna be now."

Thad held his breath and counted one, two, three, and the beginning of a fourth rotation. Then Grigoriy hit the ice and went sprawling, landing hard on his right knee and then his hip.

"Oww," Sebastian yelped, turning away and scrunching up his face.

Joaquin winced at the same time. "Yeah, that was a bad one."

Thad frowned as he watched Grigoriy struggle to get back up. "Wow. I wonder if he'll be able to finish the program."

Grigoriy skated slowly for a minute, wincing. Then his music picked up speed, and he began to skate along with it.

"He's a brave soul," Thad said.

"No more than you are, skating in Sacramento after that shoulder injury," Sebastian said.

"I suppose," Thad answered.

Joaquin nodded at the TV. "For Grigoriy, it must be the Russian winters. Their blood is thicker than ours is."

"He's been training in the States," Sebastian said, rolling his eyes.

The three men laughed, and Thad felt the tension flowing out of his body like water. His eyes went back to the screen in front of him, where Grigoriy still seemed to skate slower than usual. When his Russian rival fell a second time, and then only landed two other lackluster jumps before his program ended, Thad's hope rose within him like a spike.

Sebastian and Joaquin looked over at Thad as Grigoriy limped off the ice. "Looks like the gold medal is yours, Thad," Joaquin said.

Thad sucked in another breath as both hope and uncertainty raged within him. "Let's see what the scores say."

Brianna and Laura joined them as Grigoriy waited in the "kiss and cry" area. Brianna gave Thad a nod. "How does it feel?" she asked as Sebastian's coach joined them too.

Thad's eyes went back to Grigoriy, and the Russian skater looked downcast and in pain. *I felt the same way after the last Olympics,* he thought. He did not have the time to answer Brianna's question before Grigoriy's marks came up: 5.5, 5.4, 5.6, 5.6, 5.5, 5.7, 5.6, 5.6, 5.5.

"Damn," Joaquin said.

"Oof," Sebastian said, nodding in agreement.

The world spun around Thad as everyone in the room looked at him. He took a step backward and nearly stumbled.

Joaquin grabbed his arm. "Easy there."

Brianna grabbed Thad's other arm. "You skate to perfection on the ice and you can't stay upright on dry land?"

Everyone laughed, and Thad came back to his senses. Then the rankings flashed on the TV in front of them, and Thad had the confirmation he was looking for: his name was listed first, and with a gold circle next to it. Sebastian's name was listed next to the silver, and Joaquin's with the bronze.

A smile lit up Thad's face as he embraced his countrymen. "Unbelievable," he said, feeling like he was forcing the word out.

The three athletes stepped outside the waiting area and into the arms of their families. All around them, the arena roared as Thad hugged his parents and Scott. Rosie was crying, and even James' eyes looked wet. Scott screamed along with the spectators around them, and Thad was sure he had never heard his brother yell so loud. His legs moved him toward the podium without any command from his brain.

It was not until he was standing on the highest part of the podium that it all began to sink in. *Olympic Gold*. His knees shook as three American flags were raised to the rafters. Loud yells went up as every single person in the arena waved American flags. Thad's face split with a grin as he looked over at Sebastian and Joaquin. They looked back at him with wonder in their eyes.

Then Japanese officials stepped forward. The gold medal caught the light of the arena, and Thad's heart stopped. Within seconds he was bending forward, and the medal was draped around his neck. His whole body felt the weight of it as his fingers curled around it. Thad's eyes sought his family out once more, and he gave them a nod as they all screamed.

Thad turned and watched as the silver was draped around Sebastian's neck. A minute later, Joaquin was wearing his bronze medal. A few tears slipped down Joaquin's cheeks, even as he smiled back at Thad and Sebastian. Thad's face hurt from smiling as he faced forward for the national anthem. As the strains of the Star-Spangled Banner rang through the arena, Thad placed his hand over his heart. The weight of the gold medal continued to pull at his consciousness. When the anthem ended, Thad turned and shook hands with Sebastian and Joaquin.

Joaquin took his hand and then wrapped him in a bear hug. "Thanks for everything. I would not be here without you."

"Likewise," Thad answered.

Joaquin grinned and went over to Laura and their mother. Another round of hugs followed before Joaquin was surrounded by Jack and several other American athletes.

Thad laughed and dove back to his own family. "Has anyone seen Emily?" The words were no sooner out of his mouth than he spotted her nearby, screaming and yelling. He laughed and moved toward her.

"Thad!" Emily screamed, and Thad was amazed that he heard her over the crowd.

It took some more pushing before Thad reached her. He wrapped his arms around her, and she hugged him back tightly. It was several long seconds before Thad realized that the rest of her family was surrounding them.

"Congratulations!" Brooke howled as she hugged him.

Ryan shook his hand as Emily hugged him again. Then Tyler and Chelsea surrounded him and examined the medal. "Keep an eye on that," Ryan joked, pointing at the gold. "You don't want it to disappear."

"It won't," Scott said as he appeared behind his brother.

"Not with this guy around," Thad agreed as he and Scott draped their arms around each other.

James and Rosie appeared at their sons' sides and Thad grinned at them. They smiled back. "My face still hurts from smiling." Thad laughed.

"I've never seen you smile like this, ever," James said.

Thad nodded. "Olympic gold? This is what I've been living for."

Chapter 22

T had slept like a log that night, and when he woke up the next morning, it was past nine o'clock. "Whoa," he said as he sat up.

Joaquin, who was already dressed and pushing clothes around in his dresser, looked over at him. "You slept like you were dead. I almost checked for a pulse a couple of times."

Thad rubbed his eyes as he looked around. "It's much later than I normally get up. Must be the jet lag."

"And the excitement, Mr. Gold Medalist." Both of their medals, hanging on an improvised peg nearby, caught the light as Joaquin spoke.

Thad smiled and pulled himself to his feet. "How long have you been awake?"

"Couple hours. There was a party down the hall that woke me up at some ungodly hour."

"I didn't hear that at all."

"Wish I'd slept like that. I'm still exhausted."

Thad groaned as he got dressed. "Me too. Every part of my body is stiff."

Thad spent that day and the next with his family until he saw them off to the airport. The round of hugs lasted so long he was sure they were going to miss their flight. "I am so proud of you," Rosie said.

James smiled. "This was the best outcome possible. You should be proud of yourself."

"I am, even if it hasn't sunk in yet."

"Then you should go back to the Olympic village and stare at your medal until it you're ready to march down the streets yelling, 'I am an Olympic champion!'" Scott teased.

The whole family laughed. "That will never happen," Thad said, even if he had to force the words out around his laughter.

"I know that." Scott gave his brother a whack.

After another round of hugs, Scott, James, and Rosie went into the airport. Thad watched until he could not see them anymore. Then he went back to the Olympic village.

He spent the next several days with Emily and her family, attending her practices and varying his meals between eating with the Burrows and with Joaquin and the other athletes. On Wednesday, he filed back into the arena with Emily's family. He sat with Emily's family on one side as Joaquin sat on his other side. Jack Wallace sat next to Joaquin too as a couple of the American hockey team's players took seats behind them.

Jack fist bumped his teammates before settling into his seat. "They're just here to see Kim skate," he told Joaquin.

Thad overheard the comment and laughed. "Then it's lucky the other skaters have at least some support."

Jack made a face and threw a Snickers bar at him.

Thad picked it up and threw it back. Soon, they were all laughing.

They got quiet when the skating started, and Thad found himself biting his nails as he waited. When Japanese skater Sakura Fujita took to the ice, Thad's heart raced. All around him, the arena roared and Japanese flags flew. *Awesome,* he thought. *She's skating on home ice. You can't get much better than that.*

"She's such a good skater," Joaquin said as Sakura began her program.

The comment made Thad wonder if his friend could read his mind. He nodded. "She's as athletic as Kim is. They both give each other a run for their money."

Sakura's skating was flawless, and it made Thad nervous. *Emily's going to have a heck of a time securing a medal,* he thought. *If Kim skates as well as Sakura just did, Emily will be fighting for the bronze.*

When Emily's name was announced next, her whole family jumped to their feet and cheered. Thad did too. All around him, everyone waved American flags. When it got quiet, though, Emily looked nervous, even as she took a breath to steady herself.

Uh oh, Thad thought. He looked over at Brooke and Ryan. They were gripping each other's hands, and they looked as nervous as Emily. Thad bit his lip and looked back at the ice. Emily charged as soon as her music started, though, and Thad smiled. *She knows she has to do well and she's attacking it,* he thought. Still, he squirmed in his seat, especially as Emily bobbled slightly on one of her triple jumps.

"Oh, no," Brooke groaned.

"Don't worry, that wasn't too bad," Thad reassured her, even as his eyes never left the ice.

Emily's eyebrows came together in determination, and certainty flowed through Thad. *She'll be fine.* He started breathing better once the rest of her program was clean and she was off the ice. When her scores came up—a mixture of 5.8s and 5.9s—Thad nodded. "She did fine," he told Brooke and Ryan. To his relief, they both nodded.

Then Jenni's name was called, and Thad clapped politely. *Even if I hope she falls,* he thought. He was disappointed when she skated well. Her marks were similar to Emily's, though, and she was two tenths of a point ahead of Emily. *Damn.*

Then Kim's name was announced, and the stadium roared. A large grin spread across Kim's face as she skated to the center of the ice, and Thad was happy for her. *She's seeing how much the crowd likes her,* he realized. *Good for her—she's in the moment.*

When Kim's music started, it was a fast tango, and soon the crowd was clapping along with her skating. Kim hit one huge triple jump after another, and the crowd cheered every time she landed. When she finished, she pumped the air with her fists, and Thad cheered with the rest of the crowd.

Jack leaned over. "If she doesn't come in first, I'm boycotting skating for the rest of my life."

Thad and Joaquin laughed and looked over at the judges. Then Kim's marks came up— seven 6.0s and two 5.9s. Kim jumped up and down and cheered as the crowd chanted her name. Thad laughed and looked at the nearest screen. Emily was in fourth, behind Kim, Sakura, and Jenni.

Thad followed Emily's family and gave her a hug when they had located her. "You skated well."

Emily nodded. "I did my best. Fourth is still a hard place to be in."

"You're so close to Jenni that you could easily overtake her."

"And I've got 'Les Mis' as my long program."

"That's the spirit!"

Two nights later, nervousness crawled through Thad as he sat back in the stands for the long program. *I hope Emily can pull this off.* Once more, he was sandwiched between Emily's family and Joaquin, with a few hockey players rounding out the group. Thad struggled to relax as he waited for the last group to skate, which included Emily, Jenni, Kim, and Sakura. He leaned forward as Jenni's name was announced. Then he looked over at Emily's family.

Ryan was wearing a purposefully blank expression. He reached over and hit Tyler and Chelsea on the knees. "No booing."

Thad laughed, even as he was impressed by Ryan's admonition. "Still teaching them sportsmanship?"

"Still trying."

They all got quiet as Jenni's program started.

What is this music? Thad wondered a minute later. *It sounds like a mashup of stuff that was popular ten years ago.* He sucked in a breath as

Jenni two-footed a landing on a triple toe loop. *I hope the judges saw that.* It was not until Jenni popped out of a triple axel that Thad really began to hope. He waited until Jenni had finished skating before looking over at Joaquin.

"She looked slow," Joaquin said.

"In addition to the mistakes on her jumps."

"Yeah."

Thad bit his lip until Jenni's marks came up, a slew of 5.7s and 5.8s.

"Emily has room!" Brooke whooped as her daughter's name was called. In front of them, Emily took a long and deep breath as she got to the center of the ice.

Thad sat on his hands so as not to bite his nails as the familiar music of "On My Own" came over the speakers. He watched Emily move from the swift parts of the program to the languid ones. Her jumps were clean and smooth, and he smiled as she went into a layback spin.

"She's gotten better at those," Brooke said.

Thad nodded in agreement. Still, he remained on the edge of his seat as Emily reeled off one jump after the other, and there were more triples than doubles. Emily landed each of them cleanly, and a large smile remained on her face throughout the program. *She's putting it all out there tonight.* By the time Emily finished skating, she had the largest smile on her face that Thad had ever seen. He stood and cheered with the rest of her family.

A few minutes later, Emily's scores came up. She had three 6.0s and the rest were 5.9s. "Yeah, Emily!" Brooke yelled.

"She'll at least get the bronze," Ryan cheered.

Then it was Kim's turn to skate, and Thad crossed his fingers for her. Once more, Kim had chosen music with solid drumbeats, and she tossed off several jumps as the tempo quickened.

"She makes it look so easy!" Joaquin yelped.

"I know," Thad agreed. "But least she's playing to her athleticism now, rather than letting it get in her way."

By the time Kim finished skating, the arena was on its feet, and all Thad saw was the red, white, and blue of waving American flags. When her marks came up, there were two 5.9s and the rest were 6.0s. The arena roared again, and Kim waved to the crowd. She was still smiling.

"Good for her," Thad said.

"Sakura is going to have a hell of a time beating her," Joaquin said.

"She'll skate well," Thad answered. "She always does."

He was right. Sakura was as solid as he had ever seen her, and her marks were also a mix of 6.0s and 5.9s. Then the rankings came up, and Thad's face got hot. Emily was in third place, and Kim and Sakura were separated by two tenths of a point.

"Oh my God," Joaquin yelped. "Those scores!"

Thad nodded as he yelled as loud as he could.

When the medal ceremony began, the whole arena screamed as two American flags were raised, with the Japanese flag in between them. Emily waited for the ceremony to be over before looking for her family. Brooke and Ryan raced over to her, and Emily jumped up and down and screamed.

Thad made his way over to them and threw his arms open. He was grinning as broadly as when he had gotten his own medal.

"I did it, Thad!" Emily yelled as she hugged him.

Thad hugged her back without reservation. "You were wonderful!"

Chelsea and Tyler mobbed Emily too, so Thad went over to Kim. "You were amazing!" he howled.

"From one gold medalist to another!" Kim held up her hand, and she and Thad high fived. After a few minutes, Kim's mother and coach surrounded her, so Thad went back to Emily.

"I can't believe we still have to skate at the exhibition gala tomorrow," Emily said as Thad took her hand. "I'll be lucky if I don't sleep through it."

"You and me both," Thad said, and they laughed.

The next morning, it was quiet as Thad and Emily walked away from the Olympic village. Emily's family trailed them at a small distance. "Too bad your family had to go home so early," she said.

"Two weeks is a long time to stay here. The hotels are expensive."

"I know, it's crazy."

Thad glanced behind them to see just how far behind them the rest of Emily's family was. When he was sure they could not hear him, he looked back at Emily.

"Uh oh," Emily said.

Thad took her hand. "Don't worry, it's not anything bad. Just that we've been through a lot together and I'm very proud of you and all you've achieved." Emily grinned at him, and Thad's heart stuttered. He tried to find words for the rest of what he wanted to say, but none came. He took a deep breath, and the damp, chilly air around them brought him back to his senses. "I've come to realize that I love you."

Emily smiled at him. Then she threw open her arms, and Thad clutched her to his chest. "I'm so glad Brianna and Mia had the sense to bring us back together," Emily said, and her words were muffled.

Thad thought of their hike in the woods, and his heart thumped in his chest. "Me too. Everything would look a lot different now if they hadn't."

Then Emily's family caught up to them. She looked over, even as she continued resting her head against Thad's chest. "What's going on, love birds?" Brooke teased.

"Oh, we were just realizing that we have to get back on the ice," Thad said.

"What?" Emily asked, finally pulling away from him and checking her watch.

"That exhibition gala won't skate itself." But Thad was smiling.

Emily laughed and took his hand. "I'm looking forward to that already."

Thad's face burned, but this time it was from happiness. "A gold medal and a solid future. These have been the best few days of my life."

About the Author

Tamar's short story about Thad's father, James, was recently published in *The Rockford Review*. She has written many other short stories, as well as award-winning novels for all ages. Her most recent book is the middle grade fantasy *The Tunnel to Darkness and Light*. Her YA novel, *Two Sisters of Fayetteville*, is an Indie Brag Medallion winner that also won an Honorable Mention for Young Adult Fiction in the Firebird Book Awards. Her other YA novels include *The Fledgling's Inferno* and *A Silent Evil*. She also writes historical fiction for an adult audience. Her short story collection set in the Old West, *The Lonely Spirit*, has won many awards, including an Indie Brag Medallion and first place in the Chanticleer International Book Awards for Short Story Collections and Novellas. Tamar's alternate history series about the Romanovs- the novels *Triumph of a Tsar, Through the Fire*, and *The Imperial Spy*- won first place for the Chanticleer International Book Awards Series Awards for Genre Fiction. Her novel *Tales of the Romanov Empire* has also been long listed and short listed for numerous awards.

Made in the USA
Middletown, DE
02 May 2024

53744884R00152